HAZARDOUS DUTY

A NOVEL

CHRISTY BARRITT

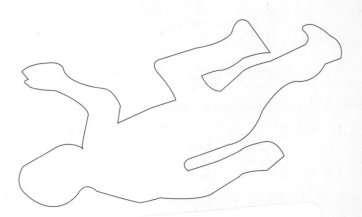

Kregel
Publications

A special thanks to:

Mary Connealy and Suzan Robertson, the two greatest critique partners ever. We've laughed and cried together. What would I do without you guys?

Captain Steve Smith of the Virginia Beach Police Department. Your insight was invaluable, your time a gift. Andy Bell, a real-life crime-scene cleaner. I hope you're enjoying yourself on the beach! Any mistakes are mine.

Thanks also to my agent for believing in me, and to Kregel Publications for seeing potential in my work. It's been a real pleasure and a true blessing to work with you.

This book is dedicated to the newest guy in my life: Eli Barritt, born June 12, 2006. Eli, you redefined love at first sight for me.

CHAPTER

ONE

Whistling a tune from Fiddler on the Roof, I used my tweezers to work a piece of Gloria Cunningham's skull out of the sky blue wall.

With a couple of tugs, the fragment broke loose. Holding it to the light, I studied the sliver that was once a part of a living and breathing woman. It wasn't much bigger than a splinter, and to the average person would look like a piece of chipped tile.

One thing was for sure: being rich definitely hadn't done this family any favors.

"Sorry, Tevye, but you were wrong on that one," I mumbled.

As I worked the rest of the wall, I tried to come up with jingles for my company:

> *"If your home is bloody*
> *Daidle deedle daidle*
> *Daidle daidle deedle daidle dum."*

Stumped for something that rhymed with bloody, I hummed "If I Were a Rich Man" and played with my options:

> *"If your carpet's gory*
> *Daidle deedle daidle*
> *Daidle daidle deedle daidle dum."*

It was my new business strategy—to save enough money to buy advertising on the radio. Ever since I came up with the idea, I'd been playing with different tunes, trying to develop the perfect one. It was amazing how many people didn't know about my services as a crime-scene cleaner.

Yeah, that's me. A crime-scene cleaner. Bonded and insured. Proud owner of my own business. A fascinating anomaly to those I meet around town.

People waiting in line behind me who strike up conversations always regret it.

"So, what do you do for a living?" the innocent bystander asks, desperate to pass time until it's her turn to be rung up.

"I mop up blood at crime scenes."

The color suddenly drains from her face. I might as well say I'm a vampire. Is there something that strange about a girl who cleans up blood for a living? I think not.

I glanced back at the wall. Fractures of bone jutted from the plaster in a spray. It looked like a mosaic gone terribly wrong.

I shook my head and continued to work. Drowning in my blue bio-hazard suit, a face mask, and gloves that were duct-taped to my sleeves, I looked like a space man at best, a Teletubby at worst. Whoever designed the suits obviously thought nothing about the importance of flattering a woman's figure. I guess they were too busy worrying about keeping people safe from diseases like AIDS and hepatitis, which could live in blood for up to a week.

I straightened as inspiration hit me. I pulled imaginary pom-poms to my waist and took a cheering stance:

> *"When blood is there,*
> *I don't care.*
> *You can call*
> *Trauma Care."*

I used my best Valley Girl voice and bounced like a cheerleader—something I had never desired to be. I was always the scientist in high school, which didn't help me win any popularity contests. I might as well have joined the chess club.

It also didn't help that as a child, while all my friends dressed up their dolls, I dissected mine. I wanted to know how the human body worked. Later in life, I developed a fascination with chemicals, a fact that Company 12 of the Norfolk, Virginia, Fire Department can attest to.

Even then it wasn't my fault. Yes, the fumes that resulted from the chemicals I mixed were deadly. Yes, the teacher meant well when he tackled me to save my life. Still, the spill and the resulting fire were all his fault. Keep your head in a crisis; that's what I say.

So much for impressing my lab partner, Bartholomew Einstein.

Yes, that was his real name. I've never particularly had good taste in guys. I'd moved between nerds and jerks so seamlessly that they should create a twelve-step program just to save me. As of late, there hadn't been anyone. It might have had something to do with the scent of blood that tends to saturate me after cleaning.

"Is that a new perfume you're wearing?" the debonair gentleman asks, raising my wrist to his nose.

I raise my head eloquently, pursing my lips in imitation of movie stars of late. "Why no, it's not. I don't wear perfume."

The handsome stranger forces his eyebrows together. "Then what is that smell exuding from you?"

I bat my eyelashes and level with him, "That, my dear, is blood. You think it smells bad? You should be around a human body that's been decaying for two weeks."

You had to have a sense of humor to do a job like this. A lot of coffee and chocolate also helped—as did having a personal counselor, aka my neighbor and best friend, Sierra. Boy, she had no idea what she was getting into when she invited me over for coffee the first time. But since I live on the floor above her, she's stuck with me.

Abandoning my workstation, I crossed the room to the built-in bookcase of the master bedroom. Against protocol, I picked up a picture displaying a happy couple smiling on a white sand beach with the sunset smeared behind them. The woman was blond and beautiful; the man, stocky and masculine.

They both looked so young, only a few years older than my twenty-seven years. They still had so much of life to share together. The husband, Michael Cunningham, was even running for a U.S. Senate seat, hoping to represent this wonderful state of Virginia. I wondered what he would do about his campaign without his trophy wife.

A gloved hand snatched the picture. I gasped and whirled around.

Harold, my assistant.

He pulled his mask up and revealed his aged, round face. "What are you doing?" His deep voice resonated in the room. He reminded me of the man who sang "Old Man River" in *Showboat*.

"Old Man River"? Hmm . . . there could be a jingle in that.

One glance at Harold's disapproving glare and I knew not to argue.

"It's your rule, Gabby. Don't get emotionally attached."

"I know. I just needed a break from cleaning." I pulled up my mask, and a red curl bounced down over my eye. I let it droop rather than touch it with my gloved hands. "How are things going on the stairway?"

Harold didn't know about the hours of research I poured into my job, trying to learn background details of the case. I wanted to know the victims. I wanted to theorize who could be the killer. Basically, I wanted to be a crime-scene investigator. But without a degree, I was forced to do everything in an unofficial capacity.

"I pulled up the carpet. The owner will have to replace it. There's just no way to get all of that blood up. It went into the padding and subfloor."

I glanced around the bedroom. "Whoever did this was a monster."

"And my mom always told me they didn't exist."

"Well, they do, and this one left us a heap of a mess to clean up. This is more than a one-day job." I leaned closer to Harold. Moisture covered his face. "You need a break?"

"I'm fine."

"Don't push yourself too hard. I understand how tough this is."

Yeah, like Harold would let a girl young enough to be his grand-daughter outlast him on a job. The man did have pride. His gaze darted across the room. "What happened in here?"

I drew in a deep breath.

"Gloria Cunningham was about to testify against a suspect in an armed-robbery trial. The perp—er, suspect—threatened her, saying if she went to court, he'd kill her. Two days before the trial, he broke into her home while she was sleeping." I spread my arm to show the room. It told the story better than words.

The crime scene had remained active for a week. I had heard about the case on the news and slipped over to the house to leave a business card. As soon as the police okayed it, Michael Cunningham's mother had called me to see if I could clean things up before her son was released from the hospital. He'd been shot in the leg while trying to save his wife.

A lot of people thought I worked for the police department, but I didn't. I was an independent contractor. The police weren't allowed to recommend services to anyone—not for anything from towing to cleaning. So I spend a lot of my days getting to know embalmers and body snatchers, my nickname for those who take the dead bodies to the morgue.

To get business, I watched the news. I followed leads by placing my card at crime scenes. As the only crime-scene cleaner in the area, I had almost 100 percent success. But drumming up jobs took a lot of time, which is why I'd been daydreaming about a radio spot that advertised my business. It would save me a lot of legwork.

I could hear Harry Connick Jr. singing it now . . . no, better yet, Julie Andrews. I closed my eyes as a melody that sounded vaguely reminiscent of "Santa Claus Is Coming to Town" came to mind:

> "If you've been shot,
> If you've been stabbed,
> If blood on your walls says, 'Someone's been bad.'
> Trauma Care is the-e-ere for you."

"Gabby?"

I quit writing advertising jingles and noticed Harold staring at me like I needed to go to the psych ward. "Well, it's back to work for us." Sincerely hoping I hadn't been humming a Christmas carol out loud, I turned back to my modern-art brain splatters.

It took me four hours to clean up the walls of the bedroom. What a bullet did to a human brain just didn't bear thinking about.

Harold finished the stairway and then cleaned the broken glass downstairs where the intruder had entered the house. With that done, he came to help me in the bedroom.

The blood-splattered coverlet had to be thrown away, as well as the sheets. We shoved them into special hazmat containers that I'd take to the hospital to be disposed of properly. Most of the carpet would have to be taken up in the bedroom, also.

I'd call Michael Cunningham's mother and see if she wanted us to subcontract the work out and have it replaced before her son returned home. Most people didn't want to be reminded of what had happened in their once-safe homes. In fact, most people ended up selling their houses after a crime because the memories were too vivid.

At 7:30, Harold tapped my shoulder and pointed to his watch. "Grandson? Baseball game? Okay if I get going?"

Had we really been here ten hours? "Sure. I can finish. Come back in the morning. Eight o'clock."

"I'll be here." He started out of the bedroom and paused. "You sure you'll be okay here by yourself? I can stay. . . ."

"No, no. I'll be fine. I just need to sand down this wall, and then I'll call it a night."

He didn't move. His brow furrowed as he stood in the doorway.

I flashed him a smile. I loved Harold. I'd only hired him a month ago, but he already worried about me like I was his daughter. Then I thought of my real father and mentally apologized to Harold for the insult.

"Really. The suspect is behind bars. It's ugly, but it's not dangerous. Besides, I'll be out of here in fifteen minutes."

"If you say so. You're the boss."

As soon as Harold left, I wished he hadn't. Blessed—or cursed, depending on your outlook—with a vivid imagination, I felt chills run up my spine as I pictured the events unfolding.

Too clearly, I could see the couple sleeping in bed. The husband hears glass breaking downstairs. Grabbing a baseball bat, he goes down to check it out, only the intruder is hiding, waiting for just the right moment to sneak upstairs and kill the sole witness to his crime.

The killer plans to escape by the ladder he left perched at the window, but the husband is too quick. As soon as the gunshot goes off, the husband is back upstairs in the bedroom. He sees the intruder climbing out the window. As he runs toward the man, the intruder takes another shot and hits Michael's knee, shattering it.

Shaking my head, I opened the closet door and sagged against it. Rows of expensive, elegant dresses hung limply. Taking my glove off, I fingered the silky material of one, pulling it to my nose. It smelled of subtle flowers.

The wife should still be wearing her beautiful dresses and spritzing her expensive perfumes. The woman's smile should still light up a room.

The dress slipped out of my hands.

"At least they have your murderer behind bars," I mumbled, stepping back.

My fingers closed over the door handle, and I started to push it shut. A spot of red on the carpet made me falter. I squinted, staring at the stain. How did that get in the closet? Blood wasn't anywhere else on this side of the room.

I slipped my gloves back on and pushed a couple of shoeboxes to the side. Mindful of carpet tacks, I tugged at the berber shag. It came up with surprising ease.

I dragged the piece of carpet into the middle of the bedroom and went back to pull up the padding. I checked the subfloor to see if the stain had soaked through. It looked okay.

Just as I was about to stand, an abnormality in the wood caught my eye. In the back corner of the closet, the subfloor was different from the rest. A small square had been cut out and replaced.

Could it just have been a leaky pipe replacement?

I moved toward the spot.

My breath caught.

A speck of blood stained the wood.

The carpet in that same area hadn't had any blood. I was sure of it.

Taking a knife from the belt at my waist, I pried under the wood. The board lifted.

With shaky hands, I pulled it back. Tucked between the floorboards, I saw a metal box.

I pulled out the container as if it were a priceless, fragile piece of art. Its contents clanged in the silence.

It was heavy. Too heavy for jewelry and trinkets.

Leaning down until my face was even with it, I clicked the latch. With a squeak, the box opened.

CHAPTER

TWO

A gun.

My heart rate quickened. The murder weapon had never been found. Could this be it?

But why would the intruder stow his gun inside the Cunninghams' closet? For that matter, how would he do it if he shot at the husband while climbing out the window? It didn't make sense.

Unless the intruder didn't shoot the wife.

Unless there wasn't an intruder at all.

A minute ago, I'd been sweating inside my hazmat suit. Now I shivered. The room temperature felt like it had dropped to subzero.

Buying a gun to kill your wife: $3,000.

Hiring Trauma Care to clean afterward: $1,500.

Having that same cleaner uncover evidence that frames you: priceless.

I latched the box and stripped out of my suit. The sweatshirt and jeans I wore underneath were much more comfortable. I would worry about the rest of this job tomorrow morning. Right now, I had to get to the police station.

I placed the box into a bag normally used for waste material. At the last minute, I grabbed the board with the blood on it. It needed to be tested to see if the blood was the wife's. I slid it into the bag and started toward the door.

The sound of glass shattering stopped me cold.

What if it was the killer coming back for the gun? My heart thudded, vibrating my entire body.

The suspect's behind bars.

But what if it's the wrong suspect?

Standing in the brightly lit room, I felt naked with nowhere to go.

My stomach tightened.

Without carpet on the stairs, surely I would hear someone coming up.

Wouldn't I?

There was no sound. No more glass breaking, no footsteps.

I sniffed.

What was that smell? Was someone burning leaves outside? Maybe the smell had drifted in through a now-broken window.

You have to get out of the house.

My astuteness never failed to astound me. I didn't get straight As in high school for nothing.

My grip tightened around the bag.

Desperate to be concealed, I flicked off the light switch. The utter darkness paralyzed me. I decided I'd rather see trouble coming and fumbled with the switch until the white bulb flared.

I darted across the room, found a flashlight in my toolbox, and sprinted back to the door, evidence still in hand.

Sweat beaded on my forehead. At least I was getting warmer. My cold chill had dissipated.

After turning on my flashlight, I flicked off the lights again. A white beam cut through the darkness, calming my racing heart.

I didn't want to go downstairs.

Gutless. You want to solve crimes, and you're scared of your own shadow. It's probably nothing. A kid who hit his baseball through the window. Besides, it's been at least ten minutes since it happened, and you haven't heard a thing since then.

I hunted around until I found my backbone, then stepped from the room. My gaze swept the hallway along with the beam of the flashlight.

Nothing.

C'mon, go, move. Don't just stand here.

At least ten doorways stood between the stairway and me in the expansive hallway. Any of them could be a potential hideout for an intruder. Why did the Cunninghams' bedroom have to be at the back of the house, so far away from the front door?

I smelled something that reminded me of a gas station. Could it be . . . ?

A light danced in the recess of the stairway. Or was it my own shadow?

The flashlight trembled in my hands, but I forced myself to keep going. My gaze darted from doorway to doorway. I waited for one to jerk open and a masked intruder to attack me.

An orange finger beckoned from the stairs.

My throat went dry.

No wonder I wasn't cold anymore.

The house was on fire.

The flashlight dropped from my hands and bounced against the carpet. It teetered with a final thud and flickered out. Eerie, smoldering darkness swallowed me. I had to get out of this house like the von Trapps had to get out of Austria.

Flames blocked the stairway in front of me. A house this size had to have two stairways. It was just a matter of finding the other one before the fire found me.

Clutching the bag, I raced down the hall.

I darted up two steps at the end of the hallway and pushed open the door. This should be the room over the garage. I dodged a pool table and scrambled across the carpet toward a door on the other side. I stumbled into it, fumbling with the knob. Finally, I pulled the door open.

Stairs.

Taking them by twos, I practically flew to the first floor. My hand covered the door handle. Searing pain caused me to jerk back.

My hand blistered.

I dropped the bag containing a gun that I might potentially die for. Ignoring the blistering ache of my left hand, I pulled the sleeve of my sweatshirt over my right hand and twisted.

The door swung open, and roaring orange and yellow flared in my face. I staggered backward, tripping over the stairs as white hot smoke seared my lungs. I fell, my chest heaving.

The fire greedily reached for me, consuming anything in its path.

In the distance, a siren squealed, a mellow, whining cry that underscored the crackling roar of the blaze. Fire trucks. But would they be too late?

For the first time in years, I wished I believed in prayer. But I knew better. I only had myself to rely on.

I spotted another door on my left. I grabbed my evidence and, on my elbows and knees, crawled to my escape hatch and opened it.

The garage. Flames danced around the walls, but a pathway straight in front of me was clear.

Taunting, greedy voices mocked from the raging flames behind me.

"No!" I slammed the door shut. But the wooden block wouldn't hold the flames back for long. I had to keep moving.

I stumbled to my feet and, clinging to the bag, staggered across the garage toward the outside door. Smoke crept inside and blinded me. I coughed, trying to get a deep breath.

My knees buckled.

I dropped to the ground, coughing.

Only a few more steps.

I pulled my sweatshirt over my mouth and nose. On my hands and knees, I dragged myself over the rough cement floor. I lurched forward, inch by inch. Glowing ash sizzled in the reddish glow of the fire as it devoured the wall beside me.

I glanced over my shoulder to ensure the bag remained intact. My eyes burned from the gritty air. The plastic started to melt. The metal box poked through. I swung it around and hugged it to my chest.

Two more steps, Gabby.

The house crackled around me, groaning with the fire. The devilish, ravenous flames were winning.

My head started to spin. I couldn't breath. The flames around me began to blur.

CHAPTER

THREE

No, you can make it, Gabby. Keep going.

My hand connected with a wall. Clinging to the box as if it were a lifeline, I reached upward and felt a doorknob. Using my last ounce of strength, I twisted it, feeling the burned flesh on my palm rip. I tumbled outside and sprawled face first on the sidewalk along the side of the house. I gulped in the fresh air.

Keep moving, Gabby. The fire's licking your heels.

I pulled myself off the ground and stumbled onto the lawn. The whole house howled with demonic fury because I'd gotten away.

Fire trucks. Help. I reeled toward the sound.

"Someone's coming out of the house," a voice yelled in the distance. Hands grasped my arms, holding me up. "Is there anyone else inside?"

I coughed, the words smoldering in my throat. Finally, I shook my head.

"It was just you?"

I nodded.

Paramedics rushed toward me and strapped an oxygen mask over my face. I was lowered onto a stretcher, still hugging my bag, and whisked to a waiting ambulance.

An hour later, my hand was bandaged, and my breathing had returned to normal. The EMTs had wanted to take me to the hospital, but I insisted I'd be fine. I climbed out of the ambulance and stared at the scene.

Firefighters, paramedics, and neighbors mingled in the front yard. Ash, gritty and sulfurous, rained down like blackened snow. It filled my senses until I could taste it. The flames were now out, but orange still glowed in the remains.

A shudder rippled through my body. Someone had set the house on fire with me inside.

I'd been in some tough scrapes before. Like in seventh grade when I was young and naive and I got my science experiments mixed up at a slumber party. I somehow convinced the girls to brush their teeth with baking soda and to rinse with vinegar. I later heard that was the solution used to unclog toilets. Needless to say, half of them went to the emergency room when the concoction started sizzling and exploding like a volcano inside their mouth. At least their teeth were sparkly white as they told the doctors what had happened.

Okay, so maybe that didn't compare to this situation. I'd almost been grilled like a hot dog at a cookout. None of my past experiences began to touch the fact that just now I'd almost died in the line of duty.

"Are you the woman who came out of the house?" someone asked behind me.

I turned and sucked in a deep breath. When had Brad Pitt moved to Virginia Beach? I swallowed. "Yes, I am."

"I'm Detective Parker. We heard someone was inside the residence, and since this is a former crime scene, we need to question you." His dark eyes looked me over as if sizing me up. "What were you doing in the residence?"

I straightened my shoulders. "I'm a crime-scene cleaner."

He nodded and lowered his head, but I saw the slight twitch of his eyebrows. He clicked his pen against his pad of paper. "Working late?"

I shrugged. "I like to get the job done right and quickly."

"You always work alone?"

"No, my assistant left about an hour earlier."

"I'll need his name."

I gave it to him.

The detective's eyes traveled to the bag in my hands. "Souvenirs?"

"Evidence." My gaze locked with his.

Parker put a hand on his hip and cocked an eyebrow in disbelief. "We searched every corner of that house."

"You sure about that?" I dangled the bag.

His eyes narrowed, and he took my arm, leading me toward a sedan parked haphazardly on the side of the road. "Let's talk in my car. Reporters are already starting to swarm."

I climbed in the passenger's side, the smell of smoke assaulting me. It was a different vapor from the scent outside but equally as grimy and thick. Cigarettes.

Parker plopped into the driver's seat and slammed the door. Reaching into his pockets, he pulled out some gloves and snapped them on. "Let me see what you found."

I opened the bag, careful not to touch my buried treasure. "This board on top has a speck of blood on it. But there wasn't any blood on the carpet above it."

He dipped his head in a side nod. "It could be old."

"It could be new."

His gaze met mine. "I can't argue with that. How do you know so much about this?"

"I went to college. Just because I spend my life cleaning doesn't mean I'm an idiot." I reserved the part about dropping out only one semester away from graduating and turning to this job because it made me feel like the forensic specialist I had studied to be.

His jaw twitched. "Of course."

He took the board and studied the bloodstain. "I'll have it tested to see who it belongs to, though I don't know how much it will tell us about the case."

"That's not the best part," I said. Only touching the metal box with the plastic, I held it up.

The detective raised a brow. "What's this?"

"This is what was under the bloodstained wood in the corner of the closet. There's a gun inside."

"A gun?"

"Maybe the murder weapon."

He shook his head. "That wouldn't make sense."

"Have you found the murder weapon yet?"

"No."

"Maybe I have."

He sighed. "Look, Nancy Drew. This isn't your case. There's nothing wrong with a couple hiding a gun in their closet. It sounds like a safe thing to me."

"First of all, I'm not Nancy Drew. I'm Gabby St. Claire, crime-scene cleaner. Second, I believe I've stumbled on some evidence you missed, Detective. Even if it is the family gun, your search should have turned it up, which makes me wonder what else your crime-scene unit missed. And blood splattered near a gun is always suspicious."

He studied me a moment before nodding. A grin spread across his face, and I relaxed my shoulders.

"Well, Gabby St. Claire, you've established that you are indeed a professional." He held out his hand, some of his earlier formalities gone. "Why don't you call me Chip?"

After contemplating a moment, I awkwardly took it with my unbandaged hand and pumped up and down. Gracefully, of course.

As I pulled away, I dared to ask my next question. "What kind of gun was the murder weapon?"

He shook his head and clicked his tongue. "You are not an official part of this investigation."

"Oh, come on. I'll find out eventually."

When he opened the metal box, I had my answer.

He glanced up at me, his gaze containing a shadow of hidden emotion. "You're going to have to tell me exactly where you found this." He pulled a note pad out of the breast pocket of his dark suit.

I recounted what had happened, all the way up until I escaped from the burning house. He nodded and grunted, jotting quick notes.

"You have any enemies?"

I tilted my head, wondering where he was going with the question. "Why?"

"Someone tried to kill you tonight, Gabby."

I shook my head. "No, someone tried to burn down a crime scene."

The detective clicked his pen and sighed. "Anyone you can think of who might want to hurt you?"

"No. My being there was an accident. Whoever did this didn't know I was inside."

"You're going to be around in case we have more questions, right?" the detective more stated than asked.

"Of course."

He looked me over. "You're free to go. I'll be in touch."

I nodded, reluctant for some reason to leave the evidence I'd found. For a moment, I'd felt like part of the investigation, like I was on the case. Like I was really someone instead of just a house cleaner.

I climbed out of the car and ambled across the street, my eyes focused on the scene around me. The flashing lights. The smoldering flames. Men in uniform milling around, mumbling theories to each other. Reporters trailed by TV cameras, trying to get the inside scoop. The smell of smoke, thick and choking.

That house could have been my grave.

Just a couple of hours earlier, things had seemed so normal. I was just doing my job. Now, I was thankful to be alive.

I circled to the back of the house, toward my white business van. I tried to park it out of sight to give people privacy. Most people didn't want to remind others of what had gone on in their home. Besides, it paid to be discrete.

I halted as my five-month-old van came into sight. It stood on four melted tires, and the front windshield was shattered. It wasn't going anywhere.

"Everything okay?" A fireman came up from behind and looked between me and the wrecked vehicle. As soon as I saw the man, I wanted to duck. I would never forget that face. He looked like someone had grabbed his nose, pulled it, and the rest of his face had molded like Play-Doh with the action. His teeth were perfectly straight . . . and yellow, just like a cob of corn. Yep, this was the same firefighter who had visited my high school that dreadful day after my experiment caught it on fire.

"No, everything's not okay." I pointed toward the remains of my only wheels. "That's mine."

"We figured as much. It's not in any condition to be driven."

I made sure I was looking away when I rolled my eyes. I pulled my arms over my chest. The edges of my sweatshirt were singed. White ash coated me. I probably looked like death.

What did it matter? At least I was alive.

Then I realized that all of my equipment was gone. I would have to start over.

I would deal with that later. Now I had to find a way home. The detective seemed like a good person to ask. As I went back toward his car, I saw he was still inside. He didn't see me approaching as he chatted on his cell phone, holding the metal box in his hands.

Without gloves.

I pounded on the window.

He glanced up and closed his cell phone. His window rolled down. "Everything okay?"

"You shouldn't be touching that without gloves." I pointed to the box.

He looked down at the evidence and pulled his hand back as if he'd touched fire. He ran his fingers through his thick, light brown hair. "My prints will be ruled out when the crime-scene unit tests it. No big deal."

He glanced up with a level gaze.

I stared at him, my mouth starting to gape open. "That's not proper procedure. Your sloppiness could compromise a piece of evidence that could change the entire direction of this case."

He leaned toward me and lowered his voice. "Things like this happen all the time. I know to a young idealist this seems like the worst thing that could happen, but believe me, it's not."

A young idealist? He didn't know anything about me. And if he thought I was going to let this slide, he was wrong. But it would have to be dealt with later. Now I needed to get home before I passed out from exhaustion.

"There's nothing I can do about your blunder," I said, silently adding, *For now.* "The whole reason I came over here was because I need a ride home. My van isn't drivable."

His shoulders seemed to sag in relief. "Give me a few minutes here, and I'll take you myself."

He stepped out of the sedan. "Why don't you stay in the car and relax? I'll be back in a few minutes."

Nothing sounded better than shutting out the world around me and trying to sort my jumbled thoughts. I nodded and slid into the passenger's seat. As soon as the noise from outside muted, I dropped my head back on the headrest.

My temples throbbed. Maybe a trip to the hospital wasn't a bad idea. My body suddenly felt fragile and weary. I closed my eyes, trying to block out everything that had happened. But with a curiosity like mine, that would be as impossible as buying oceanfront property in Arizona.

CHAPTER FOUR

The sound of the door opening, accompanied by a whiff of smoky air, jostled me awake. Incessant beeping told me the keys still hung from the ignition.

"Sorry. That took longer than I expected." Parker slammed the door and glanced over at me. "You sleeping?"

I stretched, wishing it was all a nightmare. My gaze swept over the scene outside. Only two vehicles were parked near the house now. The orange glow of timbers arched like massive dinosaur bones against the black sky. Puddles in the ruined lawn reflected the embers that still clung to life.

I pulled my gaze from the scene. "I guess I was more exhausted than I realized."

"I'll get you home."

I fought a yawn. "What time is it?"

"Just past midnight."

A few minutes later, we were cruising down the road. I mumbled out directions to my house, and we pulled out of the lush Virginia Beach neighborhood, heading toward the neighboring city of Norfolk.

The area had several larger cities all back-to-back that made up Hampton Roads. It was mostly suburban, with the exception of downtown Norfolk, where I lived. Hampton Roads was the perfect blend of southern hospitality and northeastern briskness, a mix of liberal and conservative. People with southern accents but quick beats between words.

Only minutes from the hustle of the business district in Norfolk nestled Ghent, an artistic, eccentric area where students and creative bohemians lived. How I'd ended up there, I wasn't sure. There was nothing creative about me, and heaven knew I'd failed as a student the day I'd dropped out of college never to return.

Something about the area charmed me, though, and one day I found myself looking at an apartment. To most people, the bruised Victorian would have been nothing special. To me, I felt like I'd found my home. I signed a contract for one-fifth of the old house. With Ghent's steady influx of patrons who visited the antique shops, pubs, and delis, life never got boring.

As Parker came to a quick stop at a traffic light, I reached for the dashboard to steady myself. My hand ached on contact, a reminder of my blisters. I leaned back, trying to clear my head.

"Did you think of anyone yet?" Parker asked.

"Excuse me?"

"Anyone who's an enemy?"

"I already told you—I don't have any enemies. At least none that I know about." I turned toward him, taking in his perfectly proportioned profile. A streetlight illuminated his chiseled cheeks and square jaw line. "You really think this was against me?"

"Can't rule it out."

"I heard glass breaking before the fire started, like a window got shattered or something."

He drummed his index fingers against the steering wheel, nodding to some silent beat. "I guess that's how they got inside. The initial opinion is that they poured gasoline all over the downstairs. That's why the house went up so quickly."

Had someone really tried to kill me? My stomach tightened at the thought. It just didn't make sense. "Here's my apartment building."

He pulled into the lot, put the car in park, and turned to face me. "Don't worry, Gabby. I'll track down whoever did this. You can count on me."

I thought of Parker touching that box and decided I'd be better off counting on myself. I got out of the car, watched him drive away, and then sank onto the steps outside my apartment building. The air had finally cooled, and the breeze felt like a balm on my face.

What a night.

I closed my eyes and imagined myself as a forensic specialist. Things would have been different tonight if I was. Parker would have respected my opinion instead of looking at me like a janitor. I would be at the lab right now, testing the evidence for fingerprints and trace particles.

If I had finished that last semester of college, I would have the career I wanted. I wouldn't have to worry about getting enough jobs to pay the bills or about getting all the blood out of the carpet. But sometimes responsibilities dictated your life, and you just had to make the best of what you had.

I'd become quite an expert in that area, if you asked me. Maybe I should just give up cleaning altogether and start enrichment seminars all over the country. I could see it now—turning lemons into lemonade. Remembering that the sun will come out tomorrow. Climbing every mountain and fording every stream. Okay, so kill the musical references, I know. But I did have to constantly remind myself to look on the bright side. Otherwise, I might just turn to the bottle like my dad had.

When Mom died, my father hadn't been able to function. I'd quit college to support him, and since then, I barely had time to breathe, let alone go back to school. Work had become a necessity, and college a luxury I couldn't afford. Sometimes, it was just a hard-knock life.

So maybe pondering a career change wasn't such a good idea. Look, you can be just like me! Picking bones out of walls. Almost getting killed. Being laughed at by detectives. But, hey, I could still smile. After all, you're not fully dressed without one, to quote one of my favorite musicals of all times.

Growing up, I bore an uncanny resemblance to Little Orphan Annie, from my curly red hair to the dash of freckles across my nose to my penchant for trouble. My mom didn't make things any better when she bought sewing patterns for the actual outfits that Annie wore. She proudly made the dresses for me, and I unknowingly wore them. Up until sixth grade, classmates had called me LOA—Little Orphan Annie. Luckily, I'd gotten older and learned to control my curls, my freckles had disappeared, and I'd developed better fashion taste. Well, the fashion taste was questionable, but I thought T-shirts, jeans, and flip-flops made a statement.

I stood and stretched, ready to go inside, take a shower, and fall into bed. It had been a long, long day.

As I stepped inside the old house, the door on my left jerked open. Sierra. My neighbor stuck her head through the orange-beaded strings hanging in the doorway. The small, second-generation Japanese-American girl jerked back, a pierced eyebrow darting up.

"What happened to you?"

I touched my frizzy locks with my bandaged hand and wondered what I must look like. "Long story."

Sierra pulled me into her apartment and led me to the rust-colored couch that rested against a brown wall. I melted against the cushions. My entire body cried out for sleep, yet my mind was surprisingly alert. Almost being killed would do that to you.

My head fell back into the cushions as the musky smell of incense soothed my nerves. I normally didn't like the scent and begged Sierra not to light the things when I was over for our weekly gossip sessions, but tonight, the scent covered the odors of smoke and blood that had seeped all the way into my pores.

Sierra plopped down in the seat across from me, leaning in close and wrinkling her nose. "You look like you've been in a war."

I told her about the crazy night I'd survived, leaving out the part about the gun. I needed to keep that quiet in order to not compromise the investigation. I knew that much from watching reruns of *Murder, She Wrote*.

"You could have been killed."

"I know."

"So, what are you going to do about all of your equipment?"

"I guess I'll call the insurance company and see what they tell me. I can still do small jobs, ones that don't require a lot of equipment."

One of Sierra's many cats rubbed against my leg. In the background, whales moaned as one of Sierra's nature CDs played. Weird as it was, it did have a soothing effect—although the soundtrack for *Les Miserables* would have been better.

I glanced at the tiny woman across from me, deciding it was time to change the subject. Don't get me wrong—I wanted to throw out theories and hypothesize what could have happened. I wanted to stick a pencil behind my ear, pull out a notepad, and start talking like a PI, complete with a saxophone droning in the background and cigar smoke filling the room. Here, I'd have to settle for whales and incense, which just wouldn't do.

I cleared my throat. "So, were you waiting up for me?"

My friend's almond eyes lit up. "I had to tell you—we have a new neighbor."

She'd been waiting for weeks for someone to occupy the vacancy. Sierra had become an unofficial social director of the building. She knew everyone's business and even their birthdays. It was slightly suspicious when you considered that she was writing a book called *Stupid People*. Maybe we were all case studies for the animal-loving vegan's latest whim.

"Have you met them yet?" I asked.

"I've only seen him from a distance. He appears normal."

Someone pounded down the wooden stairs of the building. Sierra darted to the window and moved the curtain aside. "There he is."

"He must be a night owl."

Sierra pressed her forehead into the window, twisting her head at an angle that looked extremely uncomfortable.

"What is he doing?" Sierra strained to see the man. "He's just standing in the middle of the parking lot, staring at the sky."

"Maybe he's talking to God or asking the stars for answers to life's pressing questions." Myself, I'd choose the stars over God. I'd long ago given up in believing a loving God controlled this messed-up world.

Growing up, my family had been strictly Christmas and Easter churchgoers. When I say "family," I mean my mother, brother, and me. My father said a certain very hot place would freeze over before he set foot inside a so-called "house of God" again. Funny thing was, my grandfather was a pastor when Dad grew up. He'd died of a heart attack when my father was only eighteen. Dad hadn't gone to church since then.

I think my mother wanted to attend church more faithfully, but my father wore her down about it. That was my mom—worn down. I knew when she was young—before she met my father—she'd been bright-eyed and vibrant. But my memories of her right up until she died three years ago consisted of worn circles beneath her eyes, frizzy red hair pulled into a makeshift bun, and a wardrobe that desperately needed updating. Since she had to work full-time as an administrative assistant and part-time at a grocery store in order to make ends meet, it was no surprise she looked like a poster child for those down on their luck.

So anyway, every holiday she'd dress me up (like Orphan Annie, of course), and we'd go to the services at the Baptist church down the street. I remember asking her about the big cross hanging behind the preacher. She explained to me that a man named Jesus—who was actually God in flesh—had died on one of those. She told me about creation and a flood and the first Christmas. I stored those stories right up there with Santa Claus and the Easter Bunny.

"Our new neighbor appears to be talking to himself." Sierra looked over at me. "What do you think? Mental case?"

"You never know."

"Should we go introduce ourselves?"

My head pounded, and I pushed myself farther into the cushions. "I'm not really in the mood."

"We need to confirm whether or not a psycho is living in our building. This can't wait."

"Sure it can. We already have some very strange people living here. One more won't hurt."

"I'm going with or without you."

My silence caused a sigh to leak from her lips. She turned to me halfway out the door. "Call the police if I'm not back in fifteen minutes."

The door shut.

Great, so I'm sitting around doing nothing while Sierra's being abducted by the oddball in the parking lot.

I forced myself to stand. My bones ached, and I felt twice as old as my twenty-seven years. Pieces of ash fell onto my shoulders like oversized dandruff. I flicked them off and caught a glimpse of myself in the mirror.

I almost screamed when a monster looked back. Then I realized it was me.

Smudges of black dirtied my face, matching the dark circles under my eyes. My hair sprang out like it didn't want to be part of the whole "Gabby" mess.

Shower? Save Sierra? It shouldn't have been so hard to decide.

I had to check on her, but unless the guy had antennae and was loading her in his flying saucer, I was heading for the shower as soon as I knew she was okay. Tonight of all nights, I deserved some peace.

CHAPTER

FIVE

I stepped into the breezy nighttime air, rubbing my sleeve over my face in a last-ditch effort to get rid of any smudges. An exercise in futility if there ever was one.

Across the parking lot, Sierra turned on her heel and charged toward me. Certainly the little pistol wasn't losing her courage. She had more guts than a drunken womanizer.

"I left my fondue pot on," she muttered. "Last time I did that, it caught my tablecloth on fire."

Before I could argue, she whipped past. The door to the building slammed shut. For a minute, I wondered if this was all an elaborate scheme of Sierra's so that I would be the one abducted.

I turned away, but just then, the man glanced over and waved. I didn't see any webbed fingers or extra eyeballs. It wouldn't kill me to say hello. The man would be living across the hall from me, and I didn't want to start off on the wrong foot. I stepped toward him, my brain in evaluation mode.

He was quite a bit taller than my 5′ 4″ frame. Dark hair that needed a trim brushed his ears and neck. His profile was strong but pleasant. Not bad looking for someone from another planet.

He rocked back on his heels. "Hey."

Intelligent blue eyes framed by long lashes greeted me as I got closer. The man had the lean build of a runner and an easy smile that made him seem approachable. Plus, he was wearing a Redskins sweatshirt. He couldn't be that bad.

I fingered my frizzy hair, remembering that a flirty smile from my sooty face would look like I was the center ring at a three-ring freak show.

I settled for, "You must be the new guy."

"That's me."

His eyes grazed my appearance. I forced my shoulders back, determined not to feel inferior for not looking picture perfect. *That had to be the understatement of the year,* I thought with a mental snort. I didn't even look *clean.*

"You must be . . . ," he said.

"Your neighbor across the hall. Gabby St. Claire."

"Riley Thomas." He looked up into a nearby tree. "I was in my apartment, trying to sleep—with the windows open, since my AC is broken—when I heard something squawking outside. I decided to check it out, and it turns out there's a parrot up in that tree."

"A parrot?" A squawk cut into the moment. I looked up at the Bradford pear tree beside me and saw a flash of red and yellow. "How in the world?"

"I'm guessing he's someone's pet that, er, flew the coop."

Sierra must have deemed it safe to come out. The front door slammed, and I saw her bobbing toward us in her typical bouncy fashion. Introductions went around, and as we filled her in on the bird, her eyes zeroed in on the creature.

"I do believe that would be a parrot in a pear tree," she said. "Seen five golden rings lying around anywhere?"

I groaned inwardly, feeling some of the tension leave my shoulders. I had a feeling Riley and Sierra would get along just fine if puns amused them both this much.

Sierra stared up into the leafy branches. I knew the way her mind worked. She was trying to figure out how to rescue the bird.

"I'm going to go get my birdcage," Sierra suddenly said, breaking out of her trance. She pushed her glasses up on her nose like Clark Kent about to transform into Superman. "I'll be right back." She disappeared into the apartment.

Awkward silence had me squirming. What do you say to a stranger while standing in a parking lot in the middle of the night? My brain felt as fried as my hair, and social graces weren't exactly my thing. Luckily, my new neighbor must have taken some Miss Manners classes at some point in life.

"You must have been to a campfire tonight," he started.

Maybe manners weren't his thing after all.

"It depends on how you define *campfire.*" Did a six-thousand-square-foot house count?

Thankfully, Sierra made like Houdini and magically reappeared, cage in hand. I could only imagine what she'd used the barred container for in the past. I'd known her for two years, and she'd never owned a bird.

She marched ahead, going straight for the bird, and gazed up through the branches. "I'll need to climb the tree. Can you guys spot me?"

She didn't wait for our answer. She grabbed hold of a branch and began to climb. Maybe she was part monkey, the way she swung from the limbs so effortlessly. Darwin would be proud. The squawking became louder and more frequent the closer she got, as if the bird was happy to see her.

"Does she do this a lot?" Riley whispered.

I nodded. "She's an animal-right's activist, as in full-time, it's-my-life-mission animal-right's activist."

"Sounds noble."

I smiled, knowing he'd find out soon enough just how noble it was. More like obsessive, in your face, and harebrained. But overall, lovable.

I watched as the bird hopped into the cage and Sierra slammed it shut. She lowered it to Riley and hopped from the tree, landing with a plunk in her fuchsia flip-flops.

That was the one thing Sierra and I had in common—our love of shoes. I was thinking about sending *Guinness* a notice about my flip-flop collection. I had to have one of the biggest on the East Coast, everything from camouflage to sparkles. It was the cheapest of shoe habits, in my opinion. Just $5.95 and I could add another pair to my collection.

Sierra's niece had weaned me from the platform variety. Told me they were out and then proceeded to take five pairs to the Dumpster before I could object. I guess everyone needs someone to keep them up-to-date, fashion-wise. I made sure I hid my toe socks before she saw them, though.

Sierra nodded toward Riley. "Looks like you're going to have a new roommate."

His face registered Sierra's thoughts, and he shook his head, handing the cage back to Sierra. "I'm not really a pet person."

"A bird is not a pet. It's an animal companion. The word pet is so derogatory." Sierra thrust the cage into his hands. "Just keep him until I can find out who the owner is."

"I know nothing about taking care of a bird." There was no whine to Riley's voice, only underlying confidence. "Besides, I wanted to catch the bird so I could sleep, and he was squawking outside my window. Having the bird in my apartment would defeat my goal."

"I have a book in my apartment that will help you out until we find our feathered friend a home." Sierra walked toward the building. "Follow me."

I shrugged at Riley and followed, not up for arguing. I'd stay a few minutes—until he got the bird settled—then head home.

Sierra opened the door to her apartment and pushed aside the beads. We stepped inside and she excused herself, hurrying toward her spare bedroom.

I glanced at Riley, trying to read his expression. He stared at the bandage on my hand. "What happened? That's fresh."

"Accident on the job."

"Are you a firefighter?"

"I almost was one tonight. A building I was working in caught fire. I burned myself getting out." I plopped onto the couch. "The accidental part is still in question."

Riley set the squawking bird on the vinyl dining-room table beside the front door and sat in a chair across from me. "What do you do for a living?"

"I'm a crime-scene cleaner."

"A crime-scene cleaner? Really?"

"It's a thriving business."

He nodded toward my arm. "It doesn't exactly sound dangerous. What happened to your arm, if you don't mind me asking?"

I glanced at the bandage. "I was cleaning up after a homicide when someone set the house on fire."

"A homicide? Sounds grim."

I closed my eyes and saw bits of Gloria Cunningham's skull. "You have no idea."

Before he could ask more questions, Sierra bounced into the room, waving a book in her hands. Hand her some pom-poms, and she could join the cheering squad. "I found it." She handed it to Riley. "All you need to know about taking care of a bird."

He frowned. "And why am I doing this?"

"Because otherwise, what's going to happen to that poor little birdie? They weren't bred to survive out in the wild. That bird has only known a pet shop and domestic living for all of its life."

A cartoonish-sounding cuckoo clock peeped from a distant room. I counted the chirps but came up short. It couldn't possibly be 2:00 AM.

Groaning, I stood from the couch and brushed cat hairs from my jeans. "I'm dead on my feet." I shuddered as I realized how close that had come to being the truth. "I have to get some sleep."

Riley stood behind me. "I have to go, too. I still have to unpack." He glanced at the bird and frowned. "Among other things."

Sierra handed the birdcage to him and added in a sing-song voice, "Thanks for making humanity a little more likable."

I fought a smile at the less-than-thrilled expression on his face. "Anytime."

We started up the stairs side by side. *Talk, Gabby, talk. Now is as good a time as ever to work on your people skills.* I sighed inwardly. Give me a microscope any day.

"So, have you met Mrs. Mystery upstairs in the attic apartment yet?" I asked.

"Mrs. Mystery?"

"Oh, that's not her real name. She writes crime novels, though. Rarely ever leaves her apartment, a real recluse. She's quite a character."

"It sounds like I'm going to have to learn the ropes of this place from you. So far, you're the only sane one I've met."

"And I'm covered in ash, smell like smoke, and clean up after murders."

"My standards of sane are really low."

We stopped at our landing. I took a quick glance at my new neighbor's longish face and decided I could get used to seeing that mug every day. I smiled. "Well, it's been nice to meet you, Riley Thomas. I'm sure we'll be seeing a lot of each other."

He smiled back. It lit up his entire face. It lit up something in me, too.

"I look forward to it," he said.

The bird squawked.

"And you too, Mister . . . ?" I looked from the bird to Riley. "What are you going to name him? You just can't refer to him as 'it.'"

"I think I'll call him Lucky. Because if it wasn't for Sierra, this bird wouldn't be living a pampered life inside my apartment tonight."

I laughed again. "You two have fun now. I'll see you later."

"Good night, Gabby."

Warmth spread through me as he said my name. Yes, I was going to like having Riley Thomas as a neighbor.

CHAPTER

SIX

Nightmares of fire chasing me through a dark, never-ending hallway jerked me awake each time I nodded off throughout the night. I tossed and turned underneath my daisy-print comforter as I relived the flames that nearly claimed my life.

At six o'clock, I gave up on sleep. I forced my legs over the side of the bed, pulled on a fuzzy blue bathrobe, and shuffled into my kitchen. I grabbed a cup of coffee, brewed each morning at 5:45 thanks to a timed coffeemaker, sank into my sand-colored couch, and turned on the morning news.

I took a sip of coffee. I would need at least three cups to get my mind going this morning. At the most, I'd gotten two hours of sleep. I needed eight to function.

A perky news anchor chatted about football and the latest musical to come to Norfolk.

"Come on, get on with the good stories," I mumbled, pulling my legs underneath me. I mean, really. Who wanted to see singing cats? Even I, a musical lover, had my standards.

I hoped there would be an update on the fire. Closing my eyes, I pictured the husband on camera, being taken into custody for the murder of his wife.

Of course, I would get no credit, but I would always know I'd been the one to break the case.

I smiled, fulfilled just to know I'd helped.

"Now we turn to our reporter, Jay Larson, who's at the scene of a late-night fire. Jay, what can you tell us about what happened?"

I turned the volume up. This was more exciting than opening presents on Christmas morning. Of course, Christmas at my house had consisted of fruit and underwear, but nonetheless . . .

"I'm at the home of Michael and the late Gloria Cunningham. You'll remember that three days ago, Gloria was found dead in their home, and husband Michael had a gunshot wound to his knee."

"Yes, yes, we know all this," I mumbled, taking another sip of my black coffee.

"Last night, a neighbor called the police, reporting flames shooting out of the Cunninghams' million-dollar Virginia Beach home. The fire looks like the work of an arsonist."

The camera panned back to the grim-faced news anchor. "Jay, do we know if this has anything to do with the murder trial?"

"I talked to the detective on the case last night, and he assured me that the right person is behind bars, that this was a separate incident."

I sat up straight, nearly spilling my coffee. "What?"

"That's two devastating blows for senatorial candidate Michael Cunningham this week." The news anchor slowly shook his head. "Keep us updated on the case, Jay."

There had to be a mistake. What about the gun? That had to prove something.

I had to talk to the detective.

I scrambled from the couch and threw on some jeans and a T-shirt. I'd slept on my wet hair, and it was hopeless, so I pulled my red locks into a ponytail and rushed out the door.

I stepped into the parking lot and skidded to a stop. Squinting against the already bright sunlight, I looked for something I knew wasn't there. My van. What was I going to drive?

I hurried back inside and knocked on Sierra's door. After waiting a few minutes, I knocked again. Finally, a sleepy-eyed Sierra poked her head between the door and strands of clicking beads.

"I guess you forgot that you kept me awake until two this morning?" she muttered, rubbing her eyes and scowling.

I raised my eyebrows. "*I* kept *you* awake?"

"Yes. Now, how can I help you?"

"I need to use your car."

"I thought you couldn't work because all of your equipment was destroyed."

"I can't, but I have something I need to do." I bit my lip, thinking of another tactic. "Look, I'll help you stuff envelopes for one of your campaigns the next time you need help."

"Let me get my keys."

Twenty minutes later, as I sat in rush-hour traffic on the interstate, I realized I hadn't called Harold about work today. He would be headed out to the Cunninghams' house, expecting to pick up where he left off yesterday. I grabbed my cell phone and dialed his number. His wife answered.

"He's on his way to work now, Gabby."

I bit my lip. "Did he take his cell phone with him?"

"No, I have it with me today. Everything okay?"

"Our crime scene burned down last night. I hate for him to drive all the way out there for nothing." I glanced at the clock and saw it was 7:30. I would have to stop by to talk to the detective later. "I'm on my way there now. Thanks, Mildred."

I hit *end* on my cell phone and tossed it on the seat beside me. I mulled over all the new information I had learned, trying to decipher the good from the bad.

Maybe there was a good reason for the news report this morning, I thought. It could be a ruse. Maybe they had to examine the gun first. Maybe they didn't want to rouse suspicion yet. The evidence seemed pretty cut and dried to me, though.

I didn't want to be a know-it-all. I really didn't. My best friend in college had been one, which drove me crazy, especially considering I knew more than she did. Some people were just so clueless. But know-it-all or not, I wasn't going to back down on this one.

Finally, my exit appeared, and I veered off the road. The rest of the drive was mostly back roads into a residential area where the city's most wealthy lived. Early morning sunlight filtered through oak and pine trees in the wooded neighborhood, casting dancing shadows on the well-manicured lawns.

As I pulled up to the driveway, I spotted Harold standing in front of the black skeleton of a house. In the daylight, it reminded me even more of the dinosaur exhibits I'd seen at the Smithsonian as an elementary-school student years ago.

Harold stared at it the same way I had stared at those prehistoric bones—with shock, curiosity, and mourning. He shook his head. The sight would be sure to surprise anyone coming into the situation. The beautiful mansion had been reduced to bare bones and ashes.

Wasting no more time, I hopped out of the car. The ground was still damp from the efforts to extinguish the flames last night, and my flip-flop feet sloshed as I hurried to my assistant.

I laid a hand on his thick arm, but Harold didn't look at me. The house seemed to entrance him.

"I'm sorry I forgot to call," I said.

He shook his head again. "When did this happen?"

"Last night."

"Were you still here?"

I shrugged, swatting at a bee buzzing in my ear. "Yeah, but I'm fine. I got out okay."

"You could have been killed, Gabby," he said with the sternness of a father.

I offered Harold a reassuring smile. "But I wasn't. I'm fine, except for a little burn on my hand and arm."

His gaze darted to my bandage. "I never should have left."

"No one could have known."

He stared through the skeleton at the shell of my van. "All of your equipment is gone?"

I nodded and wiped my brow with the back of my hand. The sun was already sweltering, and it wasn't even noon yet. Between the heat and the bee, I had the feeling it was going to be one miserable day. September in Virginia wasn't supposed to be like this.

"It's such a shame," Harold muttered. "Especially considering all that poor man has already been through."

Yeah, murdering your wife must be really stressful, I thought. *And he's probably the one who set the house on fire.* I kept my mouth closed. There was no need to stir up trouble.

Yet.

"I'm going to go look at the backside of the house. Need to pay my respects." Harold excused himself and crept toward the back yard. He kept his chin high, but I knew time was taking its toll on him. My heart pounded with sadness. Was this all there is? You live, you get old, you die. Science calls it the cycle of life. I call it depressing.

I let him have his time alone to process what had happened. We'd poured a lot of work into this house, and the damage was devastating. I'd also been counting on this paycheck to knock out some bills, not to mention to pay Harold. Now I'd have to dig into my meager savings.

"I can't believe someone burned the house down," someone with a high-pitched voice said. "It's such a shame."

I turned and spotted a middle-aged woman wearing black shorts, high heels, and a hot-pink top that emphasized her abnormally large chest. She was walking up the driveway, and as she got closer, I saw that her eyes looked red and puffy.

"It is a shame," I agreed. A quick glance behind me showed no other cars parked in the area. This woman had to be a neighbor.

"Are you with the police department?" The woman swept a platinum-blond hair out of her eye and glanced at me.

"No." A deep sigh heaved my chest.

"It was such a beautiful house. Just like Gloria. She was so beautiful. It's hard to believe she's gone." The neighbor shook her head and stared into the distance.

"This must be very hard on you."

"You just never think it will happen to someone you know. It should be someone else." The woman waved her hand in the air. The bee had taken notice of the woman's overbearing perfume and was bothering her now. She ducked, trying to avoid the kamikaze insect. I zoomed in on her swollen lips. Had a bee already stung her? By all appearances, yes. But my acute deductions told me it was more likely collagen injections. "At least Michael is finally out of the hospital."

I nodded, still watching the woman's impromptu dance with amusement. "Right."

I froze in mid-nod. What did she just say?

I jerked my head toward the woman. If Michael was out of the hospital, then he could have set the house on fire. He could be the arsonist. And he had motive, too. He could have been trying to destroy the evidence that would nail him.

Careful, Gabby. Stay calm. Don't scare her off.

Relaxing my shoulders, I asked, "He is? Already? I just assumed he'd be in the hospital for longer."

The woman nodded. "I did, too, but I saw him over here last night just a few minutes before the fire started. I assumed he stopped by to pick up a few things before going to stay at his mother's. It's a good thing he left when he did."

"Isn't it, though?" I shifted my weight and restrategized. "So, you're sure you saw Michael?"

"Positive. He was even on crutches, the poor guy. I almost said something to him, but I figured he didn't want to be bothered. The press won't leave him alone. They keep asking what he'll do about his campaign. Can't they give the man a break?"

I nodded and attempted a sweet, comforting smile.

He'd come back to get the gun but found me and Harold there. Had he known I was still inside? Was he in such a hurry to set the fire and destroy the evidence that he'd decided not to wait, even if it meant claiming another life?

This man needed to be behind bars.

I had to find Detective Parker and tell him.

"If you'll excuse me, I've got to run." I jangled my keys and started a slow jog to the car, barely giving notice to the woman as she fluttered her fingers.

Just as I started Sierra's car, Harold came around the corner. He approached my window in long strides, concern etched in the lines on his face.

I lowered the glass. "Harold, I remembered something I have to do. I'll call you later, okay?"

He raised an eyebrow. "Okay. Don't get yourself into any trouble, missy."

I grinned. "Never."

The car rumbled down the driveway and continued rumbling until I pulled up to the police station. I charged into the building and tapped my finger on the counter while the receptionist talked on the phone.

The attractive, overweight young woman pulled the phone away from her ear and sneered. "Can I help you?"

"I need to see Detective Parker. It's important."

She looked me over. "Is he expecting you?"

"If he's smart."

The woman raised her overplucked eyebrows and turned back to the phone. "I need to put you on hold. One minute."

Her gaze flickered back to me, and I could have been certain she was sizing me up like an ex-boyfriend's prom date. It almost made me wish I'd worn something other than my "I Love Carbs" T-shirt.

"What's your name?"

"Gabby St. Claire."

She gave me another once-over before dialing an extension. "Detective, there's a Gabby St. Claire here to see you. Says if you're smart, you'll be expecting her." The woman pulled the phone from her ear and smirked. "He says go on back. Second door on the left."

Honesty prevented me from saying *thank you*. I walked to his office, the rubber bottoms of my black flip-flops barely making a sound against the linoleum floor.

I pictured Parker's reaction when I told him what I had found out.

"You really will make a great forensic scientist one day, Gabby," he'll say, admiration shining in his eyes.

"It's all in a day's work." I blow on my fingertips and rub them against my shirt in false modesty.

"I'm hoping you and I will be seeing more of each other, and not just on a professional level." His voice is low and husky, and his eyes are smoldering.

"Why, Detective Parker, it looks like we have a relationship to investigate. Care to join me?"

I came to his door and started to knock, but before my fist connected with the wood, it opened. The detective stared at me. His gaze wasn't especially friendly, but it wasn't hostile, either.

Or was it?

I had a feeling my vision of how this meeting would play out was closer to a delusion than reality.

"Come in," Parker said, his back to me as he walked to the desk. He plopped into a beat-up swivel chair, complete with duct tape across the top. He looked at me with so much skepticism that I felt like a conspiracy theorist for a moment. "What can I help you with, Ms. St. Claire?"

I stood in the doorway, contemplating what approach I should take. Coming on too strong would irritate him. Being too nice would make me easy to ignore. *Middle of the road, Gabby. Middle of the road.* "Did you find out anything about the gun?"

"It's being tested now."

"So you haven't confirmed it's the murder weapon?"

"Not yet."

The middle of the road was getting me nowhere. I needed to zip into the fast lane. "On the news they said that the suspect is behind bars. This gun makes it clear that there could be another suspect, that the wrong person may have been arrested."

"We won't know anything until we test the gun."

I pushed away from the doorway and lowered myself into the driver's seat—er, chair—in front of Parker. I still had my trump card to play. I put my mouth in gear and charged full speed ahead.

"I learned something that shines new light on the case."

An eyebrow quirked. "Did you?"

"A witness places Mr. Cunningham at the scene of the crime right before the fire started last night. Our political superstar in the making set the fire in order to conceal the evidence."

Detective Parker leaned forward and sighed. "Ms. St. Claire, Mr. Cunningham was in the hospital last night. He's not being discharged until this afternoon."

CHAPTER
SEVEN

"What?" The neighbor said she saw Cunningham. He was a guilty man. No questions. No doubts.

No evidence to prove it.

He waved a folder. "I have the paperwork to prove it."

"That's not possible."

The detective nodded curtly. "You heard me correctly—Michael Cunningham is a victim here, plain and simple. Don't try to twist it any other way."

"But—"

"No buts, Ms. St. Claire. Just let us do our job, and you . . . you go clean houses. There's no need of you worrying over this."

"But Detective—"

"Trust that the evidence is being handled by professionals, and let it go. We've got it from here." He rose and drew in a deep breath. His gaze tried to put me in my place, which was no easy task. "Thank you for your help and concern. I'll let you see yourself out."

I opened my mouth but found myself speechless for one of the first times in my life. The next thing I knew, I was on the sidewalk, staring at the one-story red brick building.

What just happened?

I turned around, about to march back inside, but dropped my hand from the doorknob. I needed time to think this over. I needed to talk things through with someone else.

But who?

Not Harold. He'd only worry. Not Sierra. She'd find a way to turn it into a save-the-animals campaign. My dad wasn't an option. He had his own problems.

I drew in a deep breath and resigned myself to ponder it. With one last glance at the police station, I went back to the car.

I parked in the lot of my apartment building, got out, and slammed the car door, channeling my frustration by abusing Sierra's innocent car. I was too upset to go home. Instead, I hurried across the street to the Grounds, my favorite coffeehouse and hangout. The converted old Victorian housed a coffeehouse on the first floor and an Internet café and apartment upstairs. It was a hodgepodge of tables and chairs, accented by brightly colored walls with abstract art slashing through them. On Friday and Saturday evenings, acoustic music filled the shop, and on Tuesdays, poetry readings.

I walked into the dimly lit structure, immediately surrounded by the rich smell of Columbian coffee and the quiet rumble of chatting java addicts munching on Italian biscotti and French pastries. Latin music drifted through the overhead, and Swedish oak chairs scratched across the rust-colored German wood floor. It made me proud to be an American.

Sometimes, when crime was low and everyone else in the city rejoiced—as they should—I had to drag my dejected, out-of-work self here to slave away for some extra money. The owner, Sharon, was a sweetheart and more than willing to let me work odd shifts. I think more than anything, she liked to hear my on-the-job stories. But if she wanted to pay me minimum wage to rehash my days, then so be it. As long as I could keep my apartment.

I paused in the doorway and allowed the scents and sounds to ease into my lungs, to curl into my tense muscles. Coming here always made me feel better. Then I spotted Riley, sitting at an old farm table in the corner, and felt better yet. He was reading the paper and sipping from a steaming, bright yellow mug.

I watched him a minute. He looked so astute, almost aristocratic, the way he sat casually at the table, slowly bringing his steaming mug to his lips while reading the newspaper. All he needed was to raise his pinky finger, and I'd have been sold.

For a minute I pictured him doing this every morning. The thought warmed my heart in ways it shouldn't, yet the image seemed so normal, so peaceful. Riley did something to my heart—and my imagination—that frightened and compelled me.

With a quick wave to pink-haired Sharon behind the counter, I walked across the wooden floor. Without invitation, I plopped into the chair across from Riley. I was looking for a distraction, and I'd found a very nice-looking one.

Riley looked up and stared at me a moment. "Gabby." His blue eyes made me catch my breath. No man should have eyes that gorgeous, framed by lashes that long. I had to apply tubes of mascara to make mine visible. "I almost didn't recognize you without the soot."

Ah, wonderful. Those first impressions that you never have a second chance to make. "Believe it or not, I don't always look like a case study for the loony bin."

He grinned, showing perfect white teeth. How does someone with an obvious affection for coffee keep his teeth that white?

"I didn't think that at all." He reached for his mug and took a sip. "So, how are you today?"

Such a simple question. Up until twenty-four hours ago, the answer would have been easy. My biggest concern had been coming up with a catchy jingle. Now the sleuth in me itched to get out.

I'd always had a penchant for mysteries, starting in seventh grade, when I deduced that old lady Jones across the street had sneaked a dead body from her house under the guise of a rolled carpet. I decided to keep an eye on her and quickly discovered she had a habit of cleaning in the nude. I concluded that spying was better left to the professionals.

I'd moved on to tracking down who had taken a picture of bottle-cap-glasses Suzy picking her nose in the girls' bathroom at school. Sure I'd been kicked out of school for a week when I punched head cheer-leader Amy Murphy in the eye upon discovering she was the culprit, but it had been worth it. I'd solved my first crime.

I'd wanted anything to distract me from my dysfunctional home life—science experiments, who-done-it capers, and most recently, musicals. Who didn't love a happy ending? I sure hadn't had one yet, but deep inside I hoped one day the tables would turn.

Riley waited for an answer to his simple question, so I stuffed my thoughts to the side and blurted out the truth.

"I'm lousy. How about you?"

"Lousy? What's wrong?"

"Don't get me started." I waved my hands to ward off his questions, noting as they fluttered in and out of my gaze that I desperately needed a manicure. I decided that before returning home, I should buy some of those teeth-whitening strips and some mascara. Riley was putting me to shame. "Let's talk about something else. How's your feathered friend?"

Half his lip pulled up in a disgruntled, but good-natured smile. "Demanding. Every time I cook something, he squawks until he gets a piece of it. That bird can down steak, cheese, vegetables, anything."

"Didn't you just bring him home at 2:00 this morning? That's a lot of cooking for less than twenty-four hours."

"I was awake last night and needed something to eat. Then I fixed breakfast this morning and had an afternoon snack."

"Any word on your AC?"

"This weekend."

I noted the glaring sun bearing down on the pavement outside. "Bummer."

He set his newspaper aside and leaned forward, his eyes warm and friendly, reminding me of a sparkling swimming pool on a warm sum-mer day. "So, why have you had a lousy day?"

I leaned back and stared at the painting of a woman hugging her guitar as I contemplated my answer. "Work stuff."

"Find a stain you couldn't get out?"

I rolled my eyes. "If only Mr. Clean and I could fix this mess."

Riley's brows shot up, and I could see true concern on his face. "Need to talk about it?"

I drew in a deep breath. Oh man, were those magic words. "The detective on the case dismissed some evidence I found while cleaning up after a crime."

"Are you sure it was evidence?"

I caught his gaze. "I'm positive. If you saw this evidence, you'd know it, too."

"Why did he dismiss it?"

"I have no idea." My jaw clenched thinking about Detective Parker's arrogance. "It makes it so clear to me that the wrong person has been framed. This morning, I even found a witness to confirm my theory."

"Did you tell the detective?"

"Of course I told the detective." I slapped the table, and Riley's coffee cup jumped. "I might as well hand the guy a video of the murder being committed."

Riley ducked, and I realized I'd raised my voice.

"Sorry. You didn't deserve that. I'm mad at Detective Parker, and I'm biting your head off. Not fair."

Riley pulled his hands in front of his neck. "Okay, as long as my head's safe from your teeth, go on with your story."

That wrung a little laugh out of me, but I was too annoyed to stay amused. "He didn't care. Said it couldn't be true, that I should let him do his job, and I should do mine."

Riley leaned forward, resting on his folded, muscular arms. "Sounds like you have some decisions to make."

I sighed. "I know. That's the problem. I have no idea what to do."

"Give it time, and you'll know."

"I don't know if I can. Time is crucial in police work. If I let this slide, an innocent man could end up being charged with murder. He's already sitting in a cell."

Riley nodded. "You're right. Mr. Clean isn't of much use with this one."

I wished I could talk to him more, share all the details of what had happened. I couldn't, though. I barely knew the man, though I did hope that might change.

I cleared my throat. "Enough about me. How about you? What do you do for a living?"

Riley's lips pulled into a tight line, and he looked toward the front door as if he wanted to run outside. I'd always been good at blurting out just the wrong questions, and today apparently was no exception.

"I'm in between jobs right now."

I didn't ask. I didn't want to know. It was too much like my childhood. My father was constantly between jobs. My theory was that if he'd hunted for work the way he hunted for whiskey, he'd have been CEO of Goldman Sachs. His only disability was laziness.

We both glanced out the window at the same time and saw Sierra, a bag in hand, collecting something from the grass by our apartment building. Only too glad to abandon thoughts of dear old dad, I stared at Sierra.

"What is she doing?" I asked.

"I wish she was looking for Lucky's owner, but I'm thinking no. Maybe she's collecting litter."

"Care to go find out?" I asked.

He nodded toward the bare table in front of me. "Aren't you going to get coffee?"

I realized I hadn't ordered. I glanced behind me at the menu on the wall and shook my head, even though an iced mocha tempted me. "I think I've soaked up enough caffeine just from breathing the fumes. I'll pass today."

Our chairs scraped across the floor, and we headed outside toward Sierra. She used the sleeve of her white shirt to wipe the sweat glistening at her forehead as she scooped up an acorn from the weed-infested grass beside our building. Her glossy black hair was tied off her face with a rubber band, and it bounced as she glanced up and spotted us.

She wiped her brow again. "What's going on?"

"Just seeing what you're doing." I noted the bagful she'd already collected.

"A new project. Nothing exciting." Sierra looked at Riley. "How's the bird?"

"Fine."

She shifted her bag and placed her hands on her narrow hips. The skinny animal lover could eat what she wanted—no meat, of course—and never gain a pound. "You guys want to come over for some brownies tonight?"

We agreed.

"Bill is coming too." Sierra looked at Riley. "He's the radio talk-show host across the hall from me."

"I'd like to meet more of the neighbors," Riley said. "Any chance Bill wants a pet parrot?"

Sierra laughed, shook her head, then continued collecting nuts.

Riley and I walked into the building and paused at the stairs. "I guess I should finish unpacking," Riley started.

"Moving isn't fun. That's why I've vowed to stay in this apartment for as long as I can."

He sent me that disarming grin of his and leaned against the banister. I couldn't figure him out. One minute he seemed so high class, the next like the all-American boy grown up. He obviously wasn't in a hurry to get back to work.

Free spirits rarely were.

"I hope to stay here for a while, too," he said.

I followed his gaze as he glanced around the stairway, which badly needed a paint job. Various scrapes and smudges dirtied the wall. The house was kind of like its residents—eccentric, wounded, and toting lots of baggage.

Then again, who wasn't like this house once you really got to know them?

Some of what I was thinking must have shown on my face, because Riley furrowed his brow and asked, "What's that look for?"

"Just thinking about this house."

I looked around at the dark wood molding that added depth to the walls and imagined the place in its heyday. "I bet she was beautiful at one time."

"She still is a beauty. She's got character, you know? Not many places do anymore."

A man that appreciated character. What more could I ask for? "Character's a good thing."

Our eyes connected.

Riley smiled. "Absolutely."

Our gaze only held for a few seconds; then Riley looked away. "Well, I guess I should get to work. I keep putting it off, though I'm not sure why. It might have something to do with heat and that noisy bird."

We walked upstairs together. The silence stretched, and I dived into that old standby, talking about the weather. "Days don't get much hotter than this. What did the weatherman say it was outside? Almost 100 degrees?"

"That's one thing I miss about San Diego, where I moved from—it was perfect weather year round."

"Sounds nice."

"It was." He glanced at me. I only noticed because I was glancing at him. "But Norfolk is nice, too."

We reached the landing and faced each other. Before either of us could speak, a squawk cut through the air. We burst into laughter. Running into Riley had been a good thing. I already felt better.

"Your roommate is calling." I pushed a curl that had escaped from my ponytail behind my ear.

"I don't want to keep His Majesty waiting." Riley gave me one of those captivating glances again, one that beckoned me to look back. "Have a good day, Gabby."

I nodded and disappeared inside my apartment. Riley seemed like a good neighbor—friendly, warm, a good conversationalist. I pictured him traveling all over the U.S., having no place to call home and liking it that way.

That's how my dad had been before Mom "captured his heart," as he said. He'd been a professional surfer until a back injury grounded him. Then I was born, and he'd tried to settle into the whole daddy-husband routine. He'd probably started drinking to help forget his responsibilities.

My mind jumped back to the fire, the gun. The amateur detective in me itched to get out, to learn about the investigation. I paced and twiddled my thumbs, trying to distract my thoughts. It didn't work.

Keep busy, Gabby. Keep busy.

I called the insurance company, which took all of forty-five minutes—most of it spent on hold listening to Barry Manilow songs. Afterward, I arranged to have my van towed to a garage and placed a rush order for some new equipment, all of which would go to my charge card until insurance kicked in. Yuck.

I couldn't think about that. Not having a consistent income wasn't good for the budget, but I wasn't complaining. Instead, I started to ponder jingles. But my heart wasn't in it, and even humming music from *Annie* couldn't distract me.

I decided to wash dishes. I plunked a plate with hardened cheese from leftover pizza into the soapy water. Thoughts of the gun wandered back into my mind. I knew I was on to something. Why couldn't the detective see the evidence right before his eyes?

I shook my head, willing the thoughts to go away. I noticed I'd been washing the same dish for about ten minutes and decided I had to do something before I drove myself crazy. My apartment sparkled. I couldn't work most jobs until the gear I'd ordered came. I didn't want to help Sierra pick up nuts in the blazing sun. Before I could reason myself out of it, I charged across the hall and knocked on Riley's door. The door opened to reveal his dust-smudged face.

"Long time, no see." He wiped at the spot but only made it worse.

"I decided maybe I should be neighborly and help you unpack."

"That's nice of you."

I shrugged. "Not really. I just need something to keep my mind occupied."

He pulled the door open farther. "Then by all means, come in."

For the next three hours, I helped him fill a bookcase with hardbound volumes of many of my favorite books. We moved on to the kitchen and unpacked plates and silverware and dishcloths. We made small talk as we worked, chatting about everything from TV shows to favorite CDs.

Halfway through the last box of kitchen stuff, my cell phone rang. I snapped it from the clip on my belt and brought it to my ear.

"Gabby St. Claire."

A sniffle turned into a sob on the other end. My shoulders tensed. It wasn't unusual that I turned into an unofficial counselor for victims' families. "Hello?"

"Gabby, this is . . . Mildred."

Harold's wife. Had something happened to Harold? Several scenarios raced through my mind. Harold in an accident. Harold with a heart attack. Maybe one of his grandchildren had been hurt.

"What happened, Mildred?" I abandoned the half-empty box and walked into the next room.

"They've arrested Harold." A sob echoed on the phone line.

Whatever could dear, sweet Harold have been arrested for?

"Where are you, Mildred?"

"I'm at the police station. Oh, Gabby. They're saying he burned down that house you two were working in. Come quickly."

CHAPTER

EIGHT

"I'll be right there." I hung up the phone and started toward the door. I had to set the police straight. There wasn't any time to waste.

I started toward the door, but a firm hand on my shoulder halted me. Riley.

"What happened?" I glanced back and saw concern etched into the lines around his eyes.

"I have to get to the police station." I lunged forward. As I tripped, Riley's hand grabbed my elbow, steadying me. Something rippled throughout my entire body, making me temporarily forget the situation at hand.

I shook my head to clear it. Harold. Dear, sweet Harold. "My employee has just been arrested."

Riley grabbed some keys from a hook by the door and followed me. "I'll drive you."

"You don't have to do that."

"You're in no state to drive. Besides, if I remember correctly, you don't have a vehicle."

I couldn't argue with that.

We thundered down the stairs. At the door, Riley placed his hand on my back, directing me toward an older-model sedan. He opened the door, and I slid inside.

"Which police station?"

I gave him directions, but my mind was elsewhere. Why in the world would they think Harold burned down the crime scene? It just didn't make sense. It had to be a mistake.

Poor Mildred. She must be beside herself.

There was no way Harold would have set that house on fire, especially with me still inside.

The idea was absurd.

It didn't make sense.

I fanned myself against the thick humidity of the car. Riley put his hand over the vent as warm air blew out.

"The AC's been acting up. It takes a while to cool off."

"It's fine." I continued fanning my face. Cold air was the least of my concerns.

The wheels turned against the road. A motorcycle revved past, weaving in and out of traffic. A fire truck squealed two lanes over. The air conditioning finally began to add its chill to the car.

We pulled off the interstate and, two traffic lights later, turned into the parking lot. Before Riley cut the engine, I jumped from the car.

Inside, Mildred sat on a bench, her eyes red and puffy. She stood when I came into sight, and we embraced.

I lowered my friend back into her seat and grasped her hand. "What happened, Mildred?"

She dabbed her eyes. "They just came over and arrested him. Said he burned down that house and would be charged with attempted murder." Her water-rimmed eyes met mine. "Gabby, you know he loves you like a daughter. He'd never try to hurt you."

"I know." I patted her hand. Harold had all the qualities I'd always wanted in a father—honesty, a good work ethic, a genuine smile. Most importantly, he seemed to truly care about me. "I just can't figure out why they would think he's guilty. It doesn't make sense."

Another sniffle. "It happened a long time ago, Gabby."

I mentally heard the record screech to a halt. "What happened a long time ago?"

"The arson."

"What arson?"

"Oh, Gabby. Harold was arrested twenty years ago for burning down a church. He pleaded guilty and served his time."

I pulled back slightly. "That would have been helpful to know when I hired him."

"It's so hard to get a job with a criminal record. Everyone thinks the worst of him. He just wanted a chance, Gabby."

"Mildred, I would have hired him with a criminal record. You know I love Harold."

"He didn't do this, Gabby. He didn't do it." Sobs wracked the woman's body, and I hung an arm around her shoulders, trying to find the right words.

"We'll figure out a way to prove he's innocent, Mildred." I tried to soothe her, though I could hear my pitch going high. "I don't know how, but we will."

"The police can't hold him without probable cause."

I jerked my gaze to Riley, who stood at a distance. I'd nearly forgotten he'd driven me here until he spoke up.

"Probable cause?" Mildred asked, dabbing the corner of her eyes again with a rumpled tissue.

Riley stepped closer. "Probable cause is a fact or circumstance sufficient to justify thinking someone has committed a crime. Past crimes themselves aren't enough. There needs to be evidence that will connect them with a current crime."

"There's evidence of Harold all over the crime scene. We were working there all day." I thought of how Harold worked downstairs by himself for most of the day. He would have had plenty of opportunity to stick a few things in his car. I admit trust isn't something I give out easily. But I had to give Harold the benefit of the doubt. "What there isn't, is motive. Why would Harold do something like this?"

"What was his motive for the arson he was arrested for?" Riley asked.

"It was part of a robbery, only Harold didn't know that going in. He got mixed up with the wrong crowd, and before he knew it, they'd poured gasoline all over the church and lit it on fire."

"What was he charged with?" Riley asked.

"Being an accessory to a crime."

My shoulders wanted to slump, but I refused to give in to despair. "Where's Harold now?"

"Being interrogated. Has been for the past two hours. He was close to tears the last time I saw him." A new round of sobs began. I patted Mildred's back, trying in vain to comfort her. My gaze met Riley's, and I could tell he wanted to help. But what was there to do?

"There's a good chance they won't be able to hold him." Riley sat down on the other side of Mildred. "As long as he's being cooperative and they don't find evidence of anything stolen from the property in your possession, they've got nothing. They're probably just covering all the bases."

Or trying to pin this on someone. I'd already seen firsthand that Detective "Pitt" was capable of that.

"I hope so. I need him at home to help me take care of Keisha and Donovan. I'm too old to raise those grandkids alone. I'm just too old for all of this." Mildred suddenly sat up straighter. "The grandkids. How could I have forgotten? They're supposed to be home from school any minute."

"We can go meet them." I met Riley's gaze. He nodded slightly, letting me know it was okay.

"Are you sure?" Mildred asked.

"Positive." I rose. "We'll take good care of them. I promise."

With one more hug, we started to the car.

"I feel horrible leaving her alone at a time like this," I whispered.

Riley pushed the door open, and it felt like opening an oven. Waves of heat washed over us. "I would have offered to pick them up myself, but I didn't think that would go over well."

"I just hope they release Harold soon and realize this was all one big mistake."

Riley opened the car door, and I slid inside. My gaze roamed the interior. A straw wrapper stuck up between the seat and console. Dried grass wove its way into the floor mats. It seemed like Riley: simple, down-to-earth, attractive.

"You okay?" Riley asked, waiting in the driver's seat.

"I just can't believe this. It seems like a bad dream."

Riley waited a moment and then cranked the engine. It gently hummed as we pulled away from the station, leaving Harold in the hands of one of the most ignorant people I'd ever encountered—Detective Parker. I'd call Sierra later and see if she wanted to interview him for her *Stupid People* book.

"Are you pretty close with Harold?" Riley asked.

"He used to be a janitor, but he retired and wanted to do something to make a few bucks. I hired him after our first interview. He just seemed like such a gentle and kind man."

"Things will work out, Gabby. Even though it might not look like it now, they will."

"Thanks for the reassurance." I leaned the crown of my head against the cool window. "How do you know so much about police procedures? You sounded like an old pro in there."

"Just things I picked up here and there."

I didn't ask more questions, though my gut told me more details existed to the story.

I directed Riley into an older, rundown subdivision. A few turns later, he pulled the car up to a small, well-maintained brick house with bright blue shutters and colorful mums dotting the flowerbed.

It reminded me of my house growing up. Dad sold it when Mom died, and he moved into a trailer. He said he couldn't maintain the property. I believed him—he couldn't even maintain his shaving routine. Of course, he'd always gone for that beach-bum look. I always told him the look was a total wipeout and it didn't send good vibrations.

Riley and I climbed out of his car and sat on the porch to wait for the bus.

"So, I've been wondering—what made you decide to be a crime-scene cleaner?" Riley asked, his elbows resting atop his knees. Those eyes turned all their attention on me. He really should be an eye model, if such a thing exists.

I turned and leaned against the post beside me. The thick heat covered me like a sweater. Should I tell him or not? The last thing I wanted was anyone feeling sorry for me. But those eyes beckoned my trust.

"You want the long version or the short one?" I finally said.

"Whichever one you're willing to give me."

I drew in a deep breath. "I went to college to be a forensic specialist, but my last semester, I had to quit. My mother passed away, and my father couldn't support himself. There was just too much going on to go back to college. It seemed like every time I planned on it, something else happened. I had to come up with a plan . . . so here I am. A college dropout but a proud business owner."

"What did your dad say? He didn't care that you dropped out of college?"

I snorted. "All my dad's ever cared about is himself, believe me. I didn't grow up in a *Leave-It-to-Beaver* household. It was closer to *The Osbournes.*"

"Sounds tough."

"Yeah, it was. But I needed to make some money, and I wanted to do something that would keep me close to my career goals. I remembered hearing about crime-scene cleaners and decided to see if there were any in the area I could work for. There weren't."

"So you went into business for yourself?"

"I sure did. It's not an easy job, but it just makes me feel like I didn't give up everything, you know? Of course, half of my equipment is now ashes, and my only employee might go to jail." I sighed at the irony of it all. Maybe Dad was right and life was a beach.

"It will all work out, Gabby."

"I know it will. But it's still hard, you know?"

His gaze warmed me. "I do know."

I felt him studying my face. Only I didn't feel uncomfortable. There was something different about Riley. He seemed to truly care about the situation. How weird was that? He barely knew me, yet he'd gone out of his way to help. Maybe he was too good to be true. Maybe he really *was* an alien.

"Have you ever thought about taking any classes locally to finish your degree?"

If only he realized there wasn't a simple answer to that question. "I've thought about it. They say once you quit college, it's hard to ever go back. I can barely make ends meet as it is. And I basically have to be on call any time of the day or night. If I'm not, I might lose a job, and I can't afford that."

The roar of the bus coming down the road jarred us from our serious conversation. The gears ground until the yellow vehicle stopped and a set of elementary-aged twins ran to the front porch. They slowed down when they spotted me and Riley.

"Hey, guys! How are you?" I stood and plastered on my best smile.

"Hi, Aunt Gabby. Where's Nana?" Keisha asked. The girl faltered. Her wide, perceptive eyes soaked in Riley, and then her gaze turned to me. The emotions I saw there nearly broke my heart. Since my own childhood had been so screwed up, nothing pained me more than to see a child lose the innocence of youth. The kids had already been abandoned by their father, and their mother had died in a car crash before the twins turned one. They didn't need this.

I saw it on my job often enough—when someone's dad or brother or uncle died. The image of young, tear-brimmed eyes and trembling chins always got to me. As much as I tried to forget about it, I knew it was because I'd been that child not so long ago. I'd been the one wondering why my brother was gone and when he'd come back.

I softened my voice. "Nana had something come up at the last minute. She asked if my friend Riley and I would meet you. Is that okay?"

Keisha nodded.

"You mean we don't have to work on our homework now?" Donovan's brown eyes lit up, and his book bag slid from his shoulder.

"Nope, we're making an exception today." I touched the little guy's head, as he pulled his arm back and muttered, "Yes."

The next hour, we played ring-around-the-rosy and "London Bridge Is Falling Down," and gave the two kindergartners twirls around the yard. The wrinkles of worry finally disappeared from Keisha's forehead, and both of the children giggled with each new game.

After a couple of hours, I took a break and perched on the steps. My heart thudded with sadness as I realized what these children might face in the coming months. I closed my eyes and tried to erase the mental picture.

Someone plopped down beside me. I opened my eyes and spotted Riley leaning back on his palms, sweat trickling down his face. My gaze traveled to Keisha and Donovan as they chased each other around the yard, the sound of their laughter filling the air in a beautiful music.

"Praying?" Riley asked, his gaze catching mine.

A laugh caught in my throat. "No, I don't waste my time with that anymore."

"I'm sorry you think it's a waste of time."

"You don't?"

"I know it's not."

I wondered why he was so sure. He seemed smart—not the type to fall for the hocus pocus of religion. I couldn't see Riley passing around a snake or giving all his money to some kook who promised to heal the sick on national TV. Before I could ask any questions, a familiar, beat-up Oldsmobile pulled into the driveway. I held my breath. Keisha and Donovan paused as if sensing something was wrong. When I spotted two heads in the car, my shoulders relaxed.

They'd allowed Harold to come home.

Keisha and Donovan ran to the car and jumped into their grandparents' arms while Riley and I stood at a distance. I wanted to throw my arms around Harold, too, but didn't want the kids to get suspicious about the unusual display of affection.

Harold's eyes met mine as he approached on the cracked sidewalk. They were full of emotions that Harold usually concealed so well. My throat burned.

I patted his arm and whispered, "Good to see you."

"Let's sit on the porch, Gabby. Mildred's going to go inside with the kids so we can chat."

His tortured gaze shifted behind me, and I realized I hadn't introduced Riley yet. "Oh, Harold, this is my neighbor Riley. Riley, Harold."

The two men shook hands. After the front door slammed, quiet fell over the outside. Harold plopped into a wooden rocker, and I took the other one. Riley leaned against a post.

"What did they say?" I swallowed, bracing myself for whatever the news.

"I guess they didn't have enough to hold me, but I'm not off the hook yet. They're searching for anything they can find to frame me for this." His wide, watery eyes met mine. "I don't want to go back to jail, Gabby." He reached for his temples and lowered his head in despair. "I don't want to go back to jail."

CHAPTER
NINE

I cleared my throat, trying to hold myself together. I grabbed Harold's sweaty, thick hand. "Harold, why didn't you tell me that you had a jail record?"

He raised his head, but that pained expression remained. "I didn't think it was important. I was with the wrong people at the wrong time. I figured it would only work against me to tell you, especially since I didn't do anything except have a lapse in judgment."

Riley crossed his arms, his forehead wrinkled. "What did the police say?"

Harold's shoulders stooped. "They said for me not to leave the city, that they may need to talk to me again."

"They say anything about motive? About why they think you'd do something like this?" Riley continued.

Riley's stance was casual, but his voice said otherwise. He seemed interested in Harold's fate for some reason unknown to me.

"They claim maybe I stole things from the house and burned it to conceal the evidence." He shook his head. "Gabby, you know I don't want a lot in life, just a happy family and some place to keep warm. I didn't steal nothing."

"They're not going to be able to frame you, Harold. You have witnesses that saw you at Donovan's T-ball game. That will prove you're innocent. . . ." I paused as Harold swung his head back and forth. "Why are you doing that?"

His fingers laced and unlaced in front of him. This was a man who less than five hours ago I wouldn't believe could get rattled. Now, he was close to crumbling.

"I got caught in traffic. Then I decided to stop by the house and shower. You know how the smell of blood just saturates you."

I touched his arm. "I know."

"I'm the perfect suspect." Harold lowered his head into his hands again.

"I believe you're innocent, Harold."

"Now you just have to make sure the police believe the same," Riley said. He uncrossed his arms and stepped closer. "Did they say anything about a search warrant?"

"They're trying to get one right now."

"Do you have a lawyer?"

"Not yet."

Riley began pacing. "You need to get a lawyer. You should have had one in the first place. They did tell you that, didn't they?"

He shrugged. "I was so overwhelmed, I don't remember what they told me. I just knew I wanted to get home. I wanted to wake up from this nightmare."

As if on cue, a police car pulled to a stop in front of the house, followed by a black sedan.

Detective Parker, I realized. My stomach rolled with nausea.

The Brad Pitt look-alike stepped out of the car, sunglasses on and hair gelled in place.

"I guess that search warrant came through pretty quickly," I mumbled, standing. I stepped between Harold and Parker as the officers approached.

Parker's smirking gaze fell on me, and I wished I'd never mentally complimented him with the Brad Pitt comparison. "Well, if it isn't Nancy Drew. Why am I not surprised to see you here?"

"Tell me, is it your stubbornness or ignorance that prevents you from admitting the truth?"

His eyebrows shot up, and though I couldn't see his eyes, I would bet he was scowling beneath those dark glasses.

"I've told you to leave the investigation to professionals." His words were as clipped and tight as his expression.

"You guys are as professional as Bozo on his first day at the circus. Do you need me to remind you of what a lousy job you've done so far?"

Harold laid a hand on my arm, but my heart still raced with adrenaline. "It's okay, Gabby. Let them go on and search the house. They won't find anything."

Parker slipped his movie-star glasses up and gave me a smoldering glance before following the officers into the house.

"What did you mean by all of that, Gabby?" Harold's eyes contained the first touch of hope I'd seen since this ordeal started.

I should have kept my tongue in check, I realized. I sucked in a breath. It was too late to take back what I'd said. I just hoped Harold wouldn't get his expectations up. Parker obviously had breezed through school on looks alone. He offered nothing in the brains department.

"I found some evidence after you left, Harold. A gun. Some blood, too. On top of that, I talked to a neighbor this morning who said she saw someone walking around the house last night."

The hope in his gaze deepened. "And you told the detective?"

I nodded. "He doesn't seem to take what I said too seriously, though."

"This isn't an investigation for amateurs, Gabby," Riley said. His gaze drifted behind me, and I glanced over my shoulder. My scowl intensified when I saw Parker in the doorway.

"I know what I saw, and I know what that woman told me," I whispered quickly. "Something's not matching up in this case, and I'm not about to let Harold get framed."

The detective stomped onto the wooden porch, his steps reverberating against the flimsy floorboards. His eyes burned a hole through me, and his jaw clenched as he walked toward Harold. Music for "Send in the Clowns" played in my head.

"Harold, you're under arrest for arson and theft." Parker pulled handcuffs from his belt and jerked Harold to his feet.

"You've got to believe me. I didn't do this!" Harold pleaded, panic flashing in his eyes.

I stepped between the two, my hands clenched in fury. I had to stop myself from using one of those fists to punch Parker in his button nose. "What are you talking about? Harold didn't do anything, and you know it."

"We found stolen items in the trunk of the car parked in his garage." The detective shoved past me, pushing Harold along with him. "Now, don't make me arrest you, too."

Riley nudged me until I stepped back. My heart felt numb as I watched the detective lead Harold to the squad car. Harold's eyes met mine as the door slammed. The sound of Keisha weeping inside the house broke my heart.

Harold was being framed. His innocent family would pay the price. And I was powerless to do anything about it.

CHAPTER

TEN

By the time Riley and I said good-bye to Mildred, stars pinpricked the sky above. A magnetic force seemed to keep me at the house. But Mildred insisted I should go, and I knew I could do nothing more. Her sister had driven up from North Carolina to help out, so she was in capable hands.

Riley escorted me to his car. Around us, crickets sang with abandon, and the full moon offered a mocking smile. Didn't nature know the torment this family was going through? Shouldn't it mourn with us over this injustice? I mentally chanted, *Down with nature. Long live industrial development.*

I slid inside the car and dropped my aching head against the seat. Riley's door slammed, the sound reverberating at my temples. I gritted my teeth, wanting to be back with Mildred, as if she'd be safe under my care. I waited for Riley to start the car, but instead he touched my shoulder.

"You going to be okay?" he asked.

Even inside the shadowed car, I could see the concern on his face. I could hear it in the mellow tone of his voice. Still, my sarcasm fought to be voiced.

Of course I wasn't going to be okay. Harold, one of the nicest men I'd ever known, was going to jail, and somehow it felt like my fault. With a deep sigh, I fought for control and said evenly, "It's not me I'm worried about."

We sat in silence a moment. Finally, Riley started the car and pulled from the drive. I stared out the window, watching the world go by. Nothing had changed, yet everything had changed. Where was justice? Where was the loving God I had heard so much about? Harold certainly wasn't feeling the kindness and protection of a merciful God tonight.

"What do you think about all of this?" I asked, turning my gaze on Riley. "Do you think Harold's guilty?"

"Finding the evidence in the car sure makes him look that way."

I shook my head. "Even if Harold is a thief—which I don't believe—he's not a killer. Harold knew I was in the house. He wouldn't try to burn it down with me inside."

Riley leaned back in the seat, watching the road. Tight lines pulled around his mouth. "What's your theory, then?"

"I think the husband burned down the house." I paused, collecting my thoughts. "But the detective says he was in the hospital at the time of the arson."

"Which is a pretty good alibi."

"What if he sneaked out of the hospital?"

"What if he didn't? What if the neighbor is mistaken?"

I shook my head. "I don't really know what to think right now. I only know Harold. They've got the wrong man." My cell phone began playing do-re-mi. I jerked it from my belt and grumbled, "Gabby St. Claire."

A man needed a crime-scene cleaner to scrub his grandmother's house. She had died, and they had found fifteen cats inside. It was a crime against common sense, maybe even a crime against humanity, to have fifteen cats. And it surely was a crime against those poor cats. But cleaning up cat doo-doo sure was a far cry from being a forensic expert.

This is what I'd sunk to.

When you're plagued by cat hair,
Turn to Gabby St. Claire.

If you sang it to chopsticks, it even rhymed—sort of.

> *When the smell makes you hurl,*
> *Gabby's your girl.*

Forget the radio spot. I wondered if Chuck Norris and Christy Brinkley might do the infomercial for me.

> *When the litter box overflows—*

Oh, never mind. I made a mental note to buy a clothespin for my nose and said, "Yeah, I'll be there."

I had rent to pay and new equipment to buy. Now wasn't the time to get particular.

I clicked the phone shut.

"Another job?" Riley asked.

"Life goes on."

"What are you going to do about your equipment?"

"This job doesn't involve any blood, so I should be okay. I had extras of all my cleaning supplies, so I'll just have to run to the store and pick up a few things before I go in tomorrow morning."

Riley wove in and out of traffic. Something about having him in the driver's seat brought me comfort. I spent so much of my life fighting to be strong that it was nice to let someone else have control.

My mom had been weak, and I vowed never to be like her. I always said I'd never work to support someone else's habit, nor would I ever let a mythical God who told me to turn the other cheek dictate how I lived my life. At least I'd kept the latter vow. I just couldn't bring myself to cut Dad loose, though.

I did remember some good times—times when my dad had let me skip school and we drove to the beach where he taught me to body surf. Once he took me on a hike through the Blue Ridge Mountains. That was Dad at his best, when his free-spirited nature emerged. That was the Dad I loved.

I didn't quite understand the control my dad held over me. The only thing I could figure was that I'd lost my brother, then my mom. Dad was all I had left. Maybe I held on to the hope that one day he'd start acting like a father. Or maybe I was just as weak as Mom.

But unlike my mom, I refused to be trapped in a marriage with a freeloading husband. Men got one chance with me, and then they were out the door. Sierra always said I was too hard on my boyfriends, but I didn't care. No man was worth the heartache my mom went through.

I wondered about my "Riley Thomas, the freeloader" theory. He seemed smart, even knowledgeable about things. And when I was with him, I always felt better. But every once in a while, I saw that haunted look in his eyes like he was running from something. A wife and kids maybe? Responsibilities? The law?

He didn't offer much in the detail department, which in some ways made him even more intriguing. Who needed details when you had an imagination like mine? I could fill in all the blanks or at least have fun trying.

Maybe he was a famous actor trying to escape the paparazzi. Or maybe he was on the FBI's most-wanted list. Or he was an obscure prince trying to figure out what a normal life felt like.

If so, he had moved into the wrong apartment complex.

We pulled up, and no sooner had we stepped into the building than Sierra's door flew open. "Good, you're here. I thought you'd forgotten that we were having brownies tonight. Remember?" Her eyes darted between Riley and me.

"It's been a long day . . ." I started.

The last thing I wanted was to be social. I needed to be alone, to think, to strategize, to bake a cake with a file in it.

"A long day deserves a brownie." Sierra grabbed my wrist. She had a wild, hunted look in her brown eyes that made me curious . . . and slightly frightened. "Besides, you promised."

Before I could object, she pulled me through the beads adorning the doorframe. Glancing behind me, I saw Riley grin and wave good-bye.

Sierra had a spare hand and a will of iron. She snagged him by the little polo player on his shirtfront. "You too, Riley."

His grin disappeared as Sierra dragged him through the beads as well. Bill, the talk-show host, sat on the couch, mumbling about the horned, pitchfork-carrying woman who had divorced him. I never understood why he hadn't noticed her hooves and goatee when they were dating.

"He's been here two hours already." Sierra's desperate whisper sliced a thin hole in my eardrums. "I can't get rid of him." Her grip tightened on my arm until I could feel my heart beating in my fingertips.

She raised her voice and sang out with a pleasant tone so false, she should have used Fixodent to hold it in place. "Have a seat, guys. The brownies are still warm."

I sat on the edge of the couch, not willing to get comfortable since I wouldn't be staying. Riley took the chair across from me.

Bill wiped the crumbs from his dirty white shirt and extended a hand to Riley. "Bill McCormick from *America Live,* the radio show."

"Riley Thomas."

"You single?"

"Yes, sir." Riley sat rigid in the overstuffed chair, as if anxious to leave.

"Count your blessings, young man."

I slumped in my chair. Bill was drunk. The man could talk your leg off sober. Drunk, you should say good-bye to your leg, the rest of your day, and probably your mind.

"All a woman will do is mess up your life."

His words slurred together. Fresh off a nasty divorce, he was having a hard time. But tonight wasn't the night I wanted to hear about it. I didn't have any sympathy left.

"Take my advice and avoid them like the plague. They'll ruin you."

"I've got brownies." Sierra set a plate before us with a flourish, clinking her knife as she laid it on the table.

"Have any milk?" Riley asked.

I caught his eye and shook my head.

"Milk is a byproduct of a cow, and I'm a vegan."

Too late. Bill's divorce stories were like *Sesame Street* compared to Sierra giving her vegan speech.

"Cows are enslaved by humans. They are oppressed, abused, wrung dry for a few short bitter years, then killed after their faithful service."

"And, we're off," I muttered to no one. I glanced around, desperate for an out. My friend was in prison, and I was stuck here in something playing out like a bad sitcom. Watch out *Seinfeld*, here comes *The Weird and the Curious*.

"Did you know there are studies that prove people are better off not eating dairy? In the end, it will kill us all. Scientists have proved that the hole in the ozone layer is caused partly by methane gas generated by herds of captive cattle, force-fed massive, unneeded amounts of unnatural food, just so man—"

"So, how about those brownies? They're looking good," I said, hoping for a change of subject.

With a sweet smile completely at odds with her fanatic soliloquy, Sierra said, "Yes, please try a brownie. They're my special recipe."

Another time bomb. Sierra and her special recipes. Afraid to set her off on being a vegan again, I bit into the cake-like square, noting the strange texture and flavor. Holding a smile on my face that dynamite couldn't have shifted, I chewed away. What had my friend made these out of? I was used to strange ingredients, especially since Sierra didn't use milk or eggs, but there was something even stranger about these.

I took another bite. "These are good," I lied.

"I'm not telling what my secret ingredient is . . ."

I resisted the urges either to thank her for sparing me the awful truth or to beg her to tell me, so that when they asked at the emergency ward, I'd be able to clue them in as to what antidote to use.

". . . until you're finished."

Which meant if I wanted to know the antiserum, I had to finish the ghastly thing.

She sat down and grabbed a brownie. "What have you guys been up to today?"

Riley and I glanced at each other. Such a simple question. Such a complicated answer.

"Nothing exciting," I said. Arson, murder, police corruption, toxic brownies. Same old, same old.

I ate the last bite of my brownie and wiped my mouth with a napkin. "Okay, so 'fess up. What's the secret ingredient?"

Sierra grinned a little too wide. "Acorns."

Squirrel food. I looked at Sierra. Chipper, hyper, caught her climbing a tree last night. The woman was one bushy tail away from being one with her furry friends. Narrowing my eyes to study her face, I checked for any sign she'd stowed away acorns in her cheeks for later use.

Sierra chattered on. "Yep. They're not much different from peanuts. Did you know people didn't eat peanuts for the longest time? They fed them to their animals. Acorns are the same."

"There are no nuts in these, Sierra," I said, staring at the brownies. There was a big one sitting on the couch with me, but none I could detect in the brownies, and I'd been on high alert.

"That's because I ground up the acorns after I boiled them, of course, and used them like flour."

Of course she did. Why did I even ask?

"What a day." Bill reeled to his feet. "I've got to get going. I'm getting too old for this kind of excitement."

Even drunk as he was, Bill went into escape-and-evade mode once he heard about the acorns.

"Yeah, me, too. It's been a long day." I stood, Riley right behind me.

"They weren't that bad, were they?" Sierra asked, her gaze darting around the three of us like a furry little rodent. She clasped her hands together under her chin, and I braced myself for her to start clicking her front teeth together. I hoped to heaven she'd had her rabies shots.

"See you later, Sierra." I disappeared upstairs before Sierra could show me where she'd stored food away for the winter.

"That was interesting," Riley whispered as we trotted up the stairs together.

"Get used to it. Things like this happen quite a bit with Sierra." I leaned against my door and cast a soft grin at Riley. "Thanks for all of your help today. I really appreciate it."

"It's no problem." He looked at the floor. "You have mail."

I saw the brown-paper-wrapped, shoebox-sized package on the ground and picked it up. "No return address," I said, looking at the corner.

"Expecting anything?"

I shook my head. "I don't know what it could be." I reached for the heavily taped end to tear it open.

"Stop." Riley caught my hands.

Something about his tone made me freeze instantly. I raised my eyes to his, frightened.

His eyes locked on the package as he took it from me. Moving cautiously, he set the box on the ground and reached for me. "Step away from it, Gabby. Now."

He pulled me toward the stairwell. Backing up, I never looked away from the box with my name scrawled in black ink on top.

"What's wrong?"

"We're better safe than sorry. You should call the police and have the package checked out."

The implications of what he'd said solidified in my mind. "You think it might be a bomb?"

"Smell your hands."

I did as instructed. "Almonds."

"And the package made a sloshing sound. We need to evacuate the building."

"You mean everybody?"

"Yeah, everybody."

"But what if it's nothing?"

"What if it's something?"

His argument won. "I'll go get Mrs. Miller upstairs." I started toward the attic apartment.

CHAPTER ELEVEN

All I wanted was quiet. I slid down the side of Sierra's car, my knees bent up to my chest, my hands clasped between my legs. I wanted time alone to deal with the hand life had dealt me today. I wanted to mourn Harold's situation. I wanted a shower to wash away the sweat that had covered my body ever since I'd found out someone might be trying to kill me.

It appeared I wasn't going to get what I wanted.

Lucky squawked from his cage, which rested beside Riley's car. Sierra tried to comfort her nervous cats, all of whom were crammed into one large carrier. Bill paced back and forth, much more sober than he'd been two hours ago. But then, bombs had a sobering effect on people. He muttered something about having a lot to talk about on the radio tomorrow. I'd have jumped at his ankles when he paced by me and knocked him down if I hadn't been so tired. Glad my life-and-death experience could provide the listening public with entertainment.

Mrs. Miller, the writer upstairs, twisted her hands together and jabbered about losing years off her life. I didn't think that was possible. She weighed ninety pounds and dressed all in white to match her gray hair and pasty skin. And she was so wrinkled, she looked mummified. Not even an explosion could kill her. What we needed was an Egyptian curse.

Aside from the noisy tenants who scattered across the parking lot, the normally comforting sounds of Ghent annoyed me. Cars zoomed past, honking and calling out college cheers. Groups of young professionals lingered on the sidewalk. Faces pressed into the glass at the coffeehouse as spectators wondered what new loony thing was happening in their little community. The heat didn't deter the masses from coming out to enjoy Ghent's nightlife. Its patrons were fierce and loyal. And tonight, they were getting even more for their money as a bomb squad invaded the apartment complex.

Glad I could help.

The only things quiet about the night were me and Riley.

My gaze wandered across the asphalt to where he stood, staring up at the house like he wanted nothing more than to be inside. Had he been a bomb maker in a past career? Or maybe he'd been on a bomb squad. Really, I didn't know much about him. He didn't offer much in conversation. So, why did I feel as if I could trust him?

Calling the bomb squad was probably just a big mistake. What if it turned out to be new underwear from my Aunt May? Every year for Christmas, she sent me a package of white cotton panties big enough to rig as a sail and power a yacht down the coast to Cuba. Had she sent them early this year?

Or what if my father had decided to send me a box full of bills he needed help with? That'd be perfect. My father's incompetence, topic one on Bill McCormick's show. I wouldn't put it past him. The small amount of Social Security my father received went straight to Anheuser-Busch.

Food? That was my job. Lucky for him that beer had a high grain content or he'd have starved on what I'd chipped in lately.

Dad? Aunt May? Crazed bomber? I had to go with my family. The possibility seemed realistic, yet I knew the handwriting belonged to neither of those people.

What if Riley was right? What if the package contained a bomb? There was no reason for anyone to kill me.

The idea that had been zooming around in my head, looking for a functioning brain cell to land on, finally settled. Unless they knew about the gun.

But who knew about the gun? Only four people I could think of: Riley, who hadn't left my side all day. Parker, who was a policeman, for heaven's sake. Me, and despite my pathetic life, I wasn't inclined to bomb myself.

And the murderer.

The person who had left it in the cubbyhole to begin with.

Michael Cunningham.

What if he knew I'd found it and was determined to silence me?

My heart rate quickened.

What a night.

What a day, for that matter.

Could it get worse?

I tapped my foot and leaned against Sierra's car, unable to concentrate, on edge. Desperate for peace yet terrified to be alone.

How long did this take?

Midnight came and went as the bomb squad worked inside. Everyone quieted, staring with blank looks at the building.

Panties. Let it be panties.

Sierra and Bill went to the Grounds, leaving me to babysit five cats squashed into an undersized cathouse.

After our neighbors meandered across the street, Riley lowered himself onto the ground beside me. His eyes had lost some of their brightness, and creases formed in their corners.

"What do you think?" I asked.

"They're being cautious. One wrong move could be deadly."

"Or it could be nothing." Panties. Humiliating, but better than a bomb.

Riley placed his hand on my knee. His steady gaze reassured me. "It's going to be okay, Gabby."

"You always sound so sure of everything. How do you do it?"

"Simple. If something's out of my hands, I don't worry about it."

"Sounds like a good philosophy."

"I leave it in God's hands."

I chewed on the thought. What would it be like to leave something in a Higher Being's care? My career. My dad. My poor, arrested friend.

I'd never had anyone take care of me. The thought felt foreign. Those who were supposed to look out for me had only been a disappointment. It would be the same case with God.

Wouldn't it?

The front door of the building flew open, and four bomb-squad members emerged. Riley and I met them in the parking lot.

"Well?" I asked. Panties. Embarrassing bills. Anything but—

"A bomb."

A stocky, bald man stepped forward. "Your quick thinking saved lives tonight, Ms. St. Claire. There was a pipe bomb in that package."

My jaw slacked. My knees wobbled, and I fumbled behind me for the car. Riley caught me by the elbow and steadied me.

"It really was a bomb?" I couldn't believe it.

"Yes, it was a bomb," the detective said. "Wouldn't have taken the whole building out, but it could have cost some lives."

Especially mine. My gaze fluttered to Riley. "Thank you."

He offered a tight smile.

"Any idea who might have sent you this, Ms. St. Claire?" the short, bald detective asked. His words were crisp, businesslike.

I drew in a deep breath. Could this be connected with the fire? It had to be.

"You must have some idea. You hesitated," the detective said. What was his name again? Allen? Alex? Adams?

Adams, that was it.

"There is one situation. I don't know that there's a connection, but . . ." I glanced at Riley. He didn't know any of these details yet, but after everything he'd been through, there wasn't much use hiding them anymore. "You could talk to Michael Cunningham."

"As in 'the lawyer who's running for the U.S. Senate' Michael Cunningham?" Riley asked as he raked his hands through his hair, leaving it sticking up in adorable shocks. "You didn't tell me he was involved in all of this."

Why did Riley look so flabbergasted? He'd obviously heard of the man before, a surprising fact in itself. What else did Riley Thomas know?

I raised my chin. "I didn't think it was appropriate to name names."

"Why would you think Mr. Cunningham might have something to do with this?" Adams held his pen and paper, scribbling quick notes.

"I found evidence that points to him as the one who murdered his wife."

"What?" The same dumbfounded expression stretched across Riley's face. "That's a huge accusation."

I balled my hands into fists and willed myself not to slug the guy who had saved my life a couple of hours ago. "Look, if I wanted to be doubted, I would talk to Detective Parker."

"The Virginia Beach police know about the evidence you found?" Adams asked.

"Yes, but they've dismissed it."

"Why would you think he sent this package to you?" It was Riley again. His entire body seemed tense, almost making him a different person. His laid-back persona seemed gone with the wind, replaced by that of someone wound as tight as a jack-in-the-box.

"To keep me quiet." I shrugged, trying not to let Riley get to me. "It's the best I can come up with. But as I've been reminded many times, I'm not a detective, so I'm only going on a hunch. And evidence, of course."

"How would he know you're accusing him? You haven't confronted him, have you?" Riley asked.

"No, I haven't confronted him. But when he came back to the house that evening while I was cleaning, he could have seen me. That's why he burned the house down with me inside."

"You're accusing him of that also?" Riley began pacing. "I don't think you realize who you're accusing."

"I'm accusing a murderer, that's who."

"No. Michael Cunningham is expected to be the next big thing. There's talk about a presidential nomination one day."

I pulled my head back. "He hasn't even been elected senator yet."

"Exactly. He's got a lot of people high up who are rooting for him," Riley said.

If I hadn't been so tired, I might have suppressed the sigh that escaped. All of my energy was spent at this point, though.

"That's not my problem. Just because a person is affluent doesn't mean he's not guilty." I looked back at the detective, who watched our exchange like a tennis tournament, his bald head bobbing back and forth with each verbal serve. "Did you get any prints off the package?"

"A couple, but they could be yours. We're going to process everything down at the station, but we'll be in touch. Again, smart thinking, both of you. Everyone in this apartment building owes you a debt of gratitude." The detective nodded toward Riley and me in a moment of affirmation. "Who did you say the detective was who's handling your case at the Beach?"

The warm fuzzy feeling I had at the compliment disappeared. I spouted off Parker's name.

"We'll get the rest of the story from him," Adams said.

"I don't trust him."

With narrowed eyes that looked like he was closing ranks with his brother in blue, Adams said, "We'll keep that in mind, miss. Good night."

"Can we go back inside?" Bill yelled from across the street.

At least there was one grateful neighbor right now.

"It's clear," Adams said, motioning for everyone to go in.

After the bomb squad cleared the lot, Riley and I stood staring at each other. I could tell by the tight line of Riley's lips that he had something on his mind.

"Look, you haven't known me that long, and I'm not trying to tell you what do," Riley said. "But if I were you, I'd take the detective's advice and back off this one."

"And let my friend take the blame for the arson?" I took two steps forward and jutted out my chin. "I don't think so."

"Gabby, they found stolen items from the house in his car."

"Someone smart enough to stage a murder, vicious enough to murder his wife, desperate enough to shoot himself, tough enough to leave the hospital with a bullet wound in his leg, and cold-blooded enough to burn down a house with an innocent woman inside might dare to plant evidence."

"Yeah." He bent down until his nose almost touched mine. "Or maybe no one's that smart, vicious, desperate, tough, and cold-blooded. Maybe you're just reaching because you can't stand that you hired a petty thief who was stupid enough to torch the crime scene without checking that you'd left yet. Just because a person is nice doesn't mean they're not guilty."

"Are you sure about that? Criminals aren't usually all that nice." His bossiness irritated me, and as I looked at him standing there defending Cunningham, sneering at my theories, and condemning Harold, I couldn't remember why I'd ever liked the big jerk.

"Gabby, be reasonable."

"I have no intention of being reasonable," I said, tilting my nose in the air. Then I furrowed my brow, trying to remember what I'd just said. With a shrug, I decided it didn't make any difference.

"I don't want to talk about this anymore." I turned away. Then my pesky conscience reminded me that Riley had saved my life. I just didn't have it in me to be gracious right now. "Thanks for all of your help today, but I need to go to bed now. Good night."

Storming away, I took the stairs by two and hurried to my apartment. I stripped out of my jeans and T-shirt as I walked to the bathroom. Pushing my mop of strawberry blond curls out of my face with a headband, I washed my face and patted it dry with a towel.

Someone tried to kill you. Again.

I pulled on some running shorts and an old T-shirt and crawled into bed, determined to get some rest. As soon as I turned off the light on my nightstand, cold fear crept into my bones.

Someone tried to kill you. Again.

I shivered. The dark room closed in around me.

It was still better than the place where Harold was spending the night.

I pictured him sitting in a jail cell. Poor Harold. Poor Mildred. They were too kind to go through this.

Of course, Riley thought my assistant was guilty. But he didn't know Harold the way I did. Harold was a good man.

He did jail time for arson before.

Yeah, but a person could change. Harold had changed.

I pulled the covers up to my chin and drew in a deep breath, trying to slow my heartbeat. I knew what I had to do.

I would prove that Harold was innocent if it was the last thing I did.

CHAPTER TWELVE

The stench in the apartment turned my stomach. How had someone lived in this mess? Cat feces were smeared across almost every surface, and the carpet reeked with urine.

My gag reflex kicked into gear, and I pressed my mask tighter.

Staring at the mess would do nothing to get it cleaned. I might as well get to work. It would probably be an all-day task, even though it was just a one-bedroom apartment.

Mindful of my injured hand, I sprayed down the walls with a heavy-duty cleaner. I left the liquid to absorb for a few minutes as I pulled up the carpet. No amount of cleaning would remove its odor. I rolled it and tugged it, inch by inch, out the door. I turned back to the walls and wiped the white plaster down.

I sure did miss Harold. Working alone wasn't nearly as fun or productive. If I wasn't miffed with Riley, I might have asked him to come along and earn a few extra dollars.

Just the thought of Riley caused a weight to rest on my shoulders. His reaction had been so strong that I'd let my temper get the best of me.

In the light of day, I knew I'd overreacted. I scrubbed away, wallowing in equal parts cat dander and guilt. Riley had been a sweetheart up until that fatal conversation. He'd taken me to the police station, played with Harold's grandkids, and warned me about the package before I opened it. Good grief, give the man some chain mail, and he'd have brought chivalry back to life single-handedly.

Then he told me to let the detectives do the job, and I'd turned on him. Thanks for saving my life, buddy, but what have you done for me lately?

I lifted stacks of putrid newspaper off the countertops. Today's heart-stopping headlines, tomorrow's discount kitty litter. Stuffing the newspaper in garbage bags, I wondered why I should have expected Riley to be concerned about me. We'd only known each other two days. But I'd felt a connection to him from the first. Did he feel it, too? Could there be something between us?

Knowing my past track record with men, probably not. I always seemed to fall for the ones who were no good for me, the jerks. Riley was a nice guy. Except that he thought I was a moron who hired criminals. He seemed to like and respect a man I'd accused of murder. And he seemed to be unemployed. Maybe I was on track as usual.

So what was I going to do with these feelings?

Considering the stress I was under, the best answer was to do nothing.

My cell phone rang. Detective Parker.

"I just talked to the bomb squad. They told me what happened last night." His voice sounded surprisingly kind and relaxed. *Yeah, right.* I sucked in a breath, waiting for the lecture to come. "I'm glad you weren't hurt."

I raised an eyebrow. The detective sounded genuinely concerned. He must be having a good hair day. Or maybe Hollywood had called and asked him to be a stunt double. Better yet, maybe the BTK Strangler had been cleared of all charges and released. Parker seemed to like having guilty men on the street.

"Yeah, I'm glad someone stopped me before I opened the package. It could have taken out more than just me, or so I've heard."

His voice seemed to soften. "Look, I just wanted you to know we're doing everything we can to figure out who sent you the package."

I felt like I was in an episode of *The Twilight Zone*. Why was the detective being so open and nice? Quite the change from the hostile man I'd talked with yesterday. Maybe I'd just caught him on a bad hair day.

My best friend was turning into a woodland creature. A man I had feelings for thought his parrot was smarter than I am. My only employee might be going up the river. I didn't have it in me to alienate Parker just because he'd had his body snatched and replaced with someone who had manners. "Thanks. I appreciate it."

"And Gabby?" His voice sounded warm enough to toast acorns. Maybe I should introduce him to Sierra.

"Yeah?" I stopped scraping cat mess off the mopboard to pay attention to the only person on the planet still speaking to me.

"I just want you to know . . ."

I took a deep breath. Emotion clogged my throat. Well, emotion and cat hair, but who was keeping track at this point? Brad Pitt was worried about me.

"I'm here for you. Any time. Day . . ."—a long, lingering silence, full of promise, stretched between us across the phone lines—"or night."

After hanging up, I stared at the phone.

What do you know? I thought. Maybe the detective did have a heart and a brain, after all. But I'd have to watch the news for that report on the BTK Strangler, just in case.

CHAPTER THIRTEEN

The next morning, the garage working on my van called. They'd changed the tires, replaced the windshield, and done a whole bunch of other things that I didn't understand. It seemed a near miracle to get my van back so quickly. Sierra dropped me off, and I found my mode of transportation looking as good as new.

Now that I had my own set of wheels, I was determined to get some answers. Starting with Michael Cunningham.

I'd thought about it for the entire evening. Okay, I'd thought about it most of the time. Thoughts of Riley had slipped in there a few times, too. Thoughts of his smile, his eyes, his total lack of confidence in my judgment. I scowled.

It would only make sense to visit Cunningham's mother. After all, she was the one who hired me to clean his house. Strictly business. Totally innocent. Brilliantly devious. If I could oh so subtly grill the old lady, maybe I could find something to prove Harold was innocent.

It was the only thing I could come up with.

I pulled out the phone book and searched the Cs.

"Cunningham, Cunningham," I mumbled.

There it was. Susan Cunningham, 367 River Rd., Portsmouth. I knew exactly where she lived.

Stuffing the phone book back in place, I hurried to my van. As I started down the road, I pulled out my cell phone and dialed Mildred's number. She answered on the first ring. "It's been terrible, Gabby. Reporters keep calling."

"You don't have to tell them anything, Mildred."

"I know. But Harold is going to be found guilty by the press before he's even tried."

"What are they saying today? Any updates?"

"They said his fingerprints were all over the evidence."

I thought about that for a moment. If Harold hadn't stolen those things, then someone had come in the house and picked up things Harold had touched, planning to frame him for arson. It had to have happened while I was there alone, because with two of us there, no one could have sneaked in. How long had I been alone in that house with a murderer? Was my presence a surprise to the arsonist, or did they intend for the charge of arson against Harold to include murder? Did they just need to get rid of the evidence in the house and not have the patience to wait for me to leave? A man in a hurry to get back to the hospital before he was missed might be willing to kill, especially if he'd done it before.

"Of course his fingerprints were on the evidence," I told Mildred. "We were cleaning the house. He was bound to touch things along the way." Maybe he straightened a picture or picked up some fallen candlesticks after he took off his hazmat suit. I couldn't fault him for that. He had an eye for detail. I shuddered to think of a murderer watching us. Picking up things Harold had touched. Tucking them into Harold's car later that night.

Mildred sniffled. "It's not looking good, Gabby. Everything seems to point to him. It's almost like he was set up or something."

It was exactly like he'd been set up, but I wasn't going to tell Mildred that now. She had enough to worry about. "How's he doing?"

"As well as can be expected. We have a lawyer. You didn't tell me that's what your friend did for a living."

I didn't have any lawyers as friends. I religiously stuck with blue-collar workers, eccentrics whom no one else liked, and psychos. Me and lawyers didn't mesh. "My friend?"

"Yes, the young man who was with you yesterday."

"Riley?" I started forward. So much for my freeloader theory.

"Yes, Riley."

"He's a nice guy all right, Mildred."

"He certainly is. He promised he would take care of us. What an answer to prayer. We didn't have the money to hire anyone otherwise."

Warmth filled my chest. "Let me know if I can do anything for you, Mildred. You know I'm just a phone call away."

"Thanks, sweetie. With my sister here, we're doing okay, for now."

I hung up and shook my head. Riley a lawyer? Why hadn't he mentioned that? My heart softened. It was kind of him to take on this case. Perhaps I'd passed judgment too quickly.

The traffic became heavier on the interstate as rush hour began. I turned the vent toward my face to cool off, unsure if it was the heat or what I was about to do that had me sweating.

Don't think about it, Gabby. You'll only talk yourself out of it.

I turned on the radio to an AM station, hoping to catch the news. An anchor came on, and I turned the volume louder.

"A trial date has been set for William Newsome, the man accused of armed robbery and the death of Gloria Cunningham. The original trial date was set for this week, but it was delayed when Gloria Cunningham turned up dead in her home. Newsome is accused of murdering Cunningham, the only witness who placed him at the scene of an earlier crime, a convenience-store robbery."

A different voice came on the radio. "There's no question that Newsome is guilty. It's just a matter of whether or not he'll receive the death penalty." It had to be the prosecuting attorney speaking, I mused.

"In a bizarre twist, the Cunninghams' house was burned down earlier this week. Harold Morris, a cleaner who was at the home, has been accused of the crime. The motive appears to have been robbery."

I hit the off button. I couldn't listen anymore. I went through the downtown tunnel and crossed into Portsmouth. Only a few more turns and I would be there.

What would I say? *Hi, Mrs. Cunningham. Did you know there was a sale on ammo at Wal-Mart this week? I'll bet your son needs to restock.*

Any uninvestigated trail of dead bodies in your family since your son was born?

Has your son, the senator-to-be, ever tortured small animals?

Don't think about it, Gabby. Just go with it as it comes.

The more I planned, the bigger the explosion when things blew up in my face. Like when I confronted my former neighbor about his loud music. I'd planned out exactly what to say, but when the conversation was over, my neighbor promised to turn his music up louder so I could better hear his personal Top 40. I thanked him and went home. Later— like two days later—I came up with great responses that I should have used. Of course, in fairness, before he finally moved, I'd developed a taste for Metallica and the Rolling Stones that remained with me to this day, so the experience wasn't a total loss. In fact, it helped broaden my tastes and shape me into the person I am today—one who can annoyingly quote the lyrics to thousands of songs of different styles and generations. Who said I couldn't get no satisfaction?

No, the best plan seemed to be the natural one, the one that required no planning. Let 'er rip. Fly by the seat of my pants. Let the chips fall where they may.

I pondered that. Lots of ripping and flying and falling in that plan.

But I was out of time to come up with a better one. I pulled to a stop in front of an old Victorian house, a grand structure that still maintained its dignity. After cutting the engine, I stared at the house, wondering how the future would play out.

What was it that Riley had said last night? *If something's out of my hands, I don't worry about it.*

Now there was a plan. Let God handle it. That sounded good. If only there was a God.

I climbed from the van and started toward the house, my respectable black, sequin-topped flip-flops clunking against the sidewalk. Before I lost nerve, I pounded on the door. A white-haired woman cracked the door open.

"Can I help you?"

I tucked a hair behind my ear. "Hi, Mrs. Cunningham. My name is Gabby. You hired me to clean your son's house after . . ." I couldn't finish the sentence.

The woman's shoulders eased. "What can I do for you, Gabby?"

"I wanted to express my sympathy for what happened. I assure you that my associate and I had nothing to do with the house burning down."

Her red lips pulled down in a frown. "I'll leave that for a jury to decide."

"You've got to believe me, Mrs. Cunningham."

Her eyes looked weary and her motions seemed weak. The poor woman had been through a war the past month.

She shook her head. "You have to understand what a difficult time this has been for all of us."

How could such a sweet woman have raised a man like Cunningham?

"I can't imagine what you must be going through." I paused, tempted to end the conversation and hurry home. So far, no feathers had been ruffled. I mentally stiffened my backbone, determined to see this through. "I was wondering if I might offer my condolences to your son."

His mother paused and drew her brows together. "I can pass the message along to him. What did you say your name was?"

No, no, no. A message wouldn't work.

"Actually, I'd really like to talk to him myself, if there's any way possible. Uh . . . at a time like this, he needs to know people care enough to say so personally."

I did my best not to roll my eyeballs at the lameness of my statement. Even I wanted to boot myself to the curb.

The woman's lips tightened into a line. "You have to understand he's not doing that well right now."

Killed his wife, shot himself, burned his house. *Not well* might possibly have a home in the *Guinness Book of World Records* in the Understatement category.

"He's been through so much. We all have."

I wondered if by *we all*, she counted Harold and me.

"And I don't want to impose on you. There's something I really must tell him, though."

His mother pulled the door all the way open. Her features seemed too tight for her to be convinced. "Come in for a minute, and get out of this heat. I'll see what he says, but I can't make any promises. He's meeting with his campaign manager right now."

There's a man in mourning for you. *All right, men, murdered wives are real grabbers in the polls. Let's see if* Entertainment Tonight *will send Mary Hart and a camera crew to the autopsy. This could be as big as OJ.*

The AC hit me at full force as I stepped into the entryway to wait. A picture of Gloria and Michael on the wall made my stomach lurch. They looked so peaceful, so happy. What had happened to make Michael kill his wife?

How had this world gotten so mixed up?

Footsteps echoed down the wooden hallway in front of me. Michael Cunningham. His cleft chin held at a steady rise, and his eyes never wavered despite his limp.

"How can I help you?" he asked, his voice clipped and tight.

Oh, man, the chips were falling. I squared my shoulders. "I want to offer my condolences. I'm so sorry to hear about your loss."

"And who are you again?" He squinted and studied my face. Either he was a good actor, or he hadn't seen me before. But that didn't fit my theory.

"I'm Gabby. I was at your house the night of the fire."

And I know you killed your wife. You won't get away with it.

"Why exactly were you at my house?"

"I was cleaning it."

And I found evidence you tried to conceal, you little liar.

His gaze darkened. "You're the one whose company set my house on fire."

Instead of flying, the seat of my pants looked to be headed for skid marks on the driveway. I shook my head, knowing I had to take charge of the situation before it got out of hand. "No, sir, you're wrong. My employee had nothing to do with the fire."

You know you were behind it. Stop trying to hide it.

"Then why is your employee locked up? You have a lot of nerve coming here, young lady."

"Harold would never do something like this."

"Then tell me who would."

I let 'er rip. "I think you already know the answer to that question."

His gaze darkened. "What are you implying?"

"I know what you hid in your closet, Mr. Up-and-Coming Senator. Wouldn't it ruin your campaign if people found out their decorated war hero killed his wife?"

His mother gasped. Guilt pounded through me. I hadn't meant for it to happen this way. His poor mother could have a heart attack over news like this.

Cunningham stepped closer, his eyes lit with anger. "I did not kill my wife."

"Then how did the gun end up hidden in your closet? Surely William Newsome didn't leave it there since he shot you on his way out the window."

He looked ready to spit nails. "You need to leave. Now."

"Where were you on the night of the fire?" I asked, not ready to give up.

"You need to go," his mother said behind me. I heard her fumbling with the door.

Cunningham stepped closer. "I was in the hospital. Check the records."

"Why'd you send me the bomb then? You're the only person who would have sent it. Don't deny it, Michael. You know you did it."

Where were these accusations coming from? *Shut up, Gabby. Shut up.* These things were supposed to stay in my thoughts, not be spoken aloud.

Things were not going according to my nonplan.

Cunningham backed me against the door that his mother so desperately wanted to open. "You need to keep your nosy red head out of this."

I held my ground. Of course, I was trapped, so what choice did I have? "It's actually strawberry blond."

"Oh, and you're a smart mouth, too? Well, let me tell you something, Gabby St. Claire. If you don't let this go, I can make your life miserable."

"Is that a threat?" My voice trembled.

"It's whatever you want it to be."

"Michael Cunningham—watch what you say, young man," his mother scolded.

"Stay out of this, Mother!"

His mother shrunk back. I wanted to shrink back, but there was no room left to shrink. Cunningham leered in my face. Murder loomed in his eyes.

He was a man with a secret. And men with secrets shouldn't talk when they're mad because they might blurt out things they're not supposed to know, like . . .

"I never told you my last name."

CHAPTER FOURTEEN

"Get out." Veins protruded from his temples, pulsating with his anger. "Now!"

I inched sideways, away from the door, and cracked it open. "Have a good day, Mr. Cunningham."

I slipped out before he said anything else. Like he hadn't said enough. Like I hadn't said too much.

As soon as I got my van door closed, I snapped it locked. I leaned back and tried to catch my breath. What had happened in there?

Michael Cunningham was a man on the verge of losing it. He hardly seemed like the same person who was smiling with his wife in those photos.

I wanted to sit there until I quit shaking, but I glanced at the house and saw the form of a man standing in the downstairs window, the curtain pushed aside, the room brightly lit behind him. Cunningham. Watching me.

Inching into traffic, I replayed the conversation in my mind. How could Detective Parker not see that this man was a threat?

I pulled up to my apartment, frowning when I saw Riley's car. After slamming the van door, I went inside and climbed the stairs.

No sign of Riley. Why wasn't I relieved?

Just as I was about to close my apartment door, I heard his deep masculine voice behind me.

"Can we talk, Gabby?"

I glanced across the hall. Riley leaned against his door, his arms crossed over his broad chest. His hair was ruffled, like he'd been lying down, and his blue eyes sparkled, as always.

Why did he have to be so cute?

Before I could change my mind, I threw the door open and walked into my kitchen. He could take it as an invitation if he wanted.

I deposited my purse on the counter, then turned, colliding into his chest. His eyes cut into mine. Why did I feel like he could see more in one glance than anyone else in my life had seen in years?

"You look like you've just seen a ghost."

I swallowed, but kept my head high. "A killer, actually."

Riley tilted his head in what I could only describe as exasperation. "You didn't stop by to see Michael Cunningham, did you?"

"I'm not up to talking about this."

He grabbed my arm before I could walk away. "Gabby, why are you putting yourself in this position? Why can't you let it go?"

"Because I don't want to see Harold behind bars. Is that so strange? So hard to comprehend?"

His gaze softened. "No, it's not. But let me handle it. I'm his lawyer."

Forcing my shoulders to relax, I stared back at him. "Lawyer, huh? You never mentioned that in any of our conversations."

"It didn't seem important." He let go of my arm and ran his hand through his hair. "I'm trying to figure some things out, Gabby. It's not as simple as it seems."

His honesty began to warm my icy heart. "Well, it's really nice of you to take on Harold's case. He needs a good lawyer." I paused. "You are a good lawyer, aren't you?"

A smile pulled up half of his lip. "I like to think so."

I leaned my palms against the counter. "Things have just been so crazy here lately. I can hardly think."

"That's understandable. Someone tried to kill you. Twice."

I didn't need to be reminded of how precarious things had been the past couple of days. What I needed was a long, hot bath.

Riley sat in one of the wicker chairs at my glass-top table.

So much for my bath.

"How did you run into Michael Cunningham?" Riley grabbed a pencil from the coffee table and began twirling it between his fingers, his gaze meeting mine.

Oh, nuts. He wanted details. "I paid him a visit." I put the kettle on the stove. "Tea?"

"How did you know where he was staying?"

I pulled a mug from the cabinet. "I have my ways."

While waiting for the water to boil, I took a seat across from him, feeling awkward in my own house. Something wasn't right about that.

He raised an eyebrow. "Such as?"

I shrugged. "I'll trade you secret for secret. You tell me why you decided to take on Harold's case. Then I'll tell you how I found out where Cunningham was staying."

Riley nodded slowly. "Deal." He set the pencil down with a clink and pulled his hands back. "I thought about what you said, about how much Harold meant to you and how much you believed in him. I decided I wanted to help."

"That's it?"

"That's it. Plain and simple." His gaze held mine, unwavering. "Now it's your turn. How'd you know where Cunningham was staying?"

I leaned back, glaring at him. Somehow I'd expected more conversation before I spilled my guts. "Cunningham's neighbor told me." I quit and stared.

He repeated my earlier question. "That's it?"

I shrugged and did my best Gary Cooper imitation. "Yep."

"And what possessed you to pay his mother a visit?"

"I wanted to pay my condolences."

"No, really."

"Yes, really. I wanted to apologize. Then when I realized Cunningham might be there, I wanted to see how he reacted seeing me face-to-face."

"Did you get the reaction you wanted?"

"He knew my last name before I told him."

Riley's head bobbed up. "Interesting."

"He threatened me."

Riley's head froze, and his perfect eyes narrowed. "You could have been putting yourself in danger."

"In danger?" I batted my eyelashes dramatically. "How could I be in danger from an innocent man?"

"If you go around accusing people, things can get ugly." Riley sighed and began playing with the pencil again. "What time did his house burn down?"

"Harold left at seven thirty. Then I found the gun and started to pack up. I heard the glass break—I'd guess around eight thirty or nine. Why?"

Riley tapped on the table. "There's a two-hour period that Cunningham was unaccounted for at the hospital."

I leaned forward, processing the information. "How do you know that, Riley?"

"I have my ways."

I snatched the pencil away from him. "Explain."

He frowned, looking from me to the pencil as if he were considering snatching it back. "I went to the hospital today and asked around. I guess Cunningham said he was going to walk around the hospital for a few minutes to work his leg. He was gone for two hours. No one saw him."

Hope surged through me. "I could hug you."

"It doesn't prove anything."

"It proves Cunningham doesn't have an alibi. It proves opportunity. It weakens the case against Harold."

He shrugged. "If I'm going to prove Harold innocent, I need to prove someone else is guilty."

"No, you don't, my friend. All you need is reasonable doubt. I'm liking you more and more all the time."

"You'll like me more after this." Riley leaned forward and drew in a deep breath, as if the words didn't come easily. "Don't ask me why I'm offering this, but I have an interview with William Newsome tomorrow." His piercing expression met mine. "Would you care to join me?"

Newsome, the man accused of killing Gloria Cunningham. My mouth watered just thinking about the questions I had for that man.

CHAPTER FIFTEEN

"You're just here to listen, Gabby." Riley tugged at his tie, loosening it as we neared the front door of the prison. "Don't try anything smart."

"Me, smart? Not in this lifetime." My heels clicked across the cement sidewalk and I smoothed my beige suit.

Riley stopped short, held the door closed, and turned to me. "Gabby." He drew my name out until it had four syllables.

I raised my hands in the perfect imitation of a woman surrendering. "I'll be on my best behavior."

Riley stared at me a moment longer, then strained his neck against the fabric of his shirt. He pulled open the steel door to let me go in first. "So far your best behavior has scared me half to death. You have a glimmer in your eyes."

I stopped in the doorway and glanced up at him. My breath caught when I realized our close proximity. Something about his face was just lovable. It was earnest, wholesome, and staring back at me with equal intensity. I inhaled the woodsy scent of his cologne and found myself wanting more.

I had to get a grip.

He leaned closer, and I could feel his breath on my cheek. My heart nearly pounded out of my chest. I barely found my voice. "I'm hoping for answers. Is that too much?"

"No, it's not."

He looked dashing in a suit, though I knew he'd be more comfortable in jeans and a pullover. Whatever happened in his past, this suit seemed to be connected to it, as he fidgeted with every step.

"You look nice, Riley."

He looked away and adjusted his tie again, the mood broken. "Thanks." With a sweep of his hand, he waved me inside. "Let's go."

We walked into the gray prison. For one of my classes in college, we had gone to a prison to observe a forensic specialist at work. An inmate had hung himself. I remember humming tunes from the musical *Chicago* while watching in fascination as the crime-scene investigator gathered evidence.

College had been great fun, a place where I'd learned interesting facts such as tongue prints are just as unique as fingerprints, and a koala's fingerprint can't be distinguished from the fingerprint of a human.

College had been where I'd discovered the truth: science. Everything made sense—well, everything except the part about man evolving from monkeys. That was just ridiculous. It pained me to admit it, but I wasn't sure where we'd come from. The question had always haunted me, nagged at me even.

But science, that's where miracles were found. Things could be proven through tests and experiments. In some ways, I guess I worshipped science like others worshipped God. The nice thing about science was that it had never let me down. I couldn't say that much for God.

An officer directed Riley and me down a couple of hallways until we reached the visitation room. Riley and I took a seat in the end booth. I stared at the Plexiglas that would soon separate us from a criminal. When I talked to Harold next, is this the way we would communicate? I squirmed in my orange plastic chair.

"You going to be okay?" Riley asked.

"I'm just anxious for this to start."

As soon as I spoke, a slight man plopped down on the other side of the glass. Somehow, I had imagined William to be bigger, scarier.

Instead, his oversized glasses and greasy brown hair made him look more like a con artist than someone accused of murder.

"I didn't burn no house down." William didn't wait for the questions. His voice was too nasal to be tough. "I was in jail. The perfect alibi."

Riley's jaw locked into place. "Let's start by talking about Gloria Cunningham."

"I already told the police a million times, I didn't kill no lady."

"Then why was your shoe print found at the crime scene after she was murdered?"

William dipped his head lower and sighed. His eyes held arrogance. "I stopped by to talk with her earlier that night. I wanted to convince her not to testify."

"You were desperate for her not to testify," Riley stated, his jaw flexing with intensity.

William's face reddened. "Yeah, but not desperate enough to kill her, if that's what you're asking."

"Why would Cunningham think it was you then? He claims you shot him in the leg."

"He says whoever it was wore a mask. He can't prove a thing. Can't you see I'm a scapegoat? Now, I'm willing to do time for my past crimes, but I ain't doing time for this. That's premeditated murder."

I listened to the exchange with fascination, forcing myself to keep quiet. Though William looked like a slime ball, I believed him. He didn't kill Gloria.

"If you didn't do it, who did?" Riley asked.

"What do I look like, a psychic? I don't know. I just know it wasn't me." William rose, his face turning redder.

"You threatened to kill her."

"I didn't mean it. I just didn't want her to testify. It was all talk." He shook his head.

"What was your meeting like with the Cunninghams when you went over there earlier in the day?" I asked.

Riley narrowed his eyes at me. Though I'd promised to stay quiet, the question had popped out.

The warden cleared his throat, and William sat down. He shrugged as if trying to gain his cool. His gaze settled on Riley. "I walked up to the door. There was yelling inside, like the mister and missus were arguing about something. I rang the bell. The husband answered. He looked ticked. I thought he was gonna kill me right then and there. I never had a chance to say nothin'."

I could imagine the scene perfectly, based on my encounter with Cunningham yesterday. I pictured the veins at his temple, the fire in his eyes. Shudders rippled down my spine.

"Did you hear what they were arguing about?" Riley asked.

"No idea. It was all muffled, you know?"

"Did you hire someone to burn down their house?"

"Do I look like I have that kind of money? For Pete's sake, I robbed a bank trying to get some extra cash!" He shook his head like we were the morons. "I heard one of the guys cleaning the crime scene burned the house down. He had the access. Why don't you talk to him?"

My back went rigid. "He didn't do it."

Riley placed his hand on my arm and sent another warning glance.

The warden approached William from behind. "Time's up."

William eyed us both. "I didn't kill that woman. I don't know who did, but it weren't me."

When he was gone, Riley and I sat in silence.

"I wonder what the Cunninghams were arguing about," I said.

"It's irrelevant."

"Are you going to talk to Michael today? To ask him about those two unaccounted hours?"

"Yes, but I'm doing that alone," Riley said.

"I behaved myself! It was a good question."

"If Cunningham sees you, he's only going to get upset."

"And when Cunningham hears what you have to say, he's going to be furious."

Riley sighed. "I just need to handle this alone, Gabby. I already broke the rules and let you come here today."

Maybe I was asking for too much. I nodded and resigned myself to respect Riley's choice.

CHAPTER

SIXTEEN

I wasn't about to sit in my apartment and sulk until Riley got back. If he wouldn't let me come along, then I'd do some digging on my own.

As soon as he pulled away from the apartment, I grabbed my keys and climbed into the van. Contemplating my next move, I rubbed the pointy chin of my heart-shaped face.

Really, only sweet people should have heart-shaped faces, but by some freak of nature, I'd ended up with a face that looked angelic. It was an advantage in high school because I could get away with things. Like when the teacher asked who was playing Dr. Frankenstein with a lab frog, trying to bring the poor thing back to life using electricity. I didn't say a word. I just sat there with wide eyes and tilted my innocent face. He never even suspected me. At least not until he caught me trying to do the same thing with a fetal pig. Busted.

The two good things my parents had given me were a sweet face and a slim build, although people always assumed because I was skinny that I liked my body. But my stomach wasn't flat, cellulite attacked my hips, and I'd always hated my knees, so I rarely wore shorts. Come to think of it, I'd never known a woman who did like her body. Even my mom, who was a former Miss Norfolk, had constantly looked in the mirror and shook her head at the mess she'd become.

That's when Mom met Dad—during her reign as beauty queen of our historic port city. Dad was in Virginia Beach for a surfing competition and had come by the pageant, no doubt to ogle during the swimsuit competition. Mom always said it was love at first sight.

Mom had been seventeen, and Dad nineteen. I was born nine months later, out of wedlock. Instead of going to medical school as Mom had planned, she'd stayed home with me for a while. That's when Dad was making the covers of surfing magazines and getting endorsement deals. Then he hurt his back in a surfing accident, and he'd felt sorry for himself ever since.

I drove toward the Cunninghams' house, reviewing the conversation with William and my confrontation with Cunningham. I needed evidence that proved Cunningham was the murderer. Of course, I'd already discovered the gun in his house, and that hadn't helped. I could hand over a taped confession and Parker wouldn't care.

I pulled into the neighbor's driveway. I had to find out exactly what she had seen on the night of the fire. Had she only assumed the man was Michael Cunningham?

After parking the van, I walked up the gravel drive to the Tudor home, concentrating so I wouldn't twist my ankle in the heels I wore. A large expanse of lawn, typical in this wooded neighborhood, fluttered with the wind, the long grass blowing like ocean waves. The breeze offered a brief respite from the humidity.

I rang the doorbell. A minute later, the same bleached-blond Barbie doll from two days ago answered, smiling with all the beauty cosmetic surgery could buy. She squinted, as if trying to remember where she'd seen me before, though no lines formed on her forehead.

"Hi. We met a couple of days ago at the Cunninghams' house." I held out my hand. "I'm Gabby St. Claire."

"Oh, that's right." Her eyes widened in what might have looked like recognition if not for the Botox freezing her muscles. "I'm Barbara. Come on in."

I stepped inside the expansive marble entryway. "Sorry to disturb you, but I was hoping you might answer a couple of questions for me."

"Anything I can do to help. I just want whoever did this to pay."

"Me, too." I dropped the polite smile. "Barbara, you told me when we talked that you saw Mr. Cunningham at the house on the night of the arson. Are you sure it was him?"

"Oh, yes. I'm sure. I was raking leaves when I saw a car pull up—"

"His car?"

She drew her swollen lips into a thin line. "No, it wasn't his car, but I'd seen it at the house before. He started to go in the house but then stopped and walked around outside instead."

"How long was he there?"

"Probably only five minutes."

Long enough to set it on fire, I thought.

"Did you say anything to him?"

"I was going to, but . . . it's awkward, you know? What do you say to someone whose wife has just been murdered? It's not exactly a time for small talk."

"Did you see anything else at the house that night? Any unusual visitors?"

Barbara looked at her manicured hands, then raised her head. "No. All I know is that I saw flames shooting out the windows. I called 911 right away."

"What do you know about the Cunninghams? Were they a happy couple? I've heard they fought quite a bit."

"What married couple doesn't? But Michael and Gloria, they had their fair share. Sometimes their voices would drift all the way across the lawn."

"Any idea what they fought about?"

Barbara shook her head so robotically, I decided she'd be better as a Stepford wife. "No idea. I just assumed it was the stress of getting ready to run for office."

I stared at the woman in front of me, curious about her life. It seemed so different from mine with my endless struggles to make ends meet. What would it be like to have no worries?

"What does your husband do, Barbara?"

Her eyelids fluttered until she looked down. "We're separated, actually. But he's a banker."

"Thanks for your time. You've been very helpful." I stepped out the door, ready to leave.

"What was it you do again?" Barbara asked.

"I'm a crime-scene cleaner."

Just as I took a step away, a brown truck pulled up the driveway, and a deliveryman appeared on the porch. I slowed my walk.

"I've got a package for Mrs. Barbara O'Connor," he said.

Barbara signed for it and took the box. I was halfway down the steps when I froze.

"Is there a return address on that package?"

Barbara looked it over. "No, there's not."

That block handwriting on the front, the size of box. It kicked my memory into overdrive.

"Put the package down, Barbara."

She raised her eyebrows as if considering the possibility I was crazy. "Why?"

"It's a bomb."

Her face went white, but she did as I said.

"Is anyone inside your house?"

She shook her head. "It's just me. The kids are at school."

"I need you to come toward me. We're going to walk down the drive-way, away from the package. Understand?"

She nodded and tiptoed down the brick steps. Arm in arm, we hurried down the drive and stared back at the deadly delivery.

"I'm going to call the detective." I pulled the phone from my waist. "He'll send the bomb squad out."

"How do you know all of this?"

"Because someone sent me a package just like that."

Detective Parker walked up the drive, his tie flipping behind him in the wind. His scowl deepened when he saw me. Had the stunt-double job fallen through? Did he figure out there were actual killers in jail?

"You can tell me what you were doing here later," he mumbled as he brushed past.

"It's a good thing I was here," I called to his back, "or we might have another dead body on our hands."

He stopped and glared. "There is no 'our hands,' Nancy Drew. You're not a part of this investigation."

"I'm free to talk to whomever I want."

He stepped closer, his brows furrowed. "You need to stay away from Michael Cunningham."

"I just went over to offer condolences."

"Your innocent little facade might work with some people, Gabby, but not with me. You were snooping and sticking your nose where it doesn't belong."

"You afraid I'm going to find out what really happened and make you look bad?"

His jaw muscle flexed, and he leaned closer, lowering his voice. Only it didn't sound alluring, like I imagined it might. Instead it sounded harsh and arrogant. "You're going to get hurt if you don't back down."

I licked my lips. "That sounds like a threat, Detective."

"It's a warning. There are people in this world who wouldn't think twice about hurting a lady like you. Some might even enjoy it."

"If you recall, someone has tried to hurt me twice this week. Kill me, actually."

"The third time might be the charm." He turned on his Kenneth Cole heel and walked toward the house, leaving me with an ice-cold chill. What exactly did he mean by that?

My gaze followed the detective as he sauntered up the porch, acting immune to the bomb threat. The bomb squad, all dressed in black, huddled over the package on the porch. To my left, Barbara talked to two officers, giving a report of how everything happened. The woman's arms flailed, and her voice cracked. She had to use a lot of body language to make up for her total lack of facial expression.

Why would someone send Barbara a package bomb? Unless they were sending one to everyone they suspected knew too much. But what did Barbara know that someone would want to kill her for? That Cunningham had returned to his house on the night of the arson?

My head ached. How would I ever make sense of everything? Maybe Riley had found out something helpful, something that would offer insight and give my racing thoughts a rest.

I climbed back into my van and pulled out my cell phone. Riley answered on the third ring, right after Lucky squawked in the background.

"It's me. Did you find out anything good?"

"Gabby?"

Heat filled my cheeks. Why did I assume I was the only female who'd be calling him? He was an attractive guy. Certainly lots of women would find him interesting.

"Yeah, it's me. What did you find out?"

"I'd prefer not to talk about things over the phone. When will you be home?"

I glanced at the bomb squad working on the porch. How long had it taken at my house? Three hours? I had at least two hours to go, maybe more. "Probably not soon."

"Is everything okay?"

"Cunningham's neighbor got a package bomb just like the one I got," I blurted.

Did I imagine it, or did Riley sigh? "How do you know this, Gabby?"

"I was at her house when it was delivered."

After a pause, a chuckle came over the line. "You never fail to amaze me, Gabby. You're pretty remarkable, you know that?"

I'd expected another lecture similar to the one I'd received from Parker. Riley's words soothed my heart instead. "Thanks, Riley."

"Find me tonight when you get home, okay? Lucky and I will be here hanging out."

I smiled, imagining the two of them playing cards together and eating pizza. He was quickly winning a place in my heart. . . . Riley was, too.

CHAPTER

SEVENTEEN

Back at my apartment three-and-a-half hours later, I changed into some exercise pants and a red T-shirt before knocking on Riley's door, bowl of popcorn in hand.

A lot of redheads rebelled against wearing red. Not me. I was proud of my fiery curls. How could I not be when it put me in the same category as other famous redheads, greats like Lucille Ball, Pippi Longstocking, and Ronald McDonald? Well, maybe not Mr. McDonald, but still, red hair made a statement.

Riley's door opened, and he stood there, shaking his head with an amused expression on his face. I batted my eyelashes innocently. "What?"

"How do you do it?"

"Do what?"

"Find trouble."

"I've always heard I have a nose for it."

"You'll get no arguments from me." He stepped back and let me inside.

"Hope you don't mind. I brought my own popcorn. Funny how easy it is to forget to eat when you get busy." I dropped onto the couch and let the cushions absorb my weary, achy muscles. Even the smothering heat in his apartment didn't bother me.

"Have you had anything to eat today besides popcorn?"

I mentally ran through my day. "I did have a candy bar at lunchtime."

Riley stood. "Let me fix you something. You need to eat."

"Oh, no. You don't have to do that."

"I want to."

"You're not going to make acorn brownies, are you?"

Riley laughed. "Do you like stir-fry?"

The thought of real food made my stomach grumble. "I don't want you to go to any trouble."

"I don't mind. You just relax for a few minutes."

Starvation beat out guilt any day. I stretched my legs over the pine coffee table and wiggled my toes. I definitely wasn't used to being in heels all day. Nor was I used to someone looking after my needs. I could get used to this.

But I wouldn't.

I wasn't good at depending on others. In college, I'd depended on a lab partner in Physics 101 and ended up getting the first and only B of my college career. From then on, I decided to do all the work myself. I had to keep up my GPA in order to fulfill my dream of getting multiple job offers after college. I wanted to accept the one farthest away from here. Maybe Alaska or Hawaii. Anywhere but Virginia.

My gaze roamed the apartment. Riley had done quite a bit of work since I helped him unpack. No boxes were in sight.

He had a casual decorating style, one that fit him. Simple, navy blue curtains covered the windows; the couch was beige and oversized. The bookcase, dining-room table, and TV armoire were all simple designs made from pine. A striped, navy blue and beige rug warmed the wooden floor, and an acoustic guitar rested in a corner. I imagined Riley sitting around a bonfire on the beach, strumming his guitar. I liked the image. I could even see good old Dad joining in the fun.

Every once in a while, I'd run into someone who knew my father during his glory days. They'd tell me about the waves he'd conquered, the women he'd wooed, and the parties he'd thrown. The end of his surfing career had been like someone taking his T-Bird away. There was no fun, fun, fun after that. Even working at a surf shop didn't ease his restlessness. Only visits to Margaritaville made him feel better.

The scent of sizzling vegetables and soy sauce floated into the room. I abandoned popcorn on the coffee table and closed my eyes, anticipating my coming meal.

It was amazing how much life could change in one week. For better or for worse.

Better: a nice new neighbor.

Worse: my one and only employee now called jail home.

Better: I'd survived two attempts on my life.

Worse: two attempts had been made on my life.

I sighed. What a week.

"One chicken stir-fry and a glass of water." Riley's voice cut into my thoughts.

I opened my eyes and sat up straighter as Riley placed the steaming food in front of me.

"You do eat meat, don't you?"

I smiled. "I do. Looks great."

"I wish I could take the credit, but it's from a frozen mix, chicken and all." Riley sank into an overstuffed chair across the coffee table from me.

"You won't hear me complain." I took a bite, grateful that Riley had offered to do this. I owed him one. I owed him several, actually. Quiet fell as I enjoyed my meal.

A muffled song broke the silence. It almost sounded like an old rock song from the 1980s, only it wasn't coming from a radio. It was too off-key for that.

I glanced at Riley, and he shook his head. "Your friend downstairs sings in the shower. Every morning. Her voice travels up through the vent, and I get serenaded. Even Lucky is learning the words to 'We're Not Going to Take It.'"

I giggled and took another bite of food.

"So, I finally heard Bill's radio talk show today on the way home from talking with Cunningham," Riley said. "He's still talking about the acorn brownies."

"Yeah. Well, I'm still thinking about them, so who can blame him? I didn't even know you could eat acorns, let alone grind them into flour."

Riley leaned forward, hands clenched between his splayed knees. "Living in an apartment building like this, you hardly need a TV for entertainment."

"There's never a dull moment."

"Listen, missy, most of these nondull moments are your fault. Don't sound like you're innocent."

I paused, my fork in the air. "Whatever are you talking about? I'm as normal as normal can be."

Riley burst into laughter. "You've got the curiosity of a cat. There's no stopping you once you get something into your head."

"You're saying I belong here with the bin of loons? I'm not sure how I feel about that." A smile twitched the corner of my mouth.

"I like people who aren't afraid to be themselves. It's refreshing."

I scraped at the plate, chasing after every speck of the stir-fry I could get, then pushed the empty Fiestaware onto the table with a contented sigh. "That was great. Thank you."

"You're welcome."

"I've never gotten to know someone and not thought they were weird, actually. Some people just hide it better than others."

"I can't argue with that."

I stared at a print of van Gogh's *The Café Terrace on the Place du Forum, Arles, at Night* hanging above the TV. I only knew that because its title stretched across the bottom. The painting made me want to jump onto the canvas and sit in one of the cozy café chairs.

Riley leaned closer, and I knew the conversation would turn serious. "Tell me about your visit with Cunningham's neighbor."

"Barbara O'Connor is positive she saw Cunningham at the house on the night of the arson."

"Did Cunningham see her?"

"She doesn't think so." I recounted what Barbara had told me. "Did Cunningham tell you where he went during the two hours he was missing at the hospital?"

"Said he was walking the halls."

I held my breath, unsure if I wanted to hear the answer to my next question. I asked anyway. "Do you believe him?"

CHAPTER EIGHTEEN

"No, I don't."

"You mean someone's actually on my side? Someone believes me?" I tried to sound sarcastic so he wouldn't be able to tell how relieved I was.

Riley's confident gaze held mine. How was it that the slight bump on his nose, his strong, masculine jaw, and his need-a-trim hair were etched into my memory like a lifelong friend's? I'd already memorized the rolling tones of his voice, his smooth, deep laughter, the way his blue eyes crinkled when he smiled, and the stern set of his jaw when I aggravated him.

"Just because I didn't agree with you didn't mean I wasn't on your side, Gabby."

"I know, but it feels good to know I'm not losing it." I let out a deep breath. I wasn't sure that was right. Maybe it would be better to imagine someone was trying to kill me than for it to actually be true. "What happened to change your mind?"

"Most of what I asked Cunningham, he was prepared for. He breezed through his answers, not the least bit ruffled. But when I asked about those two hours, it took him by surprise. He said he wouldn't say anything else without a lawyer present."

I grabbed Riley's arm, delighting for a moment at the startled expression on my neighbor's face. "He pulled the lawyer card?"

"Like a guy with a losing hand."

"I'm surprised he had a meeting with you at all without his lawyer."

"I think I caught him by surprise, then made him so mad he forgot the first rule of guilty people—lawyer up!"

I tilted my head. "Isn't the husband always a suspect when the wife is murdered?"

"Usually. But with Newsome right there to be a prime suspect and Cunningham's so-called iron-clad alibi, they didn't look closer. And all the evidence pointed to Newsome. His shoe print was found outside their home, he threatened Mrs. Cunningham numerous times, and his hair was found in their bedroom."

I sat up straighter. "That's a huge red flag."

"Yeah. It's no wonder they suspect him."

"Could it have been planted?"

"Planted evidence? Who had one of Newsome's hairs?"

I held back a sigh. "What good does it do to speculate about all of this when the detective on the case disregards everything I tell him?"

"Why do you think he's disregarding what you say?"

"Because he's arrogant."

Riley smirked at me. "Glad to see you're keeping an open mind."

I rolled my eyes. "We had a little confrontation today. He told me the 'third time is a charm' when I mentioned I'd almost been killed twice."

Riley stayed silent for a long minute, as if he were turning things over in his mind. Finally he said, "Tell me about the bomb."

"Same makeup as the one sent to me," I said. "Same handwriting and packaging. No return address. It sounds like someone thinks Barbara knows something she shouldn't. They want her to be quiet."

"Just like they want you to be quiet."

"Which must mean I'm on the right track, right?"

"Yes, Gabby. It means you're so much on the right track that someone's willing to kill to keep you quiet."

I hardly wanted to get out of bed the next morning. The covers were a warm barrier from my hyperactive AC, and though the sunlight filtered cheerfully through the wooden blinds, telling me it was a beautiful day, there were killers out there. Staying in bed seemed like a much safer bet.

Third time's a charm.

Like a scratched record, it repeated itself over and over.

It seemed a promise that I would die.

There you go with that imagination again, Gabby. The detective was probably just trying to scare you into staying away from the case.

It wasn't completely true, though. Someone didn't send me a pipe bomb just for kicks. They wanted me hurt, out of commission, climbing Led Zeppelin's stairway to heaven.

My cell phone rang on my wicker nightstand, and I grabbed it. "Gabby St. Claire."

"I'm looking for a cleaner, and you were recommended to me," a man with a slight northeastern accent said.

I forced myself to sit up. "What do you need?"

"I work at a garage downtown. I've got a car with an awful lot of blood covering the seats. I need it cleaned so we can put it on the market."

Maybe wading ankle deep into someone else's blood would get my mind off how precarious my own life had become. Plus, I had bills piling up. I couldn't turn down any jobs unless I wanted to put in some minimum-wage hours at the Grounds. It wasn't my cup of tea, at least not today. "Sure, I can do that."

He gave me an address, and I agreed to get there as soon as possible. Slapping the covers back, I skipped taking a shower—no sense wasting a clean body on a bloodbath—and slid some jeans on, along with a white T-shirt. I pulled a baseball cap over my mop of curls. After brushing my teeth and applying light foundation, I was ready to go.

I stepped out the door the same time as Riley. "Morning," I said.

"It's actually past noon."

I yawned as we started downstairs, side by side. "I'd still be in bed if someone hadn't called with a job."

He paused. "Maybe I should go with you."

The idea tempted me. But cleaning a car was a one-person job, and I didn't want to put Riley's sainthood to the test. He'd already done so much. "I'll be fine."

"You sure? I don't mind."

"That's sweet of you to offer. I'll be okay, though." I glanced at his khakis and button-up, forest green shirt. "Besides, it looks like you already have plans."

"Just going to the library to check a few things out." He paused by my van. "Want to grab a cup of coffee together tonight?"

The offer sounded fun. "I'd like that."

He grinned. "Eight o'clock. Be there or be square."

I smiled back, already in better spirits. I was still grinning when I started my van. Ten minutes later, I pulled up to the garage. I stared at the building before getting out of the van. Grass grew out of every crevice in the cement and graffiti painted the brick walls.

I stuffed my keys into my pocket and approached the building. The door to the office hung on only one hinge, and the inside smelled musty, like it hadn't been used in awhile.

"Hello?" I called. "I'm here to clean a car."

Silence answered.

I stepped inside, taking in the cluttered office. A mug of coffee sat on an old desk calendar. I leaned in closer. Why did the calendar say 1998?

"You must be Ms. St. Claire."

My hand flew to my heart. A man in his forties with thinning hair and a blue mechanics uniform stood on the other side of the room. Between his protruding gut and huge lips, he had a unique look, to say the least. Slap on some white feathers and he could pass for Donald Duck's older brother.

"I didn't see you there," I said.

He waddled toward the door, a hesitant smile playing on his lips. "No problem. Let me show you the car."

The thought of walking farther into this building with Duck Man set off some kind of internal alarm, and I froze. Between the fire and the bomb, I had to be careful. But the man looked harmless enough. I just wouldn't throw him any stale bread, lest he and a flock of his friends surround me.

I glanced over and saw the man waiting at the door with a strange expression.

Great. I thought he might say quack, and he thought I was a quack. I really had to stop thinking of people as animals. Sierra had been a squirrel; this man a duck. If I wasn't careful, I'd start thinking of Parker as a dodo bird. Oh wait, I already did.

"You okay?"

Just to be safe, I nodded toward the calendar. "I thought my business has been slow lately. Yours must be practically dead."

He quacked up. "I just bought the place. Haven't had much of a chance to do anything with it, including go through this office."

The explanation made sense. Putting my shoulders back, I stepped forward and followed him into the garage. An old, beat-up Ford Escort came into view. Duck Man opened the driver's side door.

"I don't know what happened in here. Don't want to know, to be honest. I just know it left a mess. The body's in good condition, and with a little work, I should be able to make some money off of this girl. You think you can get her cleaned up?"

I peered inside the car. Blood saturated the passenger seat and glass embedded itself in the carpet. I should be able to get it cleaned up without much hassle. No job was too tough for Trauma Care. The post office had their snow, rain, heat, and gloom motto. I had my blood, guts, bones, and brain matter.

"I'll see what I can do."

"Great."

He started to toddle away when I cleared my throat. "Would you mind opening the garage doors so I can have some more light? The brighter it is, the cleaner I'll get the car."

"No problem."

The doors opened, and I basked in the sunlight.

I went to my van and pulled out the supplies I needed, starting with my hazmat suit and a thick pair of gloves. My bandage made the gloves fit snugly. The doctor said I could take it off tomorrow. I couldn't wait.

I sprayed the seats down and let them soak. A vacuum took up a lot of the glass, but much of it would have to be removed by hand, piece by piece. I would also wipe down the console and steering wheel, anywhere that blood may have splattered.

Taking a break, I wiped the sweat from my forehead and grabbed my water. Though the liquid wasn't cold anymore, it still tasted refreshing.

"How's it coming?" The mechanic stuck his head in the garage.

"I should be finished in about an hour or so."

He smiled but didn't show any teeth. Of course, ducks didn't have teeth.

"I'm going to grab some dinner. If I'm not back by the time you leave, could you close the doors and lock up for me? I left your check on the desk in the office."

"Sure thing." I watched the heavyset man disappear. A moment later, an engine cranked, and I watched him pull away in an old boat of a car. How appropriate.

I put the water back on the old workbench and started cleaning again. The sooner I finished, the sooner I could get out of this place.

An hour later, everything had been scrubbed and my equipment put away. The mechanic hadn't arrived back from dinner yet, but it didn't matter. I could go home and meet Riley for our coffee date. I smiled at the mere thought. I really felt like there could be something between me and Riley. He was different from most of the guys I'd been with. I could even overlook the fact that he was a lawyer, if he could overlook the fact that I was a crime-scene cleaner.

After doing a final inspection of my work, I stripped out of the stuffy hazmat suit and closed the garage door. The outside became a line of sunlight at the bottom of the door until the heavy metal slammed into the concrete.

Darkness filled the garage.

I'd left the light on. I knew I had. Had the mechanic flipped it off before he left for dinner?

My hand still on the handle, I tugged the door, urging it back up. It wouldn't budge.

Panic charged down my spine.

I'd have to feel my way to the office.

I inched forward, my shoes shuffling across the cement floor. The workbench should be to my left. If I could reach it, it could guide me until I found the door.

I could also grab a wrench while I was there. Something heavy and dangerous. I'd even settle for some garlic.

If only my eyes would adjust to the darkness, if I could see where I was going. But I might as well have been standing in a deep cave. The black felt as thick as ink.

Hand outstretched, I crept forward. Any minute, I should reach the bench.

I held my breath, waiting to feel it.

My hand slid across rough wood. A splinter dug into my finger. I jerked my hand back. I didn't have time to worry about it now.

My hands roamed the area. I remembered seeing a wrench earlier, a big one.

Metal clanked across the room.

I froze.

Someone else was in the garage.

I darted toward the door, adrenaline like hot fire in my veins. I stumbled but caught myself before touching the ground.

I had to get out of here.

Fingers clamped around my arm. I gasped, swinging to a stop. A scream caught in my throat as a gloved hand slapped over my mouth.

Warm breath pricked the hair on my neck. "You couldn't stay out of it, could you?"

Goosebumps popped over my flesh. Before panic solidified, I jammed my elbow into the attacker's gut. He doubled over, but quickly grabbed my arm again.

"You shouldn't have done that."

Had I heard that voice before? *Think, Gabby. Think.*

The man shoved a rag in my mouth. Its foul taste made me gag. Oil. Cheap cologne. Who knew what else.

"Lie on the floor." He shoved me on the gritty concrete. His knee dug into my spine, pushing the air out of my lungs. Tears stung my eyes as I realized what was happening.

He jerked my arms back so hard that sharp pain split through my joints. Duct tape squealed, then ripped and clung to my wrists over and over. Then my ankles.

What was he going to do?

Keep a clear head, Gabby. Pay attention so you can give the police a description of the man. My logic meant nothing right now. I just wanted to live.

He yanked me from the ground by my arms and shoved me. I squinted at the workbench, wishing the darkness would clear. I needed to find something to protect myself. Anything.

The man pushed me again. I slammed into the trunk of the Escort. My cheek throbbed at the impact. Keys jangled. The man pulled me back and popped the trunk.

My body rebelled. I wouldn't get in, no matter what he said.

The man thrust me forward. In one ungraceful motion, my knees buckled, and my head struck metal.

Then, everything was black.

CHAPTER

NINETEEN

A happy song cut through the murkiness in my mind. My eyes slowly fluttered open. Darkness surrounded me.

My head throbbed. Wherever I lay vibrated, hummed.

And that happy song kept playing over and over.

My cell phone.

I tried to reach for it but felt tape around my wrists. Everything rushed back. Tears pushed into my eyes.

I was in the Escort. The car was running but not moving.

I closed my eyes. The garage door was probably shut.

Carbon monoxide would kill me in this car. The mechanic would find me in the morning, if at all. With my supplies put away, why would he think I was still here?

My van was out front. He'd check if he saw it.

But what if it wasn't?

Despair bit into me.

The hum of the motor was interrupted by the sing-song ring of the cell phone again.

I was supposed to meet Riley. Was it him calling now?

I strained against the tape, trying to reach my phone. My fingers stroked it, but I couldn't grasp the plastic edges.

My arms went slack. I gulped in a breath. My heart raced. The phone was my only hope. I had to keep trying.

My wrists ached as the tape cut into them. Gritting my teeth against the pain, I pulled my arms forward.

The phone teased my fingers. Just one more inch. The tension of my arms made them feel like they would snap. With one last jerk, I tried for the phone.

The ringing stopped.

My body went slack as my mind raced.

Curling into a ball, I brought my knees forward until they pinched the rag in my mouth. I tugged it out, then licked my lips.

There had to be another way to use my cell phone.

Think, Gabby. Think.

Using my leg, I pushed against the phone, trying to nudge it from its clip. My thigh rubbed it. I had to turn my legs, get the phone closer to my knee.

I twisted. Finally the phone snapped off and skidded against the carpet.

Now I had to figure out how to pick it up.

I turned over and arched my back. My fingers scrambled over the carpet, searching for the plastic.

There it was!

I grasped the phone and felt until I hit a button. A soft, mellow light filled the space around me.

Straining my neck, I looked behind me. Carefully, I dialed 911 and pressed *send*. Placing the phone on the floor, I turned and scooted as far down as I could, in order to speak into the phone.

I vaguely made out a hello. "My name is Gabby St. Claire and I'm trapped inside a car on Granby Avenue and Eighth Street in Norfolk. Please send the police. The car's running and I'm stuck in a garage."

The dispatcher said something I couldn't make out.

"Please, I don't know how much more time I have!" I said.

I inched my way up and turned. My fingers fumbled over the phone. I hit *end* and attempted to dial Riley's number. There was no answer. Using the last of my energy, I tried Sierra.

Sierra's loud voice echoed through the trunk.

"Sierra, it's Gabby."

"Gabby? Where are you? We've been worried sick."

"I just called 911. I'm stuck in a garage in Norfolk. The car's running. I don't know how long I've been here."

Riley's voice came on the line. "Where are you?"

I gave him the address.

"We're on our way, Gabby. You hang on, understand?"

"I'm doing my best."

"No, I need you to tell me you're going to hang on. Say that for me."

Could I hang on? I had to. No other option existed. "I'm going to hang on. But I'm getting so tired."

"We're in the car now. It will only take ten minutes for us to get there. You can make it ten minutes."

I licked my lips again, wishing it didn't hurt so much to swallow. "Okay. Ten minutes."

I closed my eyes. Was this the same fear my brother felt when the kidnappers stuffed him into the trunk and drove away? A sob choked me. Poor Timmy. I imagined him calling out for Mom, his voice trembling like it always did when he became frightened. A six-year-old should never have to go through that.

The ache in my chest intensified until tears pushed to the surface.

"I'm sorry, Timmy. It's all my fault."

Just what had those men done with my brother?

My eyelids felt weighed down. My mind became fuzzy, as if I'd taken a strong cold medicine.

The third time's a charm was my last thought before I drifted into sleep.

I could see Timmy gliding through the air on the huge metal swing set, pumping his legs back and forth like he wanted to reach the sky. Red and yellow leaves rained down around him from the winter-ready trees. His laughter echoed across the playground, though I was the only one there to hear it.

I started toward him. My breath came out in icy clouds as I walked. I rubbed my cold hands together, enjoying the briskness of autumn.

Mom wanted to have a family meeting, though I didn't know why. She'd asked me to go get Timmy. As I approached, he continued flying through the air, the metal chains of the swing set creaking with each movement.

I started to yell my brother's name, but my voice disappeared.

"Gabby!"

No, I had to get Timmy. I couldn't listen to whoever called me. I had to get my brother and go home.

I was close enough now to see my brother's freckles, his missing front tooth. I'd missed seeing that six-year-old face.

"Gabby! Can you hear me?"

Someone shook me. I was no longer cold. In fact, I felt sticky. My hair clung to my neck. Grime coated my face.

"Timmy," I whispered.

"Gabby, it's me. Riley. Can you hear me?"

I looked back at the swing, but Timmy no longer played there. An empty swing undulated.

"No!" My voice echoed through the empty playground. Everything spun around me, a blur of autumn leaves and metal fences.

Someone shook me again. Heat blanketed me. My eyes pulled open. Riley.

My heart slowed.

Then everything went black again.

CHAPTER TWENTY

I woke up in the emergency room. A glance at the clock told me it was a few minutes past midnight. After doctors ran a series of tests on me, Detective Adams came in and I recounted everything that had happened. He grunted and nodded while jotting notes on a pad of paper.

"Did you get a good look at the man? I know you said it was dark, but anything will help," he said.

I shook my head. "I wish I could offer something, but I have no idea. It all happened so fast."

"I don't need to tell you to be careful, do I?"

The seriousness of the situation weighed heavily on my chest. "No, I figured that out all on my own."

"You still think this has something to do with the Cunningham case?"

"I have no doubt."

He nodded and stared at the pad in his hands. "I'll get working, then. Your friends have agreed not to let you out of their sight until someone is arrested for this."

Riley and Sierra. I smiled, feeling fortunate to have friends like them. "Could you send them in?"

He clicked his pen against the paper and stuffed the items into his blazer pocket. "Of course. I'll be in touch."

A moment later, Sierra peeked her head into the room. She tiptoed to my bed. I laughed at her antics.

"What are you doing?"

She shrugged. "I feel like I should be careful."

"Walking like that won't ensure safety."

"I was just going with the moment." Sierra's eyes turned serious beneath her glasses. "You really gave us a good scare, Gabby."

"Believe me, I really *had* a good scare. I didn't think I was going to make it out of this one." The last few minutes of being in the car raced through my mind. I shuddered. I could have died. I would have if my friends hadn't gotten there when they did.

"You didn't tell me you and Riley had a thing going," Sierra said, mock indignation on her face.

"That's because we don't."

She raised an eyebrow. "Could have fooled me."

"What do you mean?"

"You should have seen him when you were late for your date. He came down to my apartment and couldn't stay still. Then after you called?" She snorted. "He was hopeless after that. Almost killed us twice driving to the garage."

I smiled, but it slowly faded. "We're just friends. Really."

She raised a shoulder in a half shrug. "Whatever you say. Listen, I don't want to cut our time short, but he's pacing outside. The nurse said only one visitor at a time."

She disappeared out the door and Riley appeared. He approached my bed and looked at me with a strange emotion in his eyes. For a moment, my cheeks warmed. Was what Sierra said correct? Did Riley really have feelings for me?

His hands emerged from behind his back, and he pulled out a bouquet of daisies. "For you."

My heart fluttered. "You didn't need to do this. Saving my life was more than enough. I should be bringing you flowers."

He smiled. "I wanted to."

Before the conversation could go any further, the door swung open and Detective Parker stormed in. He disregarded Riley and positioned himself by my bed.

I scowled and rested the flowers over my chest. I glanced at them. Switch them to calla lilies, and I was doing a good imitation of a laid-out corpse. Not liking the image, I dropped the flowers to my side.

"Detective," I acknowledged.

"I heard what happened."

"And came to gloat?"

"No, I came to see if you were okay."

I forced a smile. "I'm fine. The third time wasn't a charm. What do you know?"

He frowned. "That wasn't how I meant it."

I stared at him, biting my tongue against a few insults. If the detective had listened to me from the start, I wouldn't be in this mess now. But no-o-o, he refused to believe anyone other than William Newsome or Harold was guilty.

"I'm Riley Thomas."

I diverted my eyes to Riley, thankful for the distraction. Riley held out his hand to the detective, who hesitantly shook it.

"Chip Parker." He glanced back at me. "I'm going to be working with the Norfolk police to figure out who's behind these attempts on your life."

"That's kind of you." I knew I should be nicer, but all I had was sarcasm. I wanted to say, "Welcome to the party, Einstein."

"I mean it, Gabby." Something in his gaze told me he was sincere, though I didn't want to believe it. "I don't like this any more than you do. Is there anything else you can tell me about your attacker?"

I decided today was a Dr. Jeckyl day. Mr. Hyde would be along soon enough, so I decided to cooperate. I went through all the details I could remember. My head hurt, and I just wanted to go home.

Parker snapped his notebook shut. "That should be a good start." He leaned forward and lowered his voice. "Look, I know we got off to a bad start. But I really am working on this case, trying to figure it all out. You hang in there, okay?"

I nodded, unsure of his sincerity. At least he seemed to be making an effort.

Parker straightened and nodded toward Riley. "Take care of her, would you? I'm doing everything I can to solve this case. In the meantime, someone needs to keep an eye on her."

"Got it." Riley's gaze followed the detective out before falling on me. "He's a piece of work, huh?"

"I can think of other ways to put it, but yes, he is."

Riley grinned. "So, did they tell you when you can go home?"

"They want to keep me overnight, just to make sure there's no long-term damage. I told them I'm fine, but they keep insisting on these tests." I offered a weak smile.

"I'm glad you're okay."

My voice turned serious. "Me, too."

Sierra stuck her head in the room. "They're saying we have to go now, that Gabby needs her rest."

Riley looked at me. "I'll be here in the morning to pick you up, okay?"

"Sounds great."

With one more glance, he followed Sierra out the door. My gaze remained on them until they disappeared. I had two of the best friends in the world.

Grimly, I pulled the daisies corpse-like onto my chest again.

Unfortunately, I also had one of the world's worst enemies.

CHAPTER TWENTY-ONE

"Why do people think this is fun?" I asked, a prisoner to my couch with Riley as warden. My sentence: a one-thousand-piece jigsaw puzzle that Riley found in my junk closet.

An old college roommate had given me the puzzle several years ago as her way of saying thanks for finding out who copied her term paper and sold it to college students across the country. I knew the only person capable of hacking into her hard drive was computer nerd Jeff Gates. I'd tracked him down to an off-campus arcade and creamed him at Mario Brothers until his ego was so low, he had no choice but to confess.

Puzzle pieces scattered across my coffee table, and the edges finally began to take shape. Riley insisted this was the only mystery I needed to worry about solving today.

"I need to call Mildred and find out how Harold's doing." I started to stand, but Riley prodded me back onto the couch.

"I talked to him today."

"And?"

"He's anxious to come home."

"When's the trial date?"

"Two weeks." Riley set a mug of coffee on the end table. "I have to figure out how those items got into the trunk of Harold's car."

"Cunningham."

I connected a corner piece with a long row of edge pieces. A strip of red formed. This was one of those mystery puzzles that contained no picture for a guide, only a riddle and colorful pieces that the makers insisted formed a scene. At the moment, I just knew it was a conspiracy, and there really wasn't any mystery picture, only a mangled blob we'd never figure out. I could see the game executives laughing deviously from their high-rise offices.

"How would he get Harold's keys?" Riley added a piece to the row.

"He picked the lock?"

"Not a skill your average senatorial candidate possesses. I don't see it."

I sighed and tapped a piece with yellow flowers against the couch. "There has to be some explanation. Maybe Harold left his keys on the table and someone borrowed them while he was working."

"It's a possibility." Riley shoved pieces around with his index finger, sorting and matching colors.

"What's the possibility it was Cunningham who tried to kill me last night?" I turned toward Riley, watching his expression closely.

"Not possible. He was giving a press conference at the time of your attack."

"Convenient." I shuffled pieces around. It had been years since I'd even attempted to figure out a jigsaw puzzle, not since the days of Barbie dolls, Cabbage Patch Kids, and make-believe crime scenes. "Is Cunningham still running for office?"

"Yep, and with all of this extra media attention, he'll probably win. People feel for him."

I straightened. "Maybe that's why he killed his wife. To get the attention, the sympathy of voters."

"There are simpler ways to gain sympathy than this plan that could totally backfire." He shifted to face me. "Why would he kill his wife?"

"She knew something she wasn't supposed to, something that would hurt the election?"

"Maybe. Killing someone is still pretty drastic."

"Being in office means power, prestige. Some people would kill for that." I watched as Riley pieced together an entire section, revealing a barn door. Finally, the picture had started to take shape.

"What if Cunningham is telling the truth? What if William killed Gloria and had one of his friends come to burn down the house?" Riley asked.

"It goes back to motive again. Why would William want to risk so much to burn the house down?"

"To conceal evidence."

"But the only evidence was the gun I found."

"Which was in a metal case."

"Which wouldn't have burned."

"But would have been revealed for the police to find."

We looked at each other, realization dawning between us.

"So, it was someone who knew the gun was there. Someone who knew Cunningham was the killer." I leaned into the couch and could hardly breathe. "Cunningham didn't start the fire."

"Someone who wanted him found out did. They couldn't tell the police about the gun or they would look guilty. So they burned the house down, realizing the evidence wouldn't burn."

I sat up straight. "What if they didn't realize I was inside? My van was parked out back, and the only light on in the house was in the bedroom. They could have assumed it was empty."

Riley nodded, abandoning the jigsaw also. "But that still doesn't explain why Cunningham was at the house that evening and why he's denying it."

"Burning down the house would only implicate him."

"This is getting even more tangled."

"Maybe his opponent knew about what was happening. Maybe he set the house on fire."

Riley let out a quick laugh. "Senator Ed Laskin? No way. He's straight laced."

I leaned toward Riley, curious. "How do you know so much about local politics? You've lived here less than a week."

That brooding expression I saw all too often settled on his face. What exactly was this weight he carried?

"I try to stay up on the local political scenes."

"Obviously." I waited for him to say more, to offer an explanation, but he remained silent. "Laskin would have the best motive."

"It wasn't Laskin."

"It couldn't hurt to check out his alibi."

He stood and started toward the kitchen. "You sure you don't want a muffin?"

I followed him. "What's wrong, Riley? Is it something I said?"

He grabbed a banana nut muffin from the cake dish displaying them. I had gotten something out of working at the coffeehouse—I'd had a crash course on Martha Stewart presentations.

"Nothing's wrong. Why would you think that?"

"You're acting strange."

"Nothing strange about getting a muffin."

I placed my hand over his arm. "Riley, you don't have to talk to me. But I'm here if you need to."

He started back toward the living room. "Nothing's wrong, but thanks."

Men. I sighed and followed him.

"So, what's next? Who are our other suspects?" I asked.

"We have to figure out who else was at the house that evening. That will tell us who the arsonist is."

We worked on the puzzle in silence for a few minutes. I marveled as the scene began to take shape. If only Gloria Cunningham's murder was as simple as this jigsaw. In essence, it was. All the pieces were in front of me. I just had to fit them together.

"Go to church with me tomorrow," Riley said.

My gaze jerked to Riley. "Church?" I shook my head. "I don't do church."

"Why not?"

"Because a mythical god has no appeal to me."

Riley popped another puzzle piece in place. "What if he's not mythical?"

"What if he is?"

"Then what have you lost?"

"Time and energy. Believe me, Riley. If there is a God, he must be severely upset with me because my life has been anything but ideal." I leaned back into the couch. "It's like everyone's looking for something to fill a void. Some people pour themselves into service clubs, and others pour themselves into church. If they're a little more self-destructive, they try drugs or drinking. It's all the same in the end—just another empty pursuit as people try to find meaning in life."

"I'm sorry you feel that way."

"Me, too," I answered, doing my best to ignore the void inside that hollowed me out. "Me, too."

I looked down at my pink T-shirt. It read, "Waiting for My Happily Ever After." It could have been my mantra. But I wouldn't find my happy ending in a church building.

Riley stayed at my apartment until five o'clock, playing board games and drinking coffee. He was playing bodyguard, and I was too shaken to run him off. Finally, I'd insisted he could go home, knowing he had work to do on Harold's case. I missed his company the moment he stepped out the doorway.

I shuffled across the room, staring at the puzzle as I passed. Riley and I had completed half of it, and the picture finally had begun to emerge. I'd enjoyed working on it more than I expected but had no desire to piddle with it anymore today.

Instead, I headed toward my bedroom to find a book to read. As I passed a mirror, my reflection stopped me. A gash slashed across my forehead. A burn mark reddened my other temple from where I'd maneuvered across the carpet last night. The bandage was gone from my hand, but huge blisters remained from my run-in with a hot door-knob. It really had been a tough week.

I kept moving. I had a box of books that Mrs. Mystery had given me, hidden somewhere in my closet. I opened the creaky door to the storage space, and my throat went dry.

The light had burned out, and I had never bothered to replace it. Now, as I stared at the cavelike darkness at the end of the long narrow space, I flashed back to the trunk.

As if someone rushed out of the dark toward me, I slammed the door and leaned against it. Gasping for breath, my heart pounded until I could feel pulsing in the burn on my face. Someone desperately wanted me dead. And unless I put an end to this, I'd be living *la vida loca* soon. How many attempts could be made on a life before one started to get a little loopy? Some would argue I was already there.

The phone jangled, and I grabbed it.

"Gabby."

Speaking of father figures.

"Hi, Dad." I braced myself.

"Did you ever think about calling to check on your old man?" His voice sounded three or four decibels too loud, like Jack Daniels turned up the knob on his volume control.

"I figured you were enjoying yourself at Aunt May's house. I didn't want to disturb you."

"How are you doing?"

I twisted the phone chord. "It's been a rough—"

"You should see the mountains here. You'd really love them, Gabby. Remember when we went hiking together that time?"

It was one of the few fond memories I had of Dad. Of course I remembered. My heart softened.

"That was a fun—"

"Listen, I don't have time to chat. I'm using May's long distance. You pay my rent yet?"

The real purpose of his call. Money. Why would I ever think he was just calling to check on me?

"Yes, Dad. I do every month."

We hung up, and I forced my thoughts away from the conversation. Dad dealt with his grief over the past by drinking. I dealt with mine by taking care of Dad. It seemed everyone did what they could to get by. Was this really all life was about? Getting by? Maybe Riley was on to something. Maybe God was the answer I'd been looking for. It would be so nice to have answers for a change instead of just more questions.

Science couldn't readily explain the meaning of life, other than survival of the fittest. I knew deep inside there was more to life than simply surviving. There had to be, didn't there?

The phone rang again, and I jerked it to my ear. "Yes?" I waited to hear my dad's voice, to hear the request for more money.

"Gabby? It's Detective Parker."

I relaxed my shoulders. "Hello, Detective."

"Listen, we've arrested a man for your attempted murder. Can you come to the station to identify him?"

Blood pounded through my veins. "I'll be there."

I quickly pulled my shoes on and grabbed my keys. As I stepped into the stairwell, I remembered my promise not to go anywhere alone. But I knew Riley wasn't home, nor was Sierra.

I quickly jotted them a note and then hopped in my van. As I drove to the station, I mentally ran through the possibilities of whom they may have arrested. Was it the mechanic, and if so, what was his tie with this case?

Cunningham wouldn't have done it himself, but he could have hired someone. That made the most sense. But would whoever he hired give him up? They'd be looking at attempted murder if they didn't.

I pulled up to the station and saw Parker waiting at the door. He looked as glamorous and camera-ready as ever. After I parked and hurried across the pavement, Parker led me inside.

"We traced him through the car you cleaned for him," he said. "He's not talking, though. Looks scared to death."

He led me down a plain hallway, past offices and a water fountain. Finally, he stopped in front of a steel door.

"You're going to go into this room for the lineup. You can see the men, but they can't see you." Parker lowered his voice. "You ready for this?"

My heart beat double time, but I was as ready as I'd ever be. "Let's do it."

CHAPTER TWENTY-TWO

Inside, darkness and chilled air greeted me. Parker put his hand on my back as the door clicked behind us. I spotted Adams waiting in a lone chair in the closet-sized room.

"Gabby, thanks for coming in." Adams rose. "Don't be nervous about this, but pay careful attention."

I held my breath as men walked into the viewing area. Each of them had similar features, but the last one caused me to draw a quick breath.

It was him. The mechanic. No doubt.

"Do you see him?" Parker asked.

I nodded and pointed to the man.

"Thanks, Ms. St. Claire," Adams said. He jotted something with his pen and paper. I'd never seen the man without the two objects, though it made me think of him more as a reporter than a detective.

"Are you going to interrogate him?"

"Yeah," Parker said. "We'll see if we can get a confession out of him."

"Can I watch?"

The detectives glanced at each other, and Parker said, "It's not a good idea."

"Please. I know about this case. I want to hear what he has to say. It might offer the clue we've been looking for."

Parker grasped my elbow and led me out of the room. "I'll tell you what. You wait in the lounge while we interrogate him. Afterward, we can talk about it. Okay?"

It was better than nothing. Parker settled me on a ratty brown couch with a cup of old coffee, then disappeared down the hall.

Chills raced across my cold skin. That man had tried to kill me. I shivered when I thought of how close he'd come to succeeding. What were the detectives getting out of him? Would they be able to make an arrest?

I couldn't sit still. I needed answers. I needed for life to return to normal. I needed my sun to come out tomorrow. I glanced down at my T-shirt. I needed my happily ever after.

It seemed like hours had ticked away as I paced. Finally, Parker stuck his head into the room. I rushed toward him. "Well?"

"Claims he was blackmailed. Doesn't know who threatened him. Said they'd tell his wife about his pregnant girlfriend if he didn't do it."

I let what he said sink in. It amounted to nothing. My shoulders slumped. "So, his wife would forgive him for killing someone before she'd forgive him for having an affair? That makes no sense."

"Whoever contacted him said you wouldn't be hurt. They just wanted to scare you. Apparently, they sent him pictures taken of him and his mistress. Threatened to send them to his wife, also."

"And he has no idea who the person is?"

"Their only contact was over the phone. We're checking his phone records now."

I lowered myself on the couch and buried my face in my hands, exhaustion weighing on me. A hand covered my shoulder. "You okay?"

"I'm not sure anymore."

Parker's fingers circled my arm and pulled me to my feet. "Come on. I'm going to get you something to eat, then get you home."

Now that he mentioned it, a warm dinner did sound nice. I walked with him into the balmy night. Though the temperature was probably 75 degrees, I shivered. Parker slipped his coat off and placed it over my shoulders. He directed me toward a red Viper.

As soon as we started down the road, I started in on my own interrogation. "How did you track down the mechanic?"

"Through the car's VIN."

"Did you arrest him?"

"With your identification and the fact that he purchased the car you cleaned, it seems pretty cut-and-dried."

"But he has no idea who blackmailed him?"

Parker shook his head. "No idea. They used an electronic voice modifier. We're checking the photos for fingerprints now, but I doubt we'll find any. Whoever's doing this seems pretty thorough."

We pulled to a stop. I glanced out the window in time to see a man reaching for my door. I gasped and jerked away.

"It's just the valet, love." Parker winked at me with an amused half smile.

Heat rose on my cheeks. "I guess I'm a little jumpy lately."

I stepped out, mumbling an apology to the boy. Parker tossed his keys to him. We entered Freemason Abby, an old church building converted into a restaurant. Stained-glass windows, rich burgundy carpet, and walnut-stained wood trim adorned the century-old building. I'd only been inside once before, and that was for a lunch special. At night, the place made me feel like someone of high society. And totally out of place in my standard jeans and flip-flops.

We were seated in the corner. Parker leaned back and stretched his arm across the wooden booth. "How are you doing, Gabby? Really."

"The BTK Strangler's free, huh?"

"What?"

"Never mind." I shook my head. "I'm okay. It's been a rough week."

He took a sip of water. "You need to take it easy. Give yourself a chance to deal with everything that's happened."

"I'll take it easy as soon as Harold's cleared of all charges."

"All the evidence is stacked against him. It doesn't look good, especially since he already has a record."

"I'll prove he's innocent if it's the last thing I do."

I was like Javert trying to track down Jean Valjean. Nothing would stand in my way.

Silence fell. Parker twirled his ice water before leaning forward, his voice low and serious. "Why do you think someone wants to kill you, Gabby?"

"Because I know about the gun."

"But I know about the gun. No one's come after me."

"Yes, but maybe the murderer can see that you're still focused on Newsome. I'm the only one pushing you in another direction. If he can shut me up, you'll let the whole inquiry about the gun drop."

He sighed and leaned back. "I didn't say I was going to let it drop."

"You've already let it drop. The only man the evidence points to is walking the streets scot-free, and you're not doing a thing about it."

The waitress set our sodas on the table. I took my straw and impaled a slice of lemon while Parker took a long sip.

"Cunningham isn't guilty, Gabby. I don't know how the gun got there, but it wasn't because Cunningham used it."

"Did you fingerprint it?"

"Yeah, and of course, his prints are everywhere. It's his gun, for goodness' sake."

"What about the blood?"

"What about the blood, Nancy Drew? It doesn't prove anything."

I shifted, tired of his nickname but even more tired of his disregard of my opinions. "Why are you so determined to protect Cunningham? Does he hold a spell over you?"

His gaze darkened. "No, because I'm a professional, and I know a killer when I see one."

"Then why does someone want me dead? Can you tell me that, Detective? If that gun I found means nothing, why does someone want to shut me up?"

He shrugged. "Maybe it's unrelated to the case."

Indignation forced my spine rigid. "You've got to be kidding me. That's your theory? Someone is trying to kill me just for fun—there's no other reason to explain the events that have happened?"

Parker glanced around the room, and I realized I'd practically shouted at him. Too bad.

He leaned toward me. "Look, I'm sorry. I'm not the most sensitive guy in the world. But I'm only trying to get you to look at things from a different angle."

I drew in a breath, willing myself to calm down. "Then tell me what other angle there is, Detective. How do you explain three attempts on my life?"

The perky waitress appeared again. "Are you ready to order?"

Parker looked at me for an answer, and I shrugged. As Parker rattled off something from the menu, I echoed his order. The waitress took our menus, and as soon as she disappeared, Parker leaned forward and lowered his voice.

"I just don't want you to get hurt, Gabby. I know you think I'm working against you. But whoever's committing these crimes isn't someone you want to mess with."

His words repeated in my mind until I realized what he said. "You don't think Newsome did it. He's in jail."

Parker remained silent.

"Admit it. I need to hear you say it."

"There's a lot you don't understand about police work."

"Help me understand, then."

He ran a hand through his gelled hair. "It's complicated."

"Try me."

"There's a lot of pressure with this case. The Cunninghams are a powerful family. The chief demanded someone be charged with the crime. Everything points to Newsome."

"But?"

His jaw flexed, and I could see the internal struggle going on. "It seems too perfect, you know?"

"So do something."

"The chief won't back down. He's convinced it's Newsome. The press is satisfied. City residents are satisfied. I should be satisfied."

"Isn't this where you step up with bravado and do what's right, no matter the cost?"

"I wish it were that easy."

"Who do you think did it?"

"I don't know."

"Cunningham."

"The angle the bullet went into his leg makes it unlikely that he shot himself."

"Maybe his wife shot him first."

He reached across the table and squeezed my hand. "Do me a favor, and let me handle it, okay? I don't need you to go chasing after a killer."

"He's chasing after me."

Parker shook his head. "You're a spitfire you know."

"A mess. A spitfire. A Nancy Drew wannabe. You have lots of names for me." I thought of another name he could throw in—Stubborn. I didn't bother to suggest it.

He grinned. "Only 'cause I like you."

"I would have thought I was your number-one enemy."

"I thought abrasiveness would discourage you. It didn't work."

The server set our she-crab soup in front of us. The conversation stayed generic for the rest of dinner. My anxieties melted as I found out more about Parker. Despite his earlier gruffness, I discovered he loved snowboarding, fiercely supported the Charlotte Hornets, and had been married once before.

The marriage part didn't really surprise me. A man who looked like Parker was bound to have a long history with women. He didn't seem like the type to settle down.

With our plates empty, Parker extended his hand. "You ready to head home?"

I stood, and a few minutes later, we were in his Viper. I looked around the car, wondering where the detective got the money for it. And for a restaurant like Freemason, for that matter. Maybe I should start singing, "Hey, Big Spender" instead of "Send in the Clowns" when he was around.

"Nice set of wheels you have here," I said.

"Yeah, she's my baby." He rubbed his hand down the console. "I've always wanted one of these—since the first time I laid eyes on one."

"New?"

We started down the road. "Yeah. Some people would say it's a waste to spend so much on a car, but I disagree. I feel like a million bucks when I'm driving this girl."

"I always wondered why someone would spend gobs of money on a car that can go from zero to sixty in a few seconds."

"Three point nine, to be exact."

"Do you just want to get to the next stoplight faster?"

Parker chuckled. "It's a guy thing. It's just the fact that we *can* get there faster."

"Ah, I see. Male egotism. Wanting to be better, stronger, more capable so you can take down the next guy. Makes perfect sense."

Parker glanced at me. "Have you always been so direct?"

"No, only around you."

"I'm flattered."

"They say flattery will get me everywhere."

"I think it's nowhere. Flattery will get you nowhere."

"They have their sayings, I have mine."

He chuckled again. "You're a mess. You know that?"

"So I've been told, Detective."

"You could call me Chip, you know."

I smiled. "I like Parker better."

As Parker drove toward the station, he ran through a list of safety precautions, from double-checking my locks to not going anywhere alone. He dropped me off at my van and promised to follow me home as a precaution. When we pulled up to my apartment, I expected him to zoom away, deed done. Instead, he cut the engine and stepped out. Low and behold, he was going to walk me to the door.

Maybe I had been too quick to judge him.

CHAPTER

TWENTY-THREE

"I'd like to check out everything in your apartment, just to be safe," Parker said.

We walked inside. "I appreciate it."

Parker took my keys and opened my apartment door. "Wait here."

I nodded as he stepped inside my apartment. Behind me, I could hear the muted sound of a TV from Riley's apartment. Lucky squawked. I wondered what my neighbor had done this evening.

Parker stuck his head out of the doorway. "It's all clear. You can come in."

He stepped aside and I squeezed past, catching a whiff of his leathery aftershave. "Would you like some coffee?" My words surprised even me.

Parker flashed his million-dollar smile. "I'd love some. But only on one condition—no talking about this case."

It sounded fair. "Agreed."

I started a hazelnut brew while Parker lingered in the living room. "You like jigsaw puzzles, I see."

"My neighbor insisted we work on it today. After my scare yesterday, people haven't wanted to let me out of their sight."

Parker leaned in the kitchen doorway. "They've got the right idea. You're lucky to have friends like that."

Riley's and Sierra's faces flashed through my mind. "Yes, I am."

"They say the best protection against crime is a nosy neighbor."

"Then we should be pretty safe here in this building."

Parker reached for my hand. "How are your burns?" He gently rubbed the skin around my wound.

"They're healing."

He touched the skin at my temple. It had been rubbed raw from thrashing around in the trunk. "You're going to have some badges of courage, it appears."

I never thought of them like that. "You have any?"

He touched his arm. "Yeah, a couple. I was shot in the arm my first year doing patrol. A murder suspect fled the crime scene. I chased him. Backup still hadn't arrived. I went into an abandoned building. Couldn't see a thing. Before I realized the situation I had put myself in, I had a bullet in my arm." He lowered his voice. "It's why I don't want you involved in this case. I know how dangerous it is. If that man hadn't been a bad shot, I wouldn't be here."

"I want to be a forensic scientist," I blurted out. "I know you think I'm just nosy, but I want to solve crimes for a living. This isn't a passing phase."

He stepped closer. His eyes held a new emotion, one that surprisingly intrigued me. "Then what's stopping you?"

"Time. Money."

"You don't seem like the kind of person who lets anything stop you once you have your mind set."

The smell of coffee filled the room, and I turned to pour some, grateful for the distraction. Parker's cell phone beeped as I handed him a mug.

"Excuse me." He stepped into the living room. A few seconds later, he snapped the phone shut and approached me. "I have to go."

"Everything okay?"

"There's a homicide at the Beach." He nodded toward the untouched coffee mug. "Rain check?"

I nodded and slipped his jacket off my shoulders. "Rain check."

When my alarm went off the next morning, I could hardly move. Exhaustion zapped my energy, and I played with the idea of spending the day in bed. A sense of urgency wouldn't allow me to, though. I didn't have any time to waste in proving Harold innocent.

I pulled on some shorts and a T-shirt and set out on a morning jog. Running always seemed to steady my emotions and clear my head. I'd engaged in the activity after watching the movie *Forrest Gump*. Forrest said he ran to put the past behind him, which sounded like a good idea to me. And that's all I had to say about that.

Sunday mornings weren't as busy in Ghent. The normal buzz of cars and pedestrians were absent as people slept in or lingered in front of their TV sets. I passed a few regulars out walking their dogs or taking a late-morning run.

With each rise and fall of a foot, my tension eased. I wondered what Riley was doing at church. His car wasn't in the parking lot, so I assumed that's where he'd gone. I could picture him in a massive cathedral, the organ playing and people trying to appear holy.

Only Riley didn't seem like that.

But that still didn't mean Christianity was for me. Life hadn't pointed me toward a loving God. If there was a God, he was a harsh dictator who enjoyed watching his children suffer, more akin to Adolf Hitler than Mother Teresa. I'd stick with my faith in science. It made more sense.

I rounded the corner, enjoying pushing my muscles to the limit. Even the glaring sun didn't bother me as I moved along. Just being outside invigorated me.

I replayed last evening. I couldn't believe how much I'd enjoyed talking with Parker. He'd been an engaging conversationalist and a good listener.

I compared Riley and Parker, realizing how different they were. Riley was laid-back, good-natured. He had a boy-next-door aura about him. Parker, on the other hand, had movie-star good looks and charm he turned on and off.

My apartment came into view. I'd run two miles. Now, I needed coffee. I jogged across the street.

I ordered a large iced mocha. As I waited, several families came inside wearing dresses and suits. The church service across the street must have just gotten out.

Members of that church had left a bad taste in my mouth on more than one occasion. I'd been in several arguments with attendees who'd insisted on parking at the apartment building, effectively leaving me without a space, though signs clearly stated that parking was for residents only. And Sharon, the coffeehouse owner, dreaded Sundays, she'd told me once. Christians were the worst tippers, often leaving tracts in place of money. They were also high-maintenance, complaining over the smallest discrepancy. They might sing about amazing grace, but they sure didn't live it.

I grabbed my order when it was up and walked to my apartment. Riley opened his door as I pounded upstairs.

"I can't take my eye off you for a minute, can I?" he asked.

"They found the mechanic who locked me in the car. I had to go identify him."

His gaze brightened. "That's great."

"He was blackmailed. He has no idea who put him up to it."

"There's always a trail."

I nodded and let my gaze travel down Riley. He wore a T-shirt and jeans. *Where's church boy's suit and tie?* I wondered. "So much for church, huh?"

He glanced down at his clothes. "I went."

"I see. Bedside Baptist?"

He chuckled. "No, a community church that meets at a school down the street, actually."

I stored away the information. Either Riley was sorely underdressed, or his church was casual.

"So, how about lunch? You owe me one since you stood me up on Friday." Riley waited for my answer.

"Give me thirty minutes."

"They're all yours."

Riley and I sat across from each other at a Mexican restaurant down the street. Cheerful mariachi music blared through speakers above as we enjoyed some chips and salsa. A mural of a Mexican fiesta colored the walls, and paper lanterns hung from the ceiling. How could you not feel happy coming to this restaurant?

"What else did they tell you about the man they arrested?" Riley asked, taking a sip of his soda.

"Nothing, really. He cheated on his wife and the blackmailer threatened to expose him unless he locked me in the trunk."

He raised an eyebrow. "He must have been desperate to keep his fling a secret."

I shrugged. "The blackmailer said I wasn't going to die. They just wanted to scare me."

A server placed our food on the table. The smell of cilantro and onions made my stomach growl. I waited while Riley silently bowed his head before digging in.

My mind drifted to Harold. I wondered what he was doing today. Sitting behind cold metal bars, missing his wife and grandkids, being blamed for a crime he didn't commit. Why was I the only one who could see it?

"Something on your mind?" Riley asked.

"I'm just trying to figure things out."

"That's a big job."

I raised my eyebrows. "Tell me about it."

I studied Riley's face, the defined etch of his cheek, the slight scruff on his chin. There was something different about him. I'd known it from the first day we met.

"Can I ask you a question?" I took a bite of my burrito.

"Shoot."

I put my fork down and wiped my mouth. "You seem like a logical person. Why do you believe in God?"

"Why wouldn't I believe in God?" He looked out the window before meeting my gaze. "Life seems pretty empty without him."

"But do you really believe that this guy in heaven made the earth in six days and rested on the seventh? That he made woman from a man's rib? That a fallen angel became Satan? It's the stuff of Greek mythology."

"Where do you think we came from?"

I shrugged. I couldn't totally accept the theories I'd learned in college. "I don't know."

Riley pushed his plate away. "Let me ask you a question then. Why don't you believe in God?"

"Because if there's a God up there, he doesn't care about me, so why should I give him my love?" I wished I could take the words back, that I could retreat somewhere and not feel vulnerable like I did at the moment. I met Riley's gaze, expecting to find condescension or pity. Neither of those emotions were present, though. Instead, compassion shone in his eyes.

"It's easy to confuse life with God," he stated.

"What do you mean?"

"I mean, sometimes we assume that life is a reflection of God. But it's not. Life is this way because God gives us a choice on how to live and, as humans, we screw things up. Therefore, we have a lot of ugliness around us. But that's not a picture of God."

I let the thought settle in my mind. "And you think I'm confusing life with God?"

"Your experiences have shaped your perspective. The truth is, when bad things happen, God grieves over them just like we do."

Something about what he said made sense. I needed time to turn it over in my mind, though. "You've given me something to think about."

"Anytime you want to talk about it, I'm here."

Somehow, I knew Riley would always be there. He gave off that aura—of rock-solid reliability—and I found extreme comfort in the fact. Deep inside, I longed for the security of steady companions. I hadn't found it in my family. And it seemed each time I made a friend, they ended up moving. Sometimes, life felt so lonely.

"Gabby," Riley started. He hesitated. "Who's Timmy?"

"Timmy?" I repeated. How had he heard about my brother?

"You said his name when I found you locked in the trunk."

"Oh." I never talked about what happened to my brother. I hadn't since the police gave up on the investigation. I knew it was my fault those men had taken him. If only I'd kept an eye on him. I glanced up at Riley's expectant gaze and shrugged. "It must have been a dream or something."

"Looked more like a nightmare."

I pushed my half-eaten burrito away and glanced at Riley's empty plate. "You ready to head back?" I stood.

His gaze stayed on me a minute as if he contemplated asking me more. Finally, he stood. "Sure, let's go."

He dropped some money on the table and we walked across the street in silence. I remembered that awful flashback I'd had of Timmy when I was locked in the car. It had seemed so real.

The sound of Riley chuckling pulled me out of my sorrowful state. I glanced over at him as he stared at a telephone pole, shaking his head. *What kind of poster has someone put up now?* I wondered, staring at the paper-covered pole.

"Sierra put up posters about Lucky." Riley shook his head. "When she said she'd find the bird's owner, I was hoping she might place a classified ad in the paper or something."

I examined the cluttered pole, filled with everything from concert information to strongest-man competitions. Right in the middle was a picture of Lucky with the word FOUND underneath.

"That's Sierra for you," I said.

We clambered inside and upstairs. I paused by my door and looked up at Riley. "Would you like to come inside a moment? I promise, no talks of murder or chasing down bad guys."

I expected him to say no, but instead he shrugged. "Sure, I'd like that."

We both sat on the couch. "Thanks for all your help lately," I told him. "In case I haven't told you, you've been a real godsend."

"You've been a godsend, too, Gabby. You've made my transition a lot easier. To tell you the truth, I wasn't sure how things were going to work out moving here."

"You never did tell me why you moved."

"I didn't, did I?"

I tilted my head. "And you're not going to."

The hesitation was obvious on his face. "It's a long story."

"I understand."

"It's not that I don't want to tell you, Gabby. I just have to work through some issues first. Tell me you understand that." He rested one strong hand on my cheek and angled my face toward his. "Please."

"I understand. At least I understand as much as I can without knowing anything."

He chuckled, and our gazes met. Riley's eyes swirled as he leaned closer.

He wanted to kiss me. I could see it. And I wanted to kiss him. I wanted to know if fireworks would explode, if our relationship would work at the next level. I wanted Riley Thomas to be mine and only mine.

His eyes continued to pull me in. Anticipation charged through my veins. I had feelings for Riley that I'd never experienced before. Even if he was a stuffy lawyer, he was still lovable and sweet and on my mind constantly.

Besides, every girl knows that if you want to know if a guy loves you so, it's in his kiss.

I closed my eyes and leaned closer. I waited to feel his lips against mine. I waited to know he returned my feelings.

Riley's hand slipped away from my cheek.

My eyes fluttered open, and I saw that Riley had turned away.

I clasped my hands in front of me. My gaze roamed the apartment, looking for a distraction, for something to cover my humiliation. Maybe I had imagined that he felt like I did. Maybe it had been wishful thinking. I mean, why would someone like Riley Thomas be interested in me? Before he could see my burning cheeks, I stood.

The light on my answering machine flashed, so I escaped from the couch to check it.

It said I had three calls. I pressed play. The first was from a charity wanting me to donate money. The second was from a lady needing her entryway cleaned. An intruder had been shot there. She wondered if I could come tomorrow morning.

The next message had been left only ten minutes earlier. I glanced at Riley as an electronically altered voice spoke through the machine.

"Listen, you want evidence? Go to the warehouse on Eighth and Main. You'll find an envelope on the lid of the Dumpster that will prove Cunningham is guilty. Come before nine o'clock, or you'll miss your chance."

CHAPTER

TWENTY-FOUR

"We've got to go," I said, reaching for my purse.

Riley grabbed my arm. "You need to call the police."

I considered calling Parker. He'd been supportive last night. But this was something I needed to do without him. "I'll be okay."

"It could be a setup, Gabby."

"I'll be careful." I softened my voice. "Look, you don't have to go. But I do."

"You think I'm going to let you go by yourself? You're crazy."

"I'm not twisting your arm," I reminded.

"You should call the police."

"But I'm not."

He sighed. "Let's go. But just for the record, I still don't think this is a good idea."

Fifteen minutes later, we pulled up to the warehouse. I almost changed my mind and decided to follow Riley's advice when the creepy building came into sight. It looked like a crime scene waiting to happen. Most of the windows were busted; litter tumbled with the wind against the building's crevices.

"You sure you want to do this?" Riley put the car in park and stared at me.

I was anything but sure. "Let's go."

Our footsteps echoed on the shadowed sidewalk as we walked toward the alley. Each footfall seemed to warn "go back, forget about this." A fast-food wrapper scraped against the ground, moving with the otherwise unnoticeable breeze that swept through the streets. My back muscles tensed. I could mentally hear *Pink Panther* music playing in the background.

"It's on the lid of the Dumpster, right?" I asked.

"That's what the message said."

The dingy trash container was only a couple of feet ahead. A few more steps and this could all be over.

My gaze darted around. No one hunkered in the dark places. Not even homeless people or a stray cat would come into this eerie place. That should have told me something.

We reached the Dumpster, and Riley reached for the top. With a loud, piercing squeak, it opened. A legal-sized manila envelope was taped under the lid.

Riley reached for it.

"Wait," I whispered. I reached into my pocket and pulled out a latex glove. Carefully, I pried the envelope loose and held it at the edges. "Fingerprints."

Riley didn't say anything. He lowered the top and stared at me. His voice barely audible, he asked, "Aren't you going to open it?"

"Not here. In the car."

"Why are we whispering?" Riley asked.

"Good question."

Mustering up all my cool, I walked back, imaginary spiders racing up and down my spine. The sooner I was gone from here, the better.

Riley placed a hand on my back, the action calming my nerves. Almost there.

Voices rang out from around the corner. I held my breath, waiting to see the source. Riley pulled me closer, and an involuntary shiver tingled through me.

Was this really just a setup?

Two teenage boys appeared, not even glancing in our direction. I released my breath.

Riley opened my door, and I slid into his car. My fingers fumbled with the lock until it clicked. It wasn't until Riley got in that my heart stopped trying to pound its way out of my chest.

"Do you have a knife?" I asked as Riley turned to stare at the package.

He reached into his pocket and pulled one out.

"You used to be a Boy Scout, right?"

Riley arched one eyebrow. "Eagle Scout."

"Of course."

Careful not to touch the letter except with my gloved hand, I slid the blade through one of the creases. Holding the corner, I let the contents slide into my lap.

Pictures.

Riley and I looked at each other, then looked back at my new clue. Naughty pictures.

With my protected hand, I picked up a glossy print and brought it closer. "Cunningham was having an affair," I mumbled.

"Who's the woman?"

"I have no idea."

Riley leaned in closer, and the woodsy cologne he wore filled my senses. I almost forgot about the pictures for a moment. Almost.

"Does the background look familiar to you?" Riley asked. "It looks like they're in an office, doesn't it?"

The first picture was shot through a window. It clearly showed two people lip-locked. The next photo was taken with a zoom lens. The two people lip-locked were Cunningham and a young, auburn-haired beauty wearing gold daisy earrings.

A professional had taken these pictures. Not a professional photographer—a professional blackmailer. The person who left the message, perhaps? The same person who had blackmailed the mechanic and tried to kill me? It proved that the cases were connected.

I studied the picture some more. "You see that tail in the corner? That's one of the mermaids the city has decorating the downtown." I leaned in closer. "It almost looks like this one has sequins on it, doesn't it? Look at it. It's not smooth like some of the mermaids."

"At least we know it was taken in this area. He has an office here, doesn't he?"

"Yes, he does." An idea formed in my mind.

"Someone went to a lot of trouble to make sure we got these," Riley said. "They must be significant."

"They're also one beaut of a motive for murder. Cunningham killed his wife because she found out he had an affair. She threatened to go public about it before the election. He couldn't let that happen because it would blow his chance at winning."

Riley shook his head. "I don't know. There have been a lot of stand-by-your-man women out there in recent years. It's the popular thing to do when you're in the limelight. Who wants to air dirty laundry to the world? If she went public, that's exactly what she'd be doing."

"Maybe she'd reached her limit."

"Do you think she had these pictures taken?"

"I have no idea."

"If she didn't, who did? Turn one over."

I did as instructed. The name of a national photo-paper company was the only marking. "Nothing."

"You know you have to turn this over to the police. You could be charged with obstructing justice if you don't."

"But according to the police, Cunningham isn't even a suspect."

"It doesn't matter. You have to at least show them."

I leaned back in the seat. "Or I'll go to jail."

"Or you'll go to jail."

I sighed. "I'll take them in first thing in the morning then."

Riley cranked the engine, and a few seconds later, the car puttered down the road. I continued to stare at the pictures. "Take a left at the next light, Riley."

He didn't ask any questions. A few turns later, we pulled up to Cunningham's office building. My eyes scanned the landscaping around it.

"There! There's the mermaid." I held up the picture. It was a perfect match. "So he was having an affair with someone at work. The plot thickens."

"It still doesn't make him a killer."

I glanced at Riley and frowned. "He's got means, motive, and opportunity."

"It won't hold up in court without more evidence. A lot of people have affairs today. Not all of them kill their wives."

I closed my eyes, tired of meeting resistance everywhere I went. Why was this so hard?

Riley's hand covered mine. "I'm not saying I don't believe you, Gabby. I just want to let you know what you're up against."

"Most people would have given up by now."

"And that's just one thing I like about you—you haven't."

I squeezed his hand. "Thanks, Riley. You've been a lifesaver." I meant it, too. I wouldn't be here if not for him.

"There's nothing else we can do now. We should head back and get some sleep. Things will be clearer in the morning."

I couldn't get the pictures out of my mind all night. I tossed and turned under my comforter, trying to come up with a plausible theory. Trying to come up with a way to convince Detective Parker I was right. If I turned those pictures in, as I had the gun, I'd be handing over my only piece of evidence.

What if usable prints were on them, though? I'd be ruining my chance to find out.

Finally, at 5:30, I ended my misery and crawled from beneath the warm covers. The wood floor was cold on my bare feet, so I scampered across the room and slipped on my pink bunny slippers. After pulling on a bathrobe, I plopped down at my computer and watched as its blue screen lit the room.

Time to do some research. I pulled up Google and typed in "Gloria Cunningham." The page filled with search results. The first several were about her murder. I clicked on an article, and it appeared on the desktop.

"Gloria Cunningham, the daughter of former U.S. Senator Brad Hall, was murdered in her home. . . ."

Her father was a senator. Which meant they'd probably had money. I tapped my fingers on the desk. He probably helped fund Cunningham's senate campaign. If Gloria threatened divorce when she found out about the affair, it would have sent Cunningham into a panic. All his financial backing would be gone.

It sounded like a motive to me.

Gloria's picture smiled from the top of the screen. No one deserved to die the way she had.

Gloria deserved justice. Harold deserved justice. I had to get busy.

I hopped in the shower and scrubbed away my worries with apple-scented soap and shampoo. I went through the rest of my morning routines, dressing in my "Brainy is Beautiful" T-shirt and waiting for time to pass so I could get started.

Someone knocked at my door.

I glanced at the oversized clock on my wall: 7:30. Who would be knocking at my door at this hour?

Moving slowly, so as not to give away my presence, I leaned against the door and peered through the peephole.

Riley.

I slid the chain lock and pulled the door open. "What are you doing here?"

"I heard you were awake and was afraid you'd go off to another crime scene by yourself. I thought I'd stop by and offer my services."

"Your services?" I questioned, cocking an eyebrow.

He shrugged. "I thought I could help. At least give you some company."

I eyed him. "This isn't a job for the fainthearted."

I wondered what was behind his smile.

"I think I'll be okay," he said.

I considered it before nodding. "I have to make a stop on my way there. I'm leaving in five minutes."

"I'll be ready."

I closed the door and smiled. I was getting used to having Riley Thomas around.

"You didn't tell me we were going to Cunningham's house," Riley said, grasping at the ceiling as I rumbled down the road. He'd never experienced my driving before, and I was quite entertained as I watched.

"We're not."

Riley looked around the neighborhood. "Isn't this where they lived?"

"Yes, but we're not going to their house. We're going to talk to their neighbor."

"About?"

"Gloria Cunningham."

The van's rumbling grew louder as it ambled down a gravel driveway toward the massive brick house at the end. As the vehicle stopped, a cloud of dust formed a halo around us. Without waiting for it to clear, I hopped out and started toward the house.

Riley quickly followed. "You did call and say you were coming, right?"

"Who does that anymore?" I asked over my shoulder.

"Everyone."

I bounced up the steps and rang the doorbell. Riley stood behind me. A moment later the door opened, and Barbara, wearing a bright pink aerobics outfit, answered.

"Hi, again."

The woman wiped the sweat from her face with a towel draped over her shoulders. "You're the crime-scene cleaner, right? What's going on?"

"Barbara, I have a few questions I'm hoping you can answer. Is this a bad time?" I asked.

Barbara looked over my shoulder. The distant sounds of an exercise tape sounded. "I'm in the middle of yoga, but I can spare a few minutes."

"Have you had any more threats on your life, Barbara?" I asked. "Anything since the pipe bomb was mailed to you?"

"No. Why? I was told the bomb was just random." Her squeaky, high-pitched voice grated at my ears. Too bad plastic surgery couldn't cure that.

"My theory is that someone thinks you know more than you do. They want to make sure you're quiet."

Her face froze, similar to my last encounter with her when she was fresh with Botox. "Why would you think that?"

"Because someone tried to kill me a couple nights ago."

Barbara gasped, her red lips forming a perfect O. Who wore lipstick when working out? "I don't know why they'd want to kill me. I don't know anything. I'm still in shock over the entire episode."

"What was Gloria like?" I continued.

"Gloria? She was very sweet, very determined. It didn't matter that her husband lived his career with every waking breath. She worked hard at her own career, not about to be Michael's shadow."

"How did Michael feel about that?"

Barbara shrugged. "I can only guess, but it seemed like he would have preferred she was his trophy. She was her own woman, you know? Not just a quiet wife who did whatever he said."

"You said when I talked to you before that Michael and Gloria had their fair share of fights?"

The woman's heavily made-up eyes drifted across the lawn to where the Cunninghams' house used to stand. "Yes, they fought. I could hear them all the way over here when my windows were open."

Riley stepped forward. "Any idea what they fought about?"

She shook her head. "I assume just normal married things. Money, children, housework. Who knows?"

"Did they seem happy?" I asked.

The woman fidgeted. "They were in a very high-stress situation. Running for office, balancing two careers. . . . It's hard to say, really."

"But you don't think so?" Riley filled in the blanks.

"They probably were doing the best they could. Anything else would just be an assumption on my part."

"Thanks for your help, Barbara."

She smiled. "No problem. I just want to see this case put to rest. It's been extremely hard on all of us."

Riley and I walked side by side to the van. We didn't speak until we were inside.

"Did you think it was strange that she didn't ask why we were asking?" Riley asked.

I shrugged. "No. Why?"

"Say someone came to your door asking about a neighbor's murder. A murder that a known criminal is being investigated for. Someone starts asking about your neighbor's personal life. How do you react?"

"With confusion."

"Exactly."

I let his implications sink in. "But she didn't act surprised at all. What does that mean?"

Riley shrugged. "It means she knows more than she's letting on."

I nodded. It meant that Barbara O'Connor knew Michael Cunningham was guilty.

CHAPTER TWENTY-FIVE

I watched in amusement as Riley inhaled once, then quickly pulled the front of his T-shirt over his nose and scrunched his eyes shut.

"What is that stench?" he asked.

"Dried blood. You should see it when pools of it dry. It becomes this gel—"

"I don't need to know any more." He raised his hands in surrender. "Let's just get to work."

The scene was tame compared to many I'd seen. Blood lay splattered across the tile by the front door. A few specks made their way to the walls beside me. Otherwise, everything appeared untouched. The job would probably only take an hour or two.

Riley climbed into a hazmat suit and pulled on goggles. The sight made me smile as I put on my own protective wear, before a tinge of sadness tugged at my heart.

Harold should be here.

If we worked hard, Harold would be released from jail and could work again.

"I feel like I should be in a movie." Riley looked his outfit over before glancing at me. "What now?"

"I'll start on the floor if you do the walls." I showed Riley how to spray the chemicals and scrub down the spots until all evidence of the blood disappeared. Then I got busy.

"What happened here again?" Riley asked, aiming the cleaner at the walls.

"An intruder was shot coming into the house. Self-defense." I let the chemicals soak on a stain and rocked back on my feet. "You can tell by the direction of the blood that he was hit from a distance—there's a wider range in the spray when that occurs. The man was standing a couple steps in front of me. The owner must have shot him from the stairs."

"Interesting."

"It's incredible how much you can tell just from the crime scene. Science is amazing."

"You should really think about finishing your degree. I can tell all of this forensic stuff fascinates you." Riley scrubbed down the walls with a bristle brush.

"Maybe one day. Until then, this pays the bills."

I watched the chemicals go to work and start thinning the red spot in front of me. A minute later, I began scrubbing.

"How did you develop your interest in this?" Riley asked.

"I used to think being a detective would be fun," I said. "But the more I studied science in school, the more I realized I would like to use my talents there. When I heard about forensics, it sounded like the perfect match."

"I agree. It does sound perfect."

I wiped the blood with a cloth. "How are those spots coming?"

"Almost gone."

I watched him work, his arms making purposeful circles on the white plaster wall. Part of his hair stood on end, as if he'd run his hands through it and it stayed.

Now it was my turn to ask some questions. "So, why did you decide to become a lawyer?"

Riley continued working, not missing a beat. "To defend the innocent and send the bad guys to prison."

"Sounds noble."

His rag sloshed against the wall. "I guess so."

"Where did you go to law school?"

"DC."

I wanted to ask more but accepted the two answers he offered, grateful for them.

The rest of our work was done in silence. When we finished, I couldn't tell the blood was ever there. It was spotless.

"Not bad work if I do say so myself." Riley stepped back.

"If you decide you don't want to be a lawyer anymore, give me a call. I'll make sure to have a position open for you."

He chuckled. "I'll keep that in mind."

Later, as we drove home, Riley brought up the very subject I'd hoped he'd forgotten about.

"Have you taken the pictures to the police yet?"

My hands gripped the steering wheel. "Not yet."

"But you're going to?"

"I don't see that it's necessary."

"Haven't we been over this?"

"Yes, but—"

"No buts, Gabby. You need to take them to the police."

It was the last thing I wanted to do.

"Don't go to jail over them."

He had a point.

"I *will* take them to the police."

It may not be today or tomorrow, but eventually, I will.

Was I lying? I sure felt guilty like I was.

You should take them in today, an inner voice said. I shook my head, not willing to give up my clue. I rubbed my temple, a headache coming on.

"Everything okay?"

I snapped my head in Riley's direction. "Everything's fine. Why?"

"Your head was wobbling there for a minute."

I sagged into the seat.

"Are you sure you're okay?" Riley leaned forward and studied my expression.

The concern in his eyes was enough to melt my heart. "No, I'm not feeling great all of the sudden." And I wasn't. My eyelids were heavy, my muscles sore. The past week was catching up with me.

"We'll get you home, and I'll see to it you rest for the remainder of the day. Understood?"

I nodded with a brief jut of the head forward. "Understood."

An hour later, I was under an afghan on the couch, my favorite movie rolling across the TV screen and a glass of ginger ale on the table beside me.

I'd insisted to Riley that he leave. I knew he had things to do, including grocery shopping. Not even ten minutes after he departed from my apartment, I heard the door close across the hall and footsteps clunking downstairs.

Les Miserables droned on in the background. I tried to get points from Javert for catching a suspect but finally gave up.

Why am I just sitting here, wasting time? I should be up doing something, making sure Harold is found innocent.

The events of the past week flooded my mind, and exhaustion weighed me down. If I didn't take a night to rest, I really was going to get sick.

I took a sip of my drink and tried to concentrate on the movie. I heard a faint rap on Riley's door across the hall. After a pause, I heard it again. Another pause, then a louder knock sounded—this time at my door.

I threw off my blanket and put the movie on pause. Peering out the peephole, a tall blond woman came into view. I would remember if I had ever seen this woman before. She was gorgeous. Definitely a model.

I cracked the door. "Can I help you?"

The woman smiled, the action making her seem more approachable and less like a superstar. "Yes, I'm looking for Riley Thomas."

Could this be a link to his past? I pulled the chain off and opened the door all the way.

"He lives across the hall."

"Oh, good. I was afraid I'd gotten the wrong address. I've just flown in from LA." The woman's voice sounded as smooth as honey. She didn't miss a beat.

I felt like the frumpiest, most uncultured woman in the world. This woman had been on a plane all day, yet she looked like she'd just stepped out of the dressing room.

I glanced at the jeans and T-shirt I wore. Well, I looked *comfortable*, at least.

"Do you know when he's to return?" the size 0 woman asked.

"I think he ran to the grocery store. He should be back any time now."

My gaze drifted behind the woman. Several suitcases lined the wall. This woman planned on staying awhile.

"Would you like to come into my apartment to wait? At least it would give you a place to sit down."

"Well, I suppose a friend of Riley's is a friend of mine. If you don't mind, that would be wonderful."

"No problem."

She stepped inside, and I saw the apartment as she did. A simple, folksy pad. I had the impulse to redecorate. Something more elegant and sleek. Expensive and lush. Anything but the colorful eclectic mix of furniture I'd picked up at flea markets and the old movie posters adorning the walls. Without frames even. Sigh.

Walking ahead, I grabbed the blanket from the couch and folded it, opening up a place to sit. "Please, make yourself comfortable. What can I get you to drink?"

"Do you have red wine?"

I bit my lip. "I have grape juice."

"Skim milk?"

This was a bad, bad idea. "Will chocolate do?"

The woman smiled. "I'll take water."

I excused myself. I wouldn't mention it was tap water. I returned with a goblet of ice-cold refreshment and set it on the table.

"I'm Veronica, by the way." The woman reached for my hand.

"I'm Gabby."

A manicured hand met my nibbled-nails excuse for a hand.

"Cute apartment."

She was being kind. "Thanks."

I sat in a nearby chair and watched as Veronica took a sip of her drink.

"Long flight?" I asked.

The woman rolled her eyes. "Terribly long. I'm not a big fan of flying anyway. And the service was just terrible. I hate to think how people not seated in first class were being treated."

First class. Must be nice.

"Riley hasn't mentioned he had a visitor coming from out of town."

The woman flashed a white, toothy smile. "It's a surprise. I can't wait to see his expression."

I leaned back, trying not to seem too eager. "So, how do you know Riley, anyway?"

A coworker or sister, maybe? An ex-girlfriend?

The woman's smile grew even brighter, and she held up her hand, showing a sparkling diamond ring. "I'm his fiancée."

CHAPTER

TWENTY-SIX

My jaw went slack. Fiancée? Riley had never mentioned a fiancée. I would have remembered an important detail like that.

Heat rushed to my cheeks. How could I have been such a fool? I'd thought there could actually be something between the two of us, and the whole time he was engaged.

Suddenly, it made sense. The coffee he invited me to wasn't a date—it was supposed to be a witnessing session. That's what lunch at the Mexican restaurant had been, too—Riley doing his good deed and evangelizing. That's all I'd been, wasn't it? A pet project for Riley. A duty to the faith. A mission to save the lost.

Veronica stared at me, waiting for a reaction.

Compose yourself, Gabby.

I cleared my throat. "When's the big day?"

"We haven't decided yet. I'm hoping for a Christmas wedding, though. My father has a place in the Pennsylvania mountains that would be gorgeous for the ceremony." Her voice sounded dreamy, like she lived a fairy tale.

My hands began to shake, and I stuffed them under my legs. "How long have you been dating? You know Riley—he's such a mystery. He never opens up about stuff like this, so please excuse my questions."

Veronica waved a hand in the air. "No problem. We've actually been together since law school—so, about four years."

"You're a lawyer, too?"

She flashed a bright smile. "Yes. Riley and I have talked about open-ing a practice together. He just needs some time after his last case. It was such a mess. . . ."

Footsteps pounded up the stairs, and both of us looked toward the door. Keys jangled. It had to be Riley.

Before I could say anything, Veronica darted across the room and threw the door open.

For a split second, I hoped this was all a misunderstanding, that Riley had no idea who this gorgeous woman was.

"Veronica?" Riley said, surprise evident in his voice.

She flew into his arms and planted kisses on his face.

I stayed seated, watching the scene play out. Riley's arms slipped around his fiancée's tiny waist. They did make a beautiful couple, I mused. And both were successful lawyers, a much better fit than a law-yer and a crime-scene cleaner.

For a moment, Riley's eyes met mine. I thought I saw regret there. But maybe he just regretted his two worlds colliding. Maybe he regret-ted what might come out of my big mouth. Maybe he regretted getting caught. I wasn't sure.

I stood from the chair and shut the door, not wanting to interrupt their moment. As soon as the lock clicked, I slid down the wall, feeling like crime-scene sludge.

Still obsessing about Riley the next morning, I decided to do some digging. I planted myself at my computer, which was tucked cozily in the corner of my living room, right in front of a window. I could look out and see a lovely iron fire escape and assorted Dumpsters at the back of various apartment buildings. But hey, it was still an office with a view as far as I was concerned.

Taking a sip of my coffee, I typed in the name *Riley Thomas* on a search engine. Pages of results pulled up.

I leaned back and scanned the links. *Riley Thomas, prosecuting attorney in the trial of Milton Jones, sweeps the victory for the state. The media dubs him a national hero.*

That sounded good. I clicked on it.

A picture of Riley—my Riley—popped up. Only he wasn't my Riley. He was dressed in a three-piece suit, with an eighty-dollar haircut, and he had eyes like a shark. The article below the picture read:

District attorney Riley Thomas has become the newest hotshot on a long list of most-sought-after lawyers in the United States. His victory with the Milton Jones case—

Where had I heard of that case?

—helped convict the killer. Sentencing will be later, but the death penalty is expected for the multiple murders of young girls in Southern California.

I gasped. That Milton Jones? That case had caught the nation's attention. It was no wonder Riley had looked familiar when I'd met him. His hair was longer now, and he'd shed the suits he'd worn for the televised trial.

Why would a successful attorney move to Norfolk, Virginia, leaving behind his high-profile career, his high-priced suits, and his high-maintenance fiancée? It didn't make sense.

I scanned the rest of the titles, looking for some answers. A profile in *People* magazine caught my eye. A click later, the article popped up on the screen.

Riley Thomas announced his engagement to Veronica Laskin, daughter of Virginia senator Ed Laskin. The two lovebirds hope to tie the knot sometime later this year.

Ed Laskin? I shook my head in disbelief. Riley's future father-in-law was the man running against Michael Cunningham. No wonder Riley knew so much about local politics. No wonder he insisted Laskin had nothing to do with this.

My broken heart hardened.

I closed the Web site, unable to take any more news today. Maybe cleaning the house would appease me. I collected trash from the bathroom and kitchen and carried it outside. Bill nearly collided with me when I opened the front door.

"You look distracted," I said.

"Big interview coming up. I'm going to ODU in a minute to get some material for it. Decided I should change my shirt." He pointed to a coffee stain on the pocket.

"Probably a good idea." I stuffed my garbage bag into the container. "What's going on at the college?"

"A big political debate between Senator Laskin and Michael Cunningham."

I paused. "Really?"

"Yeah, it's sold out."

I released the breath I held. "Too bad."

"I have an extra ticket if you're interested."

"I'm interested."

He raised an eyebrow. "I didn't realize you were into politics."

"It's my newest crusade, you could say."

Ten minutes later, Bill and I sped down the road, heading toward the university located less than a mile away. Bill rambled on about public education and taxes, but I barely heard him. I just knew this was my opportunity to find some answers.

The parking lot overflowed, and we ended up having to walk three blocks. As we approached the convocation center, it was hard to miss the red, white, and blue balloons that decorated the area. A moderator welcomed everyone as we slipped into the press area. Then the debate began.

I studied Michael Cunningham on the huge screens they'd set up on either side of the stage. He showed no signs of the traumas that had occurred. A confident smile was plastered across his face. His shoulders jutted back. His chin was raised. Way too happy for a grieving husband.

Maybe I was being too hard on him. Parker did say the man most likely couldn't have shot himself. I still wasn't convinced. I'd seen his temper up close and personal. I knew the man had potential for violence.

My attention switched to Ed Laskin as he appeared on-screen. Riley's future father-in-law. Was this man capable of murder? Laskin had held his seat in the senate for almost two decades. The talk was that Cunningham offered his toughest competition to date. Was Laskin desperate enough to kill Cunningham's wife to take him out of the running?

The man's white hair and graceful wrinkles contrasted sharply with Cunningham's youthful charisma. The younger crowd would lean toward Cunningham, I guessed.

Laskin held himself like a solider. His movements seemed measured and strong. I couldn't imagine Riley fitting into his world. Of course, what did I really know about Riley? Apparently, nothing.

The two candidates argued their sides on the issues, but my interest was in their actions, their mannerisms, their psyches. Which of these men was capable of murder? Either of them? Was their quest for power enough to end a life?

"There's no way Laskin will win this one. He's burned out, finished, old news," a woman whispered behind me.

"I just can't believe Cunningham is still in the running after everything he's been through. It takes a strong man," her companion replied.

Bill shushed them.

"Gloria would want me to continue in this race," Cunningham said. "We shared the dream of serving our country." His voice cracked, and he paused. The crowd hung on his every word. Visibly gathering himself, he went on. "Though many times I've wanted nothing more than to give up, it's not in my spirit to do so. Gloria . . ." He looked toward the sky. "I'm going to win this election for you."

The crowd went wild, though the debate rules required silence. Cunningham was convincing. Very convincing. I could see why he had people wrapped around his finger.

The debate continued. A crowd shot panned to Veronica and Riley sitting in the front row. Of course Riley would be here. Why was I surprised? Still, the sight of them together threw my emotions into a tailspin.

"Isn't that our neighbor?" Bill whispered.

"Yep."

"I wouldn't've guessed him to be a part of that crowd."

"What do you mean?" I didn't stay up on the political scene the way I should. Obviously.

"Their noses are so high in the air, they have no idea what 'middle America' is about. When Laskin talks about helping the middle class, everyone knows it's a joke."

"So, why do we keep reelecting him?"

"That's why a lot of experts don't think he'll be reelected this year. He's got a terrible track record." The reporters behind us copied Bill's earlier request and shushed us.

I turned my attention back to the big screen, set up so that even we peons in the nosebleed section could gaze upon our fearless leaders. What if Laskin was a murderer? What would that mean for Riley? If his future father-in-law was guilty, why would he be defending Harold?

Unless he purposely planned on blowing it. That thought pulled me to a stop so fast, it left skid marks on my brain.

I buried my head into my hands. That would make Riley a coconspirator. I didn't want to believe Riley could have a hand in this mess. But there was no denying that he'd lied to me. Or at least he'd kept things from me. Big things. Fundamental things. Three-carat, emerald-cut things.

When Bill wanted to slip out early to avoid traffic, I let him lead me away. My head spun with too much information to try and strike up a conversation as I plopped into his vintage Mustang.

"Whadya think?" Bill asked. "Did you get any answers?"

"More questions, actually."

"You'll have the chance to ask some of those questions tomorrow."

"What do you mean?"

"Cunningham's going to be on my show. You can call in. I'm always in need of intelligent questions."

"I have a better idea—can I go in and watch?"

CHAPTER
TWENTY-SEVEN

Later that afternoon, I realized I needed to find Cunningham's girlfriend, the one from the pictures. It appeared to be someone who worked for him. So somehow, I needed to get into Cunningham Law.

I considered dressing as a custodian. I contemplated faking a business deal. I even thought about being brazen and walking in without an excuse. As I thought through all those brilliant plans, they all ended up with me being hauled away by the cops. I needed something better.

I hopped back on the Internet and did a search on his practice. Several criminal cases that they were handling came up. I browsed through them, looking for something of interest.

Bingo.

His firm was representing a fast-food chain being sued for serving a boneless piece of chicken that had a bone in it. The person eating it had choked and would have died if it hadn't been for a fellow customer who did the Heimlich.

I remembered hearing that the chain, Wilbur's Chicken, had been accused in the past of being cruel to the chickens they raised. My next thought was so obvious that even Detective Parker would have been able to detect it.

Sierra.

She would have a heyday with this.

I hurried downstairs and knocked at her door, but no one answered. After standing there frustrated for a minute, it came to me. Of course Sierra wasn't home. The circus was in town.

Protestors gathered in front of the Scope, a massive entertainment plaza where the circus would take place. I pulled my van alongside the crowd, searching for Sierra. Finally, I spotted her locked inside a cage, wearing tiger ears and an animal-print leotard.

"Animals have rights, too! How would you like to be caged?" Sierra shouted. Everyone around her cheered in agreement.

I honked and rolled down my window. "Sierra!"

My friend turned to see who called her name. "Gabby? Where have you been? We're supposed to keep an eye on you, you know?"

My best friend was sitting in a cage with furry ears. Who needed looking after in this picture? On the other hand, that might be my only hope of getting her sprung.

"I thought you'd never offer. Get in the van."

She threw her hands in the air. "But I'm in the middle of a protest."

"Hand over the ears to someone else, She-ra. This is important."

My friend scowled. "It better be. I've been planning this demonstration for a month."

Good thing, too. Rental on the tiger outfit was always booked way ahead this time of year.

She climbed out of the cage and grabbed a bag from beside it. As Sierra shoved her ears at a friend, I held my breath, afraid she'd hand over the leotard right in public. It didn't look like there was room under it for much.

She settled for the ears, thank heavens, and a moment later she slammed the van door and looked at me skeptically. "What's going on?"

"I found out something about Cunningham Law Offices."

Her eyebrows shot up. "What?"

"They're defending Wilbur's Country Chicken in a lawsuit." I played my trump card. "In essence, they're supporting a restaurant chain that's cruel to animals. Cunningham could lose votes if your organization decided to boycott him."

"They're taking up for that butcher shop? Do you know what they do to their chickens?"

I'd only heard about six hundred times. All from Sierra. "It's awful. Don't you think you should talk to someone at the company? Tell them what it will mean if word of this gets out?"

Sierra's little orange-and-black-striped body trembled with outrage. "Onward, ho!"

We pulled away and five minutes later stopped outside of Cunningham's building. After I parked by the garage exit, Sierra turned to me. "So, why are we really here?"

Rats! I kept forgetting that inside that obsessed, animal-loving body lived a Phi Beta Kappa who had graduated from Yale near the top of her class.

"I'm trying to figure out Cunningham's motive for killing his wife."

She blinked. "You mean Michael Cunningham?"

I nodded.

Sierra pressed her head into the seat. "On second thought, I don't want to know the details. I'll trust you."

My friend opened the bag by the floor and pulled out jeans and a cotton shirt. She squirmed around in her seat, tugging on jeans.

"So who was the woman with Riley this morning? She was wearing a leather skirt." Sierra rolled her eyes. "Some people."

Another reason to hate Veronica. I was glad I'd brought Sierra along. "She's his fiancée."

Sierra paused with her arms raised over her head, shirt half on. Through the pink cotton, I heard the muffled word, "What?"

I shrugged, then realizing Sierra couldn't see me, I said, "She introduced herself to me last night."

She pulled on the shirt the rest of the way, her gaze fixed on me. "That's impossible."

"Obviously not. I saw the ring. I saw the articles announcing their engagement. I saw him hug her hello. It's real."

"It just doesn't make sense." Sierra shook her head. "I mean, I saw the way he looked at you, the way he talked about you. He can't have a fiancée."

I wanted to ask how he'd looked at me. "Not the first man who's been looking when his eyes should stay home where they belong. In fact, maybe he should go into politics. Seems to have the traits for it."

"But that woman is totally not Riley's type."

"I saw her, you didn't. Trust me. She's every man's type."

"She's too high maintenance. Riley's just a simple guy."

"No, he's actually a 'hotshot' lawyer from California—the newspaper's words, not mine."

"You've been doing research on him?"

I shrugged. "A little."

"You've got it bad, huh?"

"I just want some answers."

"Did the answers make you feel better?"

I sucked in my cheeks as I contemplated the question. "Not really."

Sierra opened her door. I would worry about Riley later. Right now, I needed to find some answers for Harold.

After a very persuasive argument with the receptionist, Sierra and I ended up in the public relations office. We sat in massive *leather* chairs across from a mahogany desk.

"I have nothing prepared," Sierra mumbled, frowning at the black animal skin making up her seat. "Are you sure you have your facts straight?"

"Yes. I read several things about it online. Michael Cunningham's law firm is defending cruelty to animals by representing the company in this case. They need to be shut down."

A young man with trendy clothes walked into the room. "Hello, ladies. How can I help you today?"

Sierra glanced at me before launching into her shock and disillusionment upon finding out the company supported restaurants that practiced animal cruelty. I would have never guessed she wasn't prepared, the way she charged ahead, talking on fast forward.

I glanced out the glass partition at the faces walking by as she continued. I searched for that hair in the picture, the earring. I wouldn't find out anything by sitting in here.

"Excuse me, could you tell me where your restroom is?" I asked.

The man gave me directions, and I left Sierra to do what she did best—nag. My gaze wandered the block of partitioned offices. It would be like searching for the proverbial needle in a haystack, I realized.

I walked past the restroom. Just who was this mystery woman? Cunningham's secretary? A vice president of the company? An intern?

The mermaid from the picture had been located on the north side of the building. That would narrow my search. I headed toward the opposite hallway. I'd walk by those offices and see what I could find.

An older woman approached. *Keep your head high, Gabby. Don't give any hints that you don't belong here.*

I smiled, and the woman continued past. I let out my breath when no questions were asked. Maybe this wasn't as tricky as I'd made it out to be.

As I walked past the offices, I saw blonds, redheads, brunettes with short hair, brunettes with curly hair, bald men, women with white hair pulled into buns, a woman with long auburn hair but a heavyset build. The mystery woman remained just that—a mystery.

A noise at the end of the hallway grabbed my attention. I looked up and saw Cunningham approaching, surrounded by a gaggle of people. I spun around before he spotted me. The maze of chest-level office partitions wouldn't offer many places to hide.

The space narrowed between us. I ducked behind a divider and bent to tie my shoe. The voices became louder. I continued playing with the strings, looping and unlooping them until I heard the click of their heels across the tile behind me.

"I can't stay," I heard Cunningham say. "I've got a meeting with my lawyer in thirty minutes."

"If there's anything we can do to help . . . ," a male said.

The crowd passed, not giving me a second glance. Relaxing, I stood and wiped off my jeans.

"Can I help you?" My gaze snapped to a bright-faced blond. Where had she come from? Her wide eyes soaked in my appearance.

"I . . . uh, I was looking for the restroom."

She pointed in the opposite direction. "It's right over there."

"Thanks," I mumbled. I hurried back to Sierra. We didn't have any time to waste—I had to follow Cunningham.

CHAPTER TWENTY-EIGHT

"You were right. I can't believe that law firm is defending that slaughterhouse of a restaurant," Sierra said.

I rubbed my neck, waiting for Cunningham to leave the building. I tried to care about the chickens, I really did. But I'd seen what was left of Gloria Cunningham, and somehow the idea of the senator defending chicken abusers didn't surprise me.

I would follow him. I would eavesdrop on his conversation. I would get answers.

I glanced at Sierra, with her feathers all ruffled. I'd give her a few seconds alone with Cunningham when I was done plucking him.

Finally, a white Mercedes pulled from the garage. Mentally thanking the state of Virginia for outlawing tinted windows, I recognized Cunningham through the glass and pulled out after him. The Mercedes wove through traffic until reaching the downtown tunnel. I stayed a safe distance behind him, never letting the car out of sight. Ten minutes later, we pulled off the interstate into downtown Portsmouth.

"He's going to the Bier Garden," I said as he entered the popular German restaurant. "You hungry?"

"Only for some good gossip."

I found a parking space, and we walked down the sidewalk to the restaurant. As we approached the door, I hung back. "Has he been seated yet?"

Sierra peered through the window. "I don't see him."

"Okay, let's go inside. But walk in front of me, just in case."

"You're not going to get me killed, are you?"

"I make no promises. But there's safety in numbers."

The cool chill of the air conditioning blasted us as we opened the door. I lingered behind Sierra, searching the diners for Cunningham. I'd seen him come in. I knew he was here somewhere.

Finally, I spotted him sitting at a corner table away from other patrons. "Can we have that booth over there?" I asked

The backs were high, and with the right angling, Cunningham wouldn't spot me.

"Sure," the hostess said.

I kept my head down as we were seated. I sat closest to the other booth, the best place to overhear their conversation. The hostess handed us menus, and I held mine up. It was just the right size to conceal my face.

"Bratwurst. Gag me. I can't see how even meat eaters can down those things. Do you know what they're made of?" Sierra scrunched her nose.

I shook my head. "Don't know. Don't want to know."

A man in a charcoal suit approached Cunningham and sat across from him.

"Thanks for meeting with me," Cunningham said.

"No problem. Glad to offer some help in times like these." The man paused. "How are you holding up?"

"It's been tough. Really tough."

"You have to give yourself time to grieve."

"I can't. I have an election to win. When I win, then I'll take the opportunity. Right now, I can't lose momentum."

"You could always run next time around, Mr. Cunningham. Who says you've got to be senator now? You already have a successful law career."

"This is all I've dreamed about since I was a boy. I've been working toward it for my entire life. Every decision I've made has been with this in mind. Nothing will stand in my way."

Including, say, your wife?

"Don't think of it as standing in your way. Think of it as healing—"

"Look, if I'd wanted a shrink, I would have hired one." Anger singed his voice. I could imagine the fire in his eyes, the same fire that blazed when I spoke with him at his mother's.

"Sorry." I could hear defeat in the lawyer's voice. "I just don't want you to find yourself in over your head."

"It's too late for that."

I had to agree with Cunningham on that one. I'd say he was in about forty thousand leagues over his head already. The waitress interrupted them. The two ordered their meals and then resumed conversation. I pressed my ear into the wooden booth, trying to hear better.

"How's everything going with the case?" Cunningham asked. "Any more evidence found to convict William Newsome?"

"A former friend of his has agreed to testify. He says Newsome talked about different ways to keep Gloria quiet. All of the evidence is stacked against him."

"That's a relief. I don't know why he doesn't simply admit to it. It would make things easier on him."

"He has no interest in doing that."

Silence. Sierra and I glanced at each other.

"A girl accused me of killing Gloria." Cunningham said it with such sorrow I almost thought that whoever the girl was, she had to be nuts.

Oh, wait—that was me.

"The gun does look suspicious. It's hard to explain." The lawyer cleared his throat. "How did it end up in your closet, Michael?"

"Can I take your order?"

I jumped and glanced up at the waitress. I desperately wanted to shush her but refrained. Could she have picked a worse time?

"Go ahead, Sierra. You first."

I strained to hear Cunningham's answer. Instead, I heard, "Well, that makes sense."

What makes sense? Argh!

"And for you, miss?"

I glanced at the menu and ordered the first thing I saw, wiener schnitzel.

"Your food will be right out."

I turned my attention back to the conversation, which had moved on to sports. I sighed and leaned back, kicking myself for missing that important piece of information. What was Cunningham's excuse for the gun? I couldn't think of a single one that made sense.

And what about William Newsome's former friend testifying against the man? Newsome did not kill Gloria Cunningham. It wasn't even a possibility.

"So, what do you think?" Sierra whispered.

I shook my head. "I have no idea. The mystery just keeps getting more confusing by the moment. None of the pieces are fitting together."

"Then maybe you need to come at it from a different perspective."

It sounded like a good idea, in theory.

The waitress placed plates of steaming food in front of us. The conversation at Cunningham's table quieted for a moment. I picked at my food, waiting for the talk to resume behind me.

The two began talking about sports again. It seemed as if the juicy conversation was over.

Sierra made a face. "You know, I never have liked German food, even when it is vegan."

"Sauerkraut balls no good?"

"It's rotten cabbage that's been deep fried. What do you think?"

"Then why did you order it?"

"My options were limited."

I shook my head. I could always count on Sierra for some comic relief. Today was no exception.

I glanced across the table and smiled as my friend took a bite and wrinkled her nose. I'd somehow have to repay Sierra for coming with me today. Somehow.

Movement at the table behind me caused me to tense. Were they getting up?

"Thanks for agreeing to meet with me. I've always appreciated your support," Cunningham said.

"Anytime, Michael. Anytime."

I ducked my head lower, trying to look natural yet conceal my face. One glance was all it would take for him to spot me. I grabbed a menu and held it up.

"What's he doing?" I whispered.

"Walking away," Sierra said.

Panic trembled at my hands. "Does he recognize me?"

My friend paused. "I can't tell. No, he's leaving. I don't think he knows who you are."

"Are you sure?"

"Pretty sure."

"That was close." I closed my eyes, thankful that was over. "Let's pay for this and get out of here."

Because of rush-hour traffic, it took us more than an hour to get home. To my chagrin, Riley's car waited in the parking lot when we pulled up.

"What's that look for?" Sierra asked.

I nodded toward the car. "He's back."

"Maybe he has a good excuse."

"He doesn't need an excuse for being engaged. It's a perfectly honorable activity." He didn't need an excuse for me being stupid enough to fall for him, either. But that was my problem.

"Do you want me to go upstairs with you?" Sierra asked. "Just in case you run into him?"

I shook my head. "I'll be okay. I'm a big girl."

I trudged upstairs, praying I wouldn't see Riley. I'd had about all the excitement I could stand for one day.

I cleared the landing without a "Riley" sighting. It looked like I'd make it to my apartment without seeing him or the lovely Veronica.

My keys jangled as I unlocked my door. No sooner had I opened it and taken a step inside than the door across the hall flew open.

"Gabby! I was hoping it was you," Veronica said.

There's not much she could have said that would have surprised me more than that. Although she'd been nothing but polite, I'd gotten the distinct impression snooty Veronica hadn't cared much for me.

Maintaining a poker face, I turned around and smiled. "Oh? And why is that?"

"I wanted to thank you for letting me wait in your apartment last night. That was really kind, especially considering I'm a stranger."

I waved it off. "It was no problem."

Riley's muscular form appeared behind Veronica, a white apron over his neck. His smile dropped when he saw me. An unreadable look replaced it.

Embarrassment? Pity that I'd thought there was something between us? Regret that he'd led me on?

"Why don't you come over and eat with us?" Veronica asked. "We've got plenty of food."

I shook my head. "I just ate, but thanks for the offer. Besides, I'll let you two lovebirds have some time together. You're probably not going to be in town long, and I'm sure you want to spend every minute together."

"Riley's going to come back to California with me, so we have time. Isn't that right, baby?" Veronica let out a soft laugh and glanced up at Riley.

Baby's smile looked forced, but he did plant a kiss on her lips.

So, it was true. Any doubts I'd clung to dissipated. There were no misunderstandings. No misconceptions. Riley and Veronica were engaged. Now Riley was moving back to California. What exactly did he plan on doing about Harold's trial? It was still a week and a half away.

I'd talk to him about that when Veronica wasn't around.

"Well, have a good evening. Enjoy your meal!"

Before they could say anything else, I slipped inside my apartment, acted like a perfect lady by not slamming the door in their faces, and leaned back, trying to control my shaky breaths.

CHAPTER

TWENTY-NINE

How would Cunningham react if he saw me? The question nagged at me as I drove to the radio station the next day. I pulled my khaki newsboy cap lower. I'd worn a respectable red shirt, jeans, and brown blazer. I'd have to stay in the background, keep my face hidden.

As I cruised down the road, I grabbed my cell phone and dialed Mildred's number. Her sister answered on the second ring and handed the phone over. Mildred's voice had lost the frantic edge it had contained when I last spoke to her.

"How are you?" I held my breath, waiting for the answer. She had to be a wreck with her husband sitting in jail and her left to wait it out.

"I'm doing just fine, Gabby."

"Just fine?"

"It's been tough, but Harold and I have both realized we just have to put the situation in God's hands."

"God's hands?" I'd been reduced to repeating everything she said as understanding eluded me.

"We know he's in control and that everything happens for a purpose. We didn't trust at first, but now we realize that trusting God is all we have. It says in the Good Book that we'll have trouble in this world. But this world is not our home—it's just a passing phase."

"So, you think God is going to get you out of this mess?" I didn't want to sound skeptical, but her reasoning frightened me.

"Whether Harold's framed or not, God is still in control. We've chosen to trust instead of worry, Gabby-girl. We're going to be just fine, however the tide turns."

At least it made her feel better, I reasoned. I guessed religion was good for that, if nothing else.

I flipped my phone shut as I pulled up to the station. I'd purposely arrived late so Cunningham wouldn't see me. I sneaked in and joined a crew of people listening to the interview. Most of the crowd wore suits and dress shoes. I smoothed my jeans and tugged my hat again.

My gaze roamed the people around me. No doubt there were producers, campaign managers, publicists among the faces, but no girl-friend. Cunningham probably had her tucked carefully away in a love nest somewhere. Did any of his staff suspect the man they supported was a killer?

Cunningham talked about changes he planned to make to better fund our state parks programs. He and Gloria had enjoyed visiting many of them. He believed in preserving nature.

Too bad he didn't feel the same way about human life.

As he droned on, I studied the people around me. A blond scribbled notes. An effeminate male mouthed the words along with Cunningham. A brunette nodded in cadence with each of the political superstar's words.

The show cut to a commercial. Everyone's shoulders seemed to relax collectively. The girlie-man glanced at me.

"Robert Brown, publicist." He extended his hand. It felt abnormally soft and sticky.

"Gabby. I'm . . . a friend of Bill's."

"Would you like a bumper sticker?" the blond asked. She held up a "Cunningham for a Better Virginia" monstrosity.

Everyone's eyes were on me. "Sure." I grabbed it and stuck it in my purse. Maybe I could use it to fix a crack in the plaster in my bedroom. Then I'd have it handy for a dartboard.

Cunningham approached the glass door that separated us from him. I spun around and flashed a smile, hoping my heart-shaped face would do its job. "I need to run to the restroom. Excuse me."

The radio blared from tiny speakers in the bathroom. I waited until the show started before emerging and taking my place in the back.

I didn't know what I expected to find out. I just hoped the answers were somewhere in this room. The brunette glanced back at me and did a double-take. My throat went dry, and I wanted to shrink. Did she recognize me? Did Cunningham have a hit list he shared with his staff? Was my face the biggest and most dominant on it? I tugged at my hat again.

"I love your necklace," the brunette whispered.

I fingered the heart-shaped pendant that used to belong to my mother. Relief rushed through me. "Thanks."

I glanced at the pretty woman and wondered what her role in this campaign was. My eyes traveled to her earrings. I froze at the golden daisies.

Cunningham's girlfriend wasn't tucked away at all. I was staring right at her. She'd changed her hair color, but the earrings gave her away.

"I like your earrings."

She touched them with her manicured fingers. "These old things? I love them, too. Wear them all the time."

I leaned in closer and nodded toward Cunningham. "So, what's your role in all this?"

The woman flashed a bright smile. "Candace Mills. Campaign manager."

When I saw the mermaid in the picture, I'd assumed the "other woman" was a coworker. I never considered she could be a member of his campaign.

"Nice to meet you." Finally, I had a name. I had a motive. And I had a killer.

I had to call Parker.

Bill wound down toward another commercial. I had to leave before Cunningham saw me. I took a step back, just as he looked up. His eyes darkened.

Ignoring the looks of those around me, I fled. I hopped in my van and pulled out my cell phone. A minute later, I rang Parker's private line.

"Can you meet me at the Grounds?"

"What's going on?" he asked.

"I found something out."

"How does seven o'clock sound?"

I glanced at my watch. It still left me with four hours to kill. I got a shot of brain freeze with that thought. Killing was too much a part of my life these last few days. Shaking off the chilly thought, I knew I'd have to make it work. "See you then."

I'd been pacing my apartment for an hour, with no clue as to what to do with myself. My hands were tied until I spoke with Parker. I sat down at my desk and tried to catch up on some paperwork for my cleaning business, but my mind was distracted.

When I heard a car door slam outside, I rushed to my window. Bill. I hurried downstairs. The talk-show host jerked his head back as I charged toward him.

"Whoa! Where's the fire?"

"Bill, I need to get in touch with Michael Cunningham's campaign manager. Do you have her contact information?"

"Somewhere."

"Can you find it?"

"What's this about, Gabby?"

"You don't want to know."

"If it's juicy, can I have first dibs?"

I grinned. "Absolutely."

A few minutes later, I dialed Candace's cell phone. She answered on the second ring.

"Candace, my name is Gabby. I met you at *America Live* earlier today."

"You were the redhead, right?" she said, her voice crisp. I could hear voices murmuring in the background and wondered where she was.

"That's me. I was wondering if I could meet you sometime."

"Concerning?"

I had to choose my words carefully. "How I can help with the campaign."

"I can put you in touch with the right person. I'm really very busy." The voices became louder, and I could tell she was distracted.

"It's important I speak with you."

"Can it be done over the phone?"

I could hear the agitation creeping into her voice and knew I had to cut to the chase. "I know about your affair with Michael."

Silence.

"I don't know what you're talking about," she finally muttered. The background noise muted. I could picture her moving away from the crowds for privacy.

"I think you do. I have pictures to prove it."

"Are you threatening me?"

"I just want to talk."

Pause.

"When?"

We arranged to meet in an hour at the seawall in Norfolk. I would give her the pictures. I swung by the local drugstore's one-hour photo to make copies before making my way downtown. After parking, I hurried through Waterside, an upscale international mall on the Elizabeth River in downtown Norfolk, and stepped onto the seawall outside of it. The heat had let up some, and it didn't feel as much like a sauna outside.

Large yachts docked in a lazy row, and a ferry paddled across the water, full of passengers waving to those on shore. I searched the various platforms along the wall, looking for Candace. Finally, I spotted the brunette standing by a bench, chatting on her cell phone.

Gone was the earlier smile. In its place, she wore a scowl. She quickly closed the phone when I approached. I gripped the envelope and braced myself for the conversation.

"Where did you get the pictures?" Her eyes gleamed with fire and anger. My eyes zeroed in on her earrings, the ones she always wore.

"Someone left them for me."

"What are you going to do with them?"

"I'm trying to figure out who killed Gloria Cunningham."

After a moment of silence, she chuckled. "That's what this is about?"

"I hardly think this is a laughing matter, especially since I'm convinced your senator-in-the-running is the person guilty of the crime."

She studied my face. "You're the crime-scene cleaner, aren't you? Michael told me about you and your silly accusations."

"He has motive."

"What?"

"You."

She let out an airy laugh. "Michael and I ended our fling months ago. Gloria could have him, for all I cared."

"You don't sound very fond of him."

"I'm not."

"Then why are you running his campaign?"

"Because this is my 'in' in the political scene. A bad relationship is not going to ruin it."

"It has to be awkward working for him after everything that's happened."

"We can separate our personal and professional lives. Politicians do it every day."

"Then why did he murder his wife?"

"He didn't. Michael can't even kill a spider, let alone murder someone."

I let her words sink in. Did she tell the truth? Or was she covering something up?

"The pictures." Candace held her hand out. I gave her the envelope. She pulled out the black-and-whites and shook her head.

"Sure enough. I always thought she had someone trailing us."

"Who's *she*?"

"Gloria."

"So, she knew about the affair?" My interest perked again.

"Affairs."

I leaned closer. "You weren't the only one?"

She laughed again. "No. Michael is quite the womanizer. I wasn't the first, and I wasn't the last."

"Who else?"

She shrugged. "I don't know. It's not like he talked to me about it."

I rose, content with the new information I'd learned. "Thanks for your help."

"I hope you'll look other places for your killer now. Leave Michael—and this campaign—alone."

Rush-hour traffic filled the streets at full force. I didn't arrive at the coffeehouse until thirty minutes later. Parker waited at a table. He rose when I walked in.

"You sounded upset on the phone."

"Cunningham was having an affair with his campaign manager. He had reason to kill his wife."

I told him about the pictures and my encounter with Candace Mills. When I finished, Parker shook his head.

"Can we talk about something other than the case? I wanted to go out with a pretty girl, not discuss work."

"But—"

"No buts, Gabby. Even if he was having an affair, it doesn't mean anything."

"It gives him motive."

"It gives him a big headache—*that's* what it gives him."

I leaned back in my chair, wondering if I had pushed his patience too far. "I overheard a conversation between Cunningham and his lawyer yesterday."

He sighed. "And?"

"All he's ever wanted was to be a senator. He's worked his entire life to get to this point. What if his wife knew about his affair and threatened to go public with it? He knew it would ruin his chances, so he had to kill her."

Parker took a sip of his coffee. "It sounds good if you're watching a made-for-TV movie. I still think William Newsome is our guy. We have evidence that puts him at the house on the night of the murder. He made threats. He has the real motive here."

"But why add murder to armed robbery? He would just be adding years to his sentence. That doesn't make sense."

"Can we talk about something else? Please?" Parker's eyes drooped, as if he'd been working too much overtime. His hair wasn't perfectly in place like in the past. Maybe he did need a break from all of his detective work.

I shoved my theories to the back of my mind and vowed to talk about something else. I waited for an idea to hit me. My thoughts revolved around Cunningham, however.

"Good coffee, huh?" I finally said, thinking it beat "nice weather we're having."

He shook his head. "You can't do it, can you?"

"Do what?"

"Think of anything else to talk about."

"Of course I can," I shot back, knowing the bravado behind my words would require some action. I cleared my throat. "You look tired. Hard week?"

"You could say that. I've only gotten a few hours of sleep."

"Why?"

"Big caseloads. Too much crime. You name it."

"Do you like being a detective?"

"Most of the time. It's hard having a family and working this job."

"Is that why you got divorced?"

He shrugged. "That and cayenne pepper."

"What do you mean?"

"My ex-wife and I got into a huge fight over cayenne pepper." He shook his head. "It sounds crazy, doesn't it? I attempted to cook a romantic dinner. I added a little pepper to the salmon. She didn't like spicy food and flipped out when she tasted it. She left that night."

"Over pepper?"

"That may have been what our fight was over. But the truth was that our lives just started going in different directions. She was always the clingy type, you know? She needed someone to be there for her, holding her hand."

"Who filed for divorce?"

"She did. Didn't even tell me until after she'd done it. I begged her for a second chance, but by that time she'd already found someone else who had lots of time to give her."

"I'm sorry."

"It's not your fault."

"It just sounds like such a sad story." I traced the rim of my cup with my finger, imagining how hard it must have been for Parker.

"Hey." Parker nudged my chin up. "You know what I like about you?"

"My persistence?"

"The fact that you stand on your own two feet, that you think for yourself."

"I thought that's what you hated about me."

"I just hate that you're trying to interfere with my investigation."

"Gabby!" I heard someone call from across the room. I glanced up and saw Veronica standing by the door with Riley beside her.

Great, now I was on the double date from my worst nightmares.

"Well, now I know why you've been gone so much," Veronica said as she approached the table.

I looked up at her beaming face and cringed. Why did she have to be so nice? It would be much easier not to like her if she were rude and spiteful.

"Gabby didn't tell me she had a man in her life," Veronica continued. My cheeks heated again, and I glanced at Riley. His eyes met mine but only for a moment.

Parker stood and held out his hand. "Chip Parker. Pleasure to meet you."

"I'm Veronica, and this is my fiancé—"

"Riley," Parker finished, looking him up and down with disdain. "We've met."

Riley gave him a curt nod. "Parker."

"Why don't you two pull up some chairs and join us?" Parker offered.

"No, I don't think—" I started.

"We shouldn't—" Riley said.

"Sure, we'd love to." Veronica pulled up a seat and placed herself between the two of us. I slumped in my chair.

I watched Riley frown before pulling up a chair on the other side. By me. Cozy, in a *Fatal Attraction* kind of way.

I tried to think of an excuse to leave, but my mind had left the building, and all I could do was envy it. I couldn't come up with an escape plan that wouldn't seem suspicious.

A sudden headache. An upset stomach. A bleeding heart.

I plastered a smile across my face. I scrubbed blood and guts off of floors for a living. I could have coffee with Riley and Veronica. "So, I never did hear how the two of you met."

Veronica beamed at her fiancé. "You tell them, Riley. You're so much better at it than I am."

Riley shook his head. "No, I insist. You tell."

She bobbed her head from shoulder to shoulder before grinning. "Well, okay, since the cat's got your tongue." Her glowing eyes fixed on me. It took everything I had not to picture a cat—a big cat, maybe a mountain lion—licking her chops.

"We were in law school together for two years and didn't even know each other. Then he got an internship with my father, Senator Laskin."

Marry the boss's daughter. Good career move. I tried not to let that show on my face.

Riley looked away before our gazes could meet, and Veronica continued, oblivious. "My dad had him over to eat one night, and that was it. Love at first sight, right Riley?"

He smiled and nodded. "Right."

Veronica looked back and forth between Parker and me. "How about you two? How did you meet?"

"We're not really dating—" I started.

"We met through a case I'm working on." Parker reached across the table and grabbed my hand.

"How romantic," Veronica gushed. "Just like in those detective movies."

Didn't the woman usually end up dead in those detective movies? Man, this was *just* like one of those.

I offered a weak smile. "Something like that."

She looked back and forth between the two of us before sliding her chair back from the table. "If you'll excuse me, I'm going to run to the restroom."

The life of the party left the three of us sitting in silence.

Parker stood next, the coward. "I'm going to get a refill. Anyone like anything?"

I shook my head. When the two of them left, awkwardness as thick as an iced vanilla latte filled the air. I cleared my throat.

"So, you're engaged? That was the big secret you didn't want to talk about? That and the fact that I'm a big pet project for you and your so-called faith?"

Riley tilted his head, weariness showing in his slumped shoulders. "It was never like that, Gabby. It's complicated. There's more to the story than you know."

"Maybe you could have showed me the Sunday school badge you got for trying to witness to the lost. That would have clued me in. And you certainly had your work cut out for you with me. You deserved a big fat pat on the back from your church friends."

He started to say something, but I was on a roll.

"Or even a simple, 'By the way, I'm engaged to a rich supermodel who has me wrapped around her little finger,' would have been helpful."

"Gabby—"

"And what about Harold? You promised to be his lawyer, and you're going back to California? That just boils my blood. You're no better than the rest of us, church boy. You can talk about God all you want, but that's all it is—talk."

I could see the pain in his eyes, but I pushed my guilt aside. He was the one who should feel guilty.

He sighed as if the weight of the world rested on his shoulders. "You're right—I am no better than anyone else. I never claimed to be. Christianity isn't about being perfect—"

"It's about being forgiven. Spare me." The cynicism in my voice even made *me* cringe.

"Gabby . . ." He faltered. "I just want you to know I'll be here for Harold's trial. I'm a man of my word."

"Could have fooled me."

"I never lied."

I nodded. "Right, you just withheld the truth. What is that called again, counselor?" I could see the strain on his face, but I didn't care.

"I didn't mean to hurt you. I wanted to tell you the whole story. I still want to."

"I know enough."

"Don't be like this."

"Like what?"

"Treating me like I'm nobody to you."

My heart thudded against my chest. I'd hoped he *would* be somebody, and my hopes had made me weak. "You are nobody to me, Riley. That's all you're allowed to be."

"This hazelnut coffee is great." Parker sat at the table and held his mug under his nose.

I'd wanted to slug Parker for leaving me with Riley. Now I wanted to pound him for coming back before I'd had my say. I didn't think it boded well for a future relationship with Parker that he inspired me mainly to violence.

"I used to think real men drank their coffee straight and plain," Parker said, not impressing me with his detective skills when he didn't notice the tension between Riley and me. "I'm a changed man."

"You know, I've got a headache." What the hey, huh? Lame excuse or not, I had to get out of there. I went with the headache story, especially since it was now the truth. "If you'll excuse me, I'm going to head home."

"You sure?" Parker put his mug down.

Oh, I was so beyond sure. "Yeah, I'm sure." I stood and grabbed my purse.

"I'll walk you back."

"Really, I'll be fine. You stay and enjoy yourself." Before anyone could say another word, I fled. As I crossed Colley Avenue, Riley called my name.

I sighed as I heard his footsteps approaching at a jog. I kept walking.

"Gabby, wait up. You shouldn't be walking alone. Someone's still trying to hurt you."

"There are lots of ways to be hurt, Riley. I'll take my chances with Cunningham."

"What about the bomb? And have you forgotten what happened in the garage?"

I stopped on the sidewalk and turned to give him a dirty look. "Things like that aren't easily forgotten."

He looked down. "Look, I'm sorry. I wasn't trying to bring back bad memories. I don't want to see you getting hurt because you're careless, either."

"Now I'm careless?" I started to walk.

"You know what I mean." He grabbed my arm, jerking me to a halt. "Let me explain things to you."

"There's nothing to explain, Riley. You don't owe me anything. I'm the one who owes you something for saving my life. So please accept that you don't have to explain. Your private life is yours."

"It's so complicated, Gabby."

"As are you, Riley Thomas." I stepped back from his grasp. "Good night. I can let myself in."

"I'd rather I walk you."

I nodded across the street to where Parker and Veronica chatted. "Get back to your fiancée. She obviously thinks you hung the moon."

I escaped inside the apartment building before he could respond. Pounding upstairs, I went full speed until I reached my door. No bomb tonight. Things were looking up. Inside, I leaned against the door and sank down to the floor.

What is wrong with you, Gabby St. Claire?

A tear rolled down my cheek. How had things gone so incredibly wrong?

Get a grip, Gabby.

Wiping my tear away, I pushed myself from the floor and reached for the light switch. Nothing happened. I tried several times, but the room remained dark.

Had a bulb burned out? I couldn't remember when I'd changed them last, so it was a possibility.

I sighed and felt my way across the room. My toe rammed into the entertainment center.

"Ouch!" I grabbed my foot and bounced into the kitchen. Just as my hand covered the light switch, I heard a voice behind me.

"I wouldn't turn that on if I were you."

I froze, trying to place the voice. Then it hit me: Michael Cunningham.

CHAPTER

THIRTY

Slowly, I turned around. As my eyes adjusted to the darkness, I spotted Cunningham seated on my couch, his arm casually draped across the back.

"What are you doing here?" I whispered, letting loose of my foot. There was a bright side to having a murderer drop by. He'd distracted me from my aching toe.

He rose and crossed the room. Fear rippled through me as he stood mere feet away. I knew the eyes of a desperate man. I looked into them now.

"We need to talk," he rasped. Sweat beaded his forehead. His eyes were bloodshot. He smelled like whiskey, a scent I knew all too well thanks to dear old Dad.

I backed up. "There's nothing to talk about."

"Drop your little investigation, Ms. St. Claire. You're only going to get yourself in trouble."

"Is that a threat?" Duh. I wanted to slap myself in the head. Could I have asked a more stupid question?

"You tell me. Why were you following me today? Who told you about Candace?"

"It doesn't matter."

He grabbed my upper arms and shook me. "Don't tell me what does and doesn't matter. Who told you?"

Okay, he hadn't pulled a gun. He hadn't sent someone with a bomb. Maybe I could still reason with him. "If you don't get your hands off me, I'm going to scream."

He drew in a breath and stepped back, running his hands through his hair. "Okay. We should both calm down."

He seemed to be trying to control himself. A good sign. "How'd you get into my apartment?"

He glanced at me, his chest rising and falling with labored breaths. "I'm the one asking questions, Gabby."

"I could have you arrested for breaking and entering."

"No one will believe your word over mine."

So far, that had been the honest truth.

"You killed your wife."

His eyebrow twitched. "No, I didn't."

"Why'd you do it?"

He twitched again. "I didn't do it. You need to start minding your own business and stop spreading these dirty little rumors."

I swallowed, wishing I'd let Riley walk me up. "What are you doing here?" My voice trembled, belying my fear.

"I'm convincing you to lay off of me. I've been through enough without you butting into my business."

"I'm just trying to find the truth. I want your wife to have justice. I want my assistant to have justice."

"Really?" The dry edge to his voice caused sweat to bead on my forehead. He was running out of interest in persuasion.

Buy time, Gabby. Buy time.

"I guess the pipe bomb and carbon monoxide weren't enough?" I said. "You had to finish the task face-to-face, huh?"

He pulled back. "What are you talking about?"

"Don't play dumb. You've been trying to get me to shut up for days now."

He shook his finger at me and laughed, as if unsure whether or not I told the truth. "It's not going to work, Ms. St. Claire. Whatever mind game you're playing isn't going to work."

I stepped back. He stepped closer.

My hands collided with the counter. I was cornered.

"Mind your own business, Gabby. I won't let you cost me this election."

"No, you'll do anything to win. Even murder your wife."

He reached for me. I grabbed the first thing I felt behind me and swung it into his head. My glass cake dish.

It shattered into small pieces.

Holding my breath, I watched as Cunningham's eyes glazed over. His knees wobbled, and he sank to the ground.

I tiptoed past and ran to my door. I had to get Parker and Riley.

Please let them be across the street still. Please.

I tore down the stairs and outside. My heart slowed when I spotted the three of them seated at the corner table. I dodged cars and hurried across the street. At the coffeehouse, I threw the door open and ran to the table.

The three of them looked up as if I'd lost my mind.

"Cunningham. In my apartment. Tried to kill me."

Riley and Parker jumped from their seats and darted out the door.

"Who's Cunningham?" Veronica asked, following behind me.

"The man your father's running against."

Riley and Parker left me in the dust, but I wasn't staying behind for long. Even though I felt near collapse, my adrenaline propelled me on. Cunningham hadn't confessed anything, but just the fact that he'd threatened me in my apartment had to prove something. Maybe Parker would finally believe me.

Sierra stood at the apartment's outside door. "The boys told me to keep you down here." She folded her arms over her chest. "What's going on?"

"Cunningham was going to kill me." I gasped for air, trying to catch my breath. "He's in my apartment. I knocked him out with my cake dish." Pyrex, the homemaker's answer to mace.

Sierra threw her arms around me. "Then this is over. You don't have to worry about someone trying to kill you anymore. They have reason to arrest him."

"Kill you?" Veronica's mouth gaped open. "Why in the world is someone trying to kill you?"

"It's a long story."

Veronica crossed her arms. "There are a lot of those going around these days."

The last thing I was concerned about was whether Veronica was keeping up with unfolding events. I glanced upstairs. "What's going on up there? Why haven't they come down yet?"

"I'm sure it's fine. They're probably just tying him up or asking questions or something," Sierra said.

"I hope they're okay," Veronica said. "It's awfully quiet."

Veronica's heels clicked as she paced the cement walkway. Sierra made a funny noise with her tongue, a clucking roll that almost sounded like a horse's trot. Cars zoomed past. The wind ruffled tree leaves. Merrymakers laughed from an unknown location.

The silence was killing me. I had to know what was going on. I had to go to my apartment.

Sierra braced herself in front of the door. "Strict orders. You're not allowed inside."

"I can't take it anymore."

Sierra's arms stretched across the wooden door. "Let them handle it, Gabby."

"She's right. You should stay down here," Veronica said.

I jerked my head toward the blond, who shrugged.

"I may not know what's going on, but I know Riley has good instincts. If he says stay, there's a reason for it."

A siren wailed in the distance. The noise grew louder until an ambulance pulled into the parking lot.

"An ambulance? Shouldn't the police come to arrest him?" I muttered.

A noise from inside pulled my attention away from the flashing lights. Through the small window atop the doorway, I spotted Riley coming downstairs. Sierra stepped away from the door, and Riley came out.

I gasped when I saw the blood on his white shirt. Had there been a struggle? Was Riley hurt? *Oh Lord, please don't let Riley be hurt because of me.* And how about Parker? Where was Parker?

"What happened?" I whispered, desperate to reach out and touch him, but not daring to do it in front of Veronica.

"We tried to save him, Gabby." Riley stepped closer. A strange emotion hovered in his eyes. Sorrow, maybe. Exhaustion? Accusation? "We did everything we could."

Wild thoughts collided in my head. Maybe he'd hit his head. He was talking crazy. "You're not making sense, Riley."

"He's dead, Gabby."

My mouth gaped open. "Dead? How could he be dead? I knocked him out with a cake dish."

As the paramedics rushed past, Parker staggered down the stairs, blood staining his clothes also. He glanced up at me and something flashed in his eyes. Anger? Regret?

"You should have let me handle it, Gabby," he whispered. I met his gaze, and he looked apologetic. "I'm going to have to take you down to the station."

I stepped back, dread pooling in my gut. Something wasn't right here. "Why do I have to go to the station?"

"For the murder of Michael Cunningham."

CHAPTER THIRTY-ONE

"How many times do I have to tell you? I didn't murder him. I have no idea who stabbed him. It must have happened after I left." I leaned back in the chair, fighting off tears.

Parker didn't believe me. Riley probably didn't believe me. I was there, and I almost didn't believe me. They thought I had killed Cunningham, and from appearances, I looked guilty.

I was so shaken, I'd even temporarily forgiven Riley, the two-faced, engaged-to-a-supermodel liar.

Riley placed his firm hand over my trembling one. "Gabby, if you didn't stab him, how did a knife end up in his leg?"

I shook my head. "I have no idea. I was only gone five minutes, from the time I ran out to get you guys until you found Cunningham."

"The knife has your prints all over it," Parker said.

"Of course it does! It's my knife!" I slapped my hand on the table and started to rise.

Riley nudged me back into my seat. "Stay calm."

"I'm being accused of murder! How can I stay calm?"

"You won't be charged with murder, Gabby," Riley said. "He obviously broke into your apartment. It looks like self-defense, if anything."

Riley's voice was so calm, so soothing. I closed my eyes and let its waves sink in. He was right. It was self-defense.

But I didn't do it.

"Someone must have sneaked into the apartment after I left." I ran my hands through my hair. "It's the only thing I can think of. Either that, or he stabbed himself."

"If it was someone else who stabbed him, then they would have been hiding in the apartment, right?" Riley asked.

My head dropped into my hands. Someone else in my apartment? Why didn't I just move into Grand Central Station? "I have no idea. Nothing is making sense right now. How would someone else have gotten in my apartment?"

"The same way Cunningham did—by the fire escape."

"But why? Why would someone else break in?" I asked.

"Maybe they were following Cunningham," Riley said.

I noted how the blood on his shirt had turned a dark brown. His hair was more rumpled than usual, and dark circles shadowed his eyes. Our time together so far had been one adventure after another. And now this.

Riley glanced at Parker. "You have no reason to hold her."

"I'd say I do," Parker said. "What would a respected candidate for the senate be doing breaking and entering into an apartment? It doesn't fit." Parker looked at me, and I could see the conflicting emotions in his eyes—compassion blended with loyalty to his job. "I want to believe you, Gabby. The evidence is stacked against you."

I wasn't going down without a fight. "I thought he was going to kill me," I said. "He said nothing would keep him from winning this election. We all know he wanted me quiet, to stay away from him. It made him desperate. Especially after what happened today."

Riley leaned toward me. His baby blues narrowed before he asked his next question. "What happened today?"

"I confronted one of the women he had an affair with."

He sighed, and for some reason, I felt guilty.

"Why would you do something stupid like that? Are you *trying* to get yourself killed?"

A tear rolled down my cheek. This couldn't be happening. I wasn't going to be Parker's scapegoat. "No, I didn't want to get killed. What I wanted was to put an end to this case."

Parker stood and began pacing. "It looks like you got your wish, Nancy Drew. Your main suspect is dead."

I slammed my fist on the table. "Well, whoever killed him isn't, so this case isn't even close to ending."

Riley put one hand over my clenched fist and held it on the table. "Enough, Gabby."

He turned to a cool Parker. "Do you have any more questions for my client? If not, I'm taking her home."

Parker sighed and stopped pacing. "Not for now. But I will later, so don't leave the state or do anything stupid."

"Understood."

Parker glared at me. "Which part? The leaving or the stupid, because I don't think you have a lot of control over that."

Riley held my fist so I couldn't swing it at Parker's smug, pretty-boy face. He took my hand and pulled me from the seat. Before we left the interrogation room, Parker's voice rang out once more. "Oh, and remember, the crime scene is off limits. Especially since you're a suspect."

With a hand on my back, Riley led the way outside to the star-sprinkled night. The air was balmy, humid without the wind, but chilly when it blew.

Inside Riley's car, I pushed my head back onto the seat and tried to maintain control. Cunningham was dead. Someone killed him in my apartment. I was the number-one suspect. Would they let me wear my cute little T-shirts and flip-flops in jail?

"I can't believe this is happening," I muttered when Riley climbed in.

"We have to figure out who stabbed him, Gabby."

I lifted my head and whirled around to face Riley. "You believe me?" I held my breath, afraid of his answer. I desperately needed someone to believe me.

He tilted my chin up. "I believe you. You may have a nose for getting into trouble, but you're not a liar. Plus, I saw your face when you found out he'd been stabbed. You were clueless."

I forced a smile. "Thanks. It's good to know someone's on my side."

"I've always been on your side, Gabby."

I felt my cheeks growing warm and scolded myself. Riley was engaged, not the kind of man who should give me warm fuzzy feelings.

His hand dropped from my chin, and he started the engine. As we drove down the road, thoughts haunted me; unanswered questions swirled in my mind, stabbing at my nerves.

"You should stay with Sierra tonight. Maybe go to a hotel or a friend's house with her."

I nodded. It wasn't like I could go back to my apartment—not that I had any desire to do that anyway. I was supposed to clean other people's crime scenes, not my own.

"Gabby, about Veronica . . ."

I'd almost been killed, if not by Cunningham, then by whoever else was in my apartment. I'd had a man murdered in my room tonight. I'd spent hours being interrogated and accused of murder. Heaven forbid I use all those little excuses to stop poor engaged Riley from talking about his girlfriend.

"It's like I said before, Riley, you don't have to explain."

"I need to, Gabby, for my sake if not for yours." He drew in a deep breath and strummed his fingers against the steering wheel. "I called off the engagement before I moved here. I needed to get away from all the pressure. I had television cameras on me all the time. The trial, my engagement, Laskin's campaign. I felt like I had to be perfect, look perfect, act perfect. I never planned for my life to end up like that."

I waited for him to continue, part of me relieved that he was opening up, part of me wanting to smother him with a pillow.

"I couldn't take it anymore. I called off the engagement, but Veronica is used to getting what she wants. It didn't sink in. When she showed up at the apartment, I'd had no idea she was coming. As far as I was concerned, we were through."

"But she thought differently?"

Riley smiled weakly. "Yes, and she's very convincing. We had been together four years. I decided to give it another chance. She promised to lay off with some of her high expectations and try again."

I nodded, though my heart was heavy. "That makes sense."

"I didn't purposely lead you on, Gabby. I was attracted to you, but I knew I needed time to get over a four-year relationship, so I didn't rush things. And now . . ."

"She seems nice, Riley. I hope you're happy together." It killed me to say the words, though they were the truth.

"Veronica's . . . high maintenance." He ran a hand through his hair. "A wonderful woman. I'm just not sure we're right for each other."

"Maybe you should be telling her this and not me."

His fingers strummed the wheel again. "You're probably right."

"When are you going back to California?" I didn't want him to leave. More than anything, I wanted him to stay if he was engaged or not.

His voice sounded strained. "I don't know. I just don't know, Gabby." He pulled up to the apartment building and cut the engine. "I never wanted to deceive you."

"You've been a good friend, Riley. If you hadn't been around, I wouldn't be alive now."

"There's one more thing you should know while I'm sharing."

My gaze fluttered to his. "Go on."

"Remember the Milton Jones trial that went on last year?"

Finally, he was going to share the entire truth with me.

"Yes, I remember."

"I was the attorney in charge of prosecuting that case."

"Why are you walking away from your career?"

He shrugged. "I never wanted to be a big-shot attorney. All I ever wanted was the peaceful American dream, picket fence, two-point-five kids, and all."

I offered a half-smile. "Veronica can help you with that."

He slowly nodded. "Yeah, I guess she can."

A movement in the distance caught my eye. "Speaking of your lovely fiancée, here she comes now."

Before Riley even opened the door, Veronica folded into his arms, tears running down her porcelain cheeks. "Are you okay? I've been so worried."

I thought maybe that question might be better directed at me, but no such luck.

"I'm fine." Riley swung the door open and gave Veronica all his strong, soothing attention. "Nothing a shower and clean clothes won't fix."

I climbed from the car to give them their moment. I had to find Sierra, provided she was still lingering around somewhere, and see if I could find a place to stay. I heard her call my name from across the street at the dark coffeehouse. I glanced back at Riley as I departed, just in time to see him glance over also, a glimmer of something in his eyes. An apology maybe?

At least some of my questions had been answered. The answers stunk, but I had them. I wasn't done, though.

"Veronica's always going to try and make Riley fit into her perfect little life." Sierra popped an organic, all-natural potato chip in her mouth. We were staying the night in Sharon's—the coffeehouse owner's—apartment. She'd graciously offered us a place to crash for the night. "You should have heard her talking after you left about how anxious she is to get him away from this town."

"She seems nice." I went to the refrigerator to get some soy milk that Sierra had been sure to bring over.

"Yeah, but high class. You said Riley wants it simple."

"He thinks he wants it simple. But isn't Veronica the girl of every guy's dream? I mean, she's beautiful, successful, rich."

"Some guys care about more than what's on the outside."

I paused midpour, trying to think of one. Giving it up as hopeless, I shrugged. "Yeah, well, it doesn't matter. Riley is engaged, and that's that. He'll probably be moving back to California, and they'll live a perfect, if not simple, life together."

"That's too bad. You guys would have made a great couple."

I plopped back down on the Hide-A-Bed, one of the metal bars underneath digging into my hip. I made a face and rubbed my injured hind side. "There are plenty of other guys out there for me. You know I've never believed in the 'there's only one right person' theory."

"Soul mates." Sierra leaned back with a little smile. "I believe it."

Part of me had to admit the idea was appealing. The thought that there was only one perfect person for you and the two of you had to find each other. It made for a good movie script, but real life didn't seem to work that way.

"I would take you for a dreamer, too, Gabby."

I stood up just for the sake of moving. "I stopped dreaming a long time ago, Sierra." *Right about the time my brother was kidnapped,* I thought.

Sierra frowned. "You know, those who don't dream age more quickly. You should at least get an animal companion. They'll add a few years to your life to make up for your pessimistic attitude."

"I'm not a pessimist."

"Could have fooled me with your comments of late."

I sighed. "Can we talk about something else?"

"Sure, how about Detective Parker? He would be a good distraction from Riley."

I swallowed, my throat feeling raw. "Parker thinks I'm guilty. He thinks I killed Cunningham."

"Who did stab Michael Cunningham?" Sierra asked.

"That's the question of the hour."

"Somebody else had to be in your apartment, Gabby. It's the only thing that makes sense. What if they came up the fire escape after you left? If they were following Cunningham and saw him sneaking into your apartment?"

"But why would they kill him?"

"They had a vendetta against him."

"But why?"

Sierra blew the hair out of her face. "Maybe it was a scorned lover."

According to Candace Mills, he had a lot of those. I sat up straighter. "You may be on to something, Sierra."

"Don't sound so surprised."

"I need to look at the crime scene." I propelled myself off the bed toward the door.

Sierra staggered behind me. "I don't think that's a good idea. You could get arrested if you cross the police line. I watch enough TV to know that."

"I just want to see the evidence." I paused on the steps outside Sharon's place above the coffeehouse and stared at my apartment building across the street. The police were gone and the press seemed to have crawled back into their holes for the time being. No one would know if I sneaked up to my apartment for a quick look.

"They've probably taken the evidence to the station, don't you think?" Sierra asked from behind me.

There was evidence, and then there was evidence. I had no doubt the blood splatters would still be there. I shushed her as she followed me across the street. "Whatever you do, don't tell Riley I did this."

"Tell Riley you did what?"

I looked up and saw him leaning against the side of the apartment building. "What are you doing? Why aren't you with Veronica?"

"I'm waiting for you."

"Why?"

"Because I knew you'd come back."

I stepped toward the entrance, but Riley's arm darted across the door before I could enter. "You're not allowed to go in there."

"I need to clear my name. I have to see my apartment."

"You don't want to see it."

"Why?"

"It's bloody."

"I see blood all the time. It's part of my job."

"Yeah, but not in your own apartment."

"I'll be fine."

Sierra piped in from behind. "Don't argue with her. You'll never win."

As if planned, Parker pulled into the parking lot. I groaned as he climbed from his car and approached.

"What are you doing here?" Parker had changed clothes, but he still wore the exhaustion of the evening in the circles under his eyes.

"I need to get into my apartment."

I could have been certain he sighed without moving even one facial muscle. "I figured you would."

Why did everyone act like they knew me so well? I raised an eyebrow. "Are you going to let me go in?"

"If I'm there supervising you, at least you won't get arrested."

I could have hugged him. Instead, I charged past Riley and into the eerily quiet building. I assumed everyone followed behind me as I tiptoed into what used to be home sweet home. Now it just felt like the place I lived; there was nothing sweet about it.

"I could get in trouble for doing this, you know," Parker called from behind.

"You don't think I did it. Otherwise, you wouldn't be here now."

Parker's hand covered my shoulder. "Are you sure you want to do this?"

I couldn't turn to look at him. He'd see the truth in my eyes. "I'm sure."

With shaky hands, I unlocked my apartment and ducked under the crime-scene tape. As the kitchen came into view, I stopped in my tracks. Red blood pooled on the floor, fingerprint dust was everywhere, a patch of my rug had been cut out.

I drew in a shaky breath and pointed to the corner where the pedestal of the cake dish stood, stale muffins atop it. "That's where he cornered me. He started to reach for me when I grabbed the glass top and swung it into his head. He collapsed in front of me."

"The block of knives are on the other side of the kitchen, so someone had to walk past him to grab one," Riley said.

I stared at the tiled floor. "In the process, they'd crunch the glass that was scattered all over the floor."

"Some might even get caught in their shoes," Sierra said.

I held my head higher. "And maybe one of those pieces fell out when the intruder escaped."

While Parker lingered in the background, the rest of us began searching the floor for a telltale speck of crystal. I climbed onto the fire escape. The nighttime sky made it hard to see.

"Riley, toss me the flashlight from my desk drawer."

He did as I asked. I twisted the top, and a pinpoint of light spotted the wall in front of me. I studied every inch of the escape landing, but there was nothing.

Maybe I should check the metal stairs.

I stepped onto the first foothold, and the structure started downward with my weight. I held my breath until it slammed into the next landing. Crouching to keep my balance, I examined the first step.

Nothing.

Lowering myself, I flinched. A piece of hair was caught in a metal crevice. I jerked back and the strand snapped. Out of curiosity, I shined my light on the spot. There was my short, strawberry blond hair.

I leaned in closer.

And there beside it was a long blond strand.

CHAPTER

THIRTY-TWO

Using a pair of tweezers, I carefully pulled the hair from the fire escape and placed it in a plastic zippered bag.

Parker squatted in front of me, studying my every move. "I think you'll make a pretty good forensic specialist one day, Gabby."

The first smile I'd felt in days stretched across my face. "Thanks." I held up the bag. "Let's get this to the station."

"Any ideas about whom it belongs to?" Sierra asked from the window.

"Not Candace. Lately, she's a brunette," I said, climbing back into my apartment. "Maybe it's someone we haven't met yet. There were other women in the picture. I'm just ready to have this finished, once and for all."

"Amen," Riley echoed behind me. He dug into his pockets and pulled out his keys. "Come on. I'm driving. It's time to put closure to this."

When we arrived at the station, Parker took me back to the crime lab. I handed the bag over to the lab tech, a middle-aged Latina named Lela, and explained how I came across it.

She glanced at Parker, who nodded in affirmation, and then held the bag up to the light. "If you look at the end, you can see that the hair came out at the root. We should be able to get some DNA off of this." The slender woman glanced up at me. "Where did you say you found this?"

I told her.

She shook her head. "We checked all over the apartment. Sometimes another set of eyes will find what we missed."

I glanced back at Riley and Sierra as they chatted by the doors and decided to keep the conversation going. "Is it unusual for the forensics team to miss evidence? Does that happen a lot?"

"Not a lot. But we're not God. We can't see everything. It sounds like you were thorough, though. There isn't going to be a good, unbroken chain of evidence, so this won't hold up in court. But if we find whoever this belongs to, he or she had better have a rock-solid alibi for last night. Good job."

"Thanks." I stared at the lab equipment and wanted nothing more than to wander around, exploring all of the technology and wonders of science. I wanted to ask Lela questions, to quiz her about her job. I didn't want to leave the crime lab, I realized.

My eyes zoomed in on the gold cross hanging around Lela's neck. Could she be a Christian? Could she have found common ground between faith and science?

She caught me staring and touched her necklace.

"Sorry," I mumbled, looking away.

"No need to apologize. Are you a Christian, too?"

"No. I can't prove there's a God. I look at Christians and how screwed up they are, and it compounds my belief that God is a myth."

"Just because God is perfect doesn't mean that Christians are. You know that—you are a scientist, right?"

"As soon as I finish my degree I will be."

"Then you realize that the universe is fine-tuned for our existence." Lela continued to mix solutions together in test tubes as we spoke. "You know that if certain physical properties were even slightly different, we wouldn't be here. Besides, you don't really think that a tree is just as significant as you are, do you?"

The fact was, sometimes I did believe that, and the thought depressed me. I shrugged.

She continued, "Einstein said that science without religion is lame, religion without science is blind."

"Einstein said that?"

"He was a Christian, as were Newton, Boyle, Copernicus, and Galileo."

Why didn't I know that?

"Don't confuse life with God, Gabby—or Christians. We make a mess of things because it's our nature. But you can look at the orderliness of the world and see that someone's in control."

Wasn't that what Riley had told me at lunch that day? That I was assuming that life was a reflection of God? It was a coincidence that these two people had said the same thing. Or was there really such a thing as a coincidence?

Lela pushed a hair behind her ear. "Let me know if you ever want to chat, okay? About science or God or both."

I nodded. "I would like that."

Riley appeared behind me and touched my shoulder. "You ready?"

That was a great question, I realized. On many levels.

All night, I tossed and turned on the Hide-A-Bed. The hair kept nagging at me, taunting me. Whose was it? Who had I met concerning this case who had long blond hair?

I sat up in bed. Veronica? She had long blond hair. And she had a connection to the campaign. Her father had some tough competition in the election since he was running against Cunningham. But was Veronica a killer?

No. I shook my head. I had left her in the coffeehouse when I ran to my apartment, and she was still there when I got back. She couldn't have killed Cunningham.

There could be any number of other women who Cunningham had an affair with who had hair like that. I couldn't ignore that possibility.

I sank back into the bed again. Which put me back at square one.

Frustrated, I took a long, hot shower. Despite the humidity, I played with my hair, trying to get all the waves out of it by blow-drying it straight. I applied some of Sharon's makeup with care. Anything to waste time.

I needed to get a change of clothes from my apartment. Sierra still snoozed in bed, I realized. Though tempted to wake her and make her keep me company in my blood-splattered apartment, I shook my head. I could handle it by myself.

Gripping my keys with a white-knuckled fist, I forced myself upstairs. I paused by my door. Last night with Parker, Riley, and Sierra, I'd handled it okay, but now I was alone with no one to distract me from the memory of Cunningham's desperate eyes and the blood from his wounds. I didn't want to experience the horror that had taken place in my apartment again. I didn't need any reminders of the gruesome crime.

But I did need a clean shirt.

After drawing a deep breath, I twisted the lock, and the door opened. My gaze was drawn to the splatter of red across the kitchen floor. I closed my eyes.

Michael Cunningham. Murdered. In my apartment.

I shuddered.

How had my life turned into such a mess?

I looked away and saw the light on my answering machine beeping. Keeping my gaze focused, I stepped across the room and hit play.

"Gabby, it's your dad. Just wanted to remind you I'll be home next week. I need to borrow some money. Ernie's birthday is coming up, and I need to buy something."

He always came up with some excuse to buy alcohol. I knew his tricks. And I needed to start making some changes. Dad needed to get help, but he wasn't going to accept it from me. He would have to hit rock bottom before he realized how dire his situation was.

Glass crunched beneath my feet as I hurried past the kitchen to my bedroom. I grabbed some clothes from my dresser and started to retreat. A textbook resting on my bookshelf caught my attention. I hadn't touched it in years.

Hugging the clothes to my chest, I crossed the room and slid the book from its snug home. It was from one of my forensic classes at college. I ran my hand over its smooth cover and remembered the excitement I'd felt as I'd studied this book.

I stuck the book on top of my clothes and hurried back to Sharon's. After I dressed, I sat on the couch and looked over the textbook. I remembered Lela's words to me last night. I remembered the feel of being in a crime lab.

Maybe it was time to make some life changes, I realized. But first, I had to ensure I didn't go to jail for a crime I didn't commit.

An hour later, I decided to go visit Harold. It had been a few days since we'd spoken, and so much had happened.

I walked into the jail and went to the front desk. "I'm here to see Harold Morris."

The bald man looked over a sheet and shook his head. "He's out on bail."

"He is?"

"Just released this morning."

After thanking the guard, I hurried to my van and drove to Harold's house. When I pulled up, he was playing with Keisha and Donovan in the front yard. I threw the vehicle into park and ran across the yard to embrace him.

"How? When?" I started, at a loss for words.

"Riley bailed me out this morning."

"He did?" Why hadn't Riley mentioned this to me? He had obviously known when I spoke with him earlier.

"He's been the biggest blessing to me, a real answer to prayer."

Riley's words came back to me. *Don't confuse life with God,* he'd said. Was that what I was doing? Was I transferring my view of life onto God? Could it be true that God wasn't harsh and unfair like life?

Harold squeezed my arm. "You're an answer to prayer, too, you know."

I laughed. "Me? An answer to prayer?" I'd never heard that one before.

"God's been using you, Gabby, even if you haven't realized it."

My cheeks flushed. I needed to change the subject before the strange emotion that welled in my gut became evident. I cleared my throat. "So, how are you doing?"

"Okay. Better now that I can spend some time with my family before the trial."

"Do you have any idea how that evidence got into your trunk, Harold?"

He shook his head. "None."

"When was the last time you opened it before the fire?"

"I went grocery shopping the Saturday evening before we cleaned the house. That's the last time I remember."

"So, sometime between Saturday evening and Monday when you were arrested, someone put it there."

"I've thought about it over and over as I sat in the jail cell. I just can't figure it out."

"Can I look at your trunk, Harold? Maybe there's some kind of clue there."

"Look all you want." He tossed me the keys. I popped the trunk open and examined the carpet for anything out of place. A leaf embedded itself in the carpet. Some pine straw. An old jack.

"Do you have a flashlight?"

He disappeared inside and returned with one in hand. I examined the crevices, searching for something to give me a clue. The police hadn't searched the trunk, I'd bet. They'd found the stolen goods and deemed Harold a criminal.

If—when—someone else put the loot in Harold's car, they had to leave something behind. As humans, we leave traces of ourselves everywhere, from hair to fingerprints to skin flakes. I'd just read about it in my textbook earlier. With enough patience, I could find something.

Had someone picked the lock? I studied it but didn't see any signs of tampering. They could have gotten hold of his keys somehow. But that seemed too risky.

I walked around the car and tugged on the doors. They were all unlocked.

"Do you usually lock these?" I asked.

"Call me an old-fashioned country boy, but no, I don't."

I slid inside the back seat and tugged at the seats. They pulled down to allow for extra luggage room. What if the murderer/arsonist had pulled the seat down, put the items in the trunk, then let the police do the rest of the work?

It seemed plausible. And if that was the case, evidence could be in the back seat, too.

I shined the light on the floor, then in the crevices of the seat. Nothing. I continued to move the beam of light through the car. As I studied the window across from me, I froze. Slowly, I crawled across the car, closer to an almost invisible thread stuck in the door.

Bingo.

A long blond hair dangled there.

I dropped off the hair at the station and briefly spoke with Detective Adams. He assured me he was doing everything he could. He also let me know that aside from my apartment, the rest of the building was no longer a crime scene. I left the station, grabbed a few things at Sharon's house, and then went to Sierra's place to crash. As I sat on her couch, I began to flip through the pages of my old textbook.

I closed my eyes and replayed my conversation with Candace. She'd said Cunningham had had multiple affairs. I would bet one of those affairs was with a woman with long blond hair.

Something nagged at me. There was a connection I knew I wasn't making. I reviewed all of the blonds I'd met in connection with Cunningham. There was the woman at his office, his publicity director. Both seemed like possibilities, but my gut told me not to pursue those leads. There was someone else. . . .

I snapped the textbook shut. Everything clicked, and I could clearly see the big picture. I knew to whom the hair belonged. Now I just had to prove it.

CHAPTER

THIRTY-THREE

I rushed upstairs and knocked at Riley's door. Veronica answered, her smile disappearing when she spotted me.

"I need to talk with Riley. It's urgent."

Her gaze darkened. "We were just packing his things. Can't it wait until another time?"

"No. I need to speak with him now." I pushed past her and into Riley's apartment. I found him in the kitchen. He paused from packing his pots and pans.

"Gabby." A wrinkle formed between his eyebrows.

"I know who killed the Cunninghams and burned their house down."

Riley set the box down and turned toward me. "Who?"

"I'll tell you on the way. Right now I need you to come with me."

"Shouldn't you just tell Parker?"

"No. I've already developed a bad track record with him. You're Harold's lawyer. You should be there."

He glanced behind me. I felt Veronica standing there.

"I'll be right back." He wiped his hands on a dishcloth and stepped toward the door. "It won't take long."

"Don't walk out on me again, Riley." Veronica pushed past me and caught his arm. "If you leave, I won't be here when you get back."

I cringed at the desperation in her voice. Where was the poised woman from earlier?

"Veronica, don't do this." Riley touched her shoulder, and she jerked back.

"You're going to go with her, aren't you?" she demanded.

"We'll talk when I get back, okay? Don't do anything irrational."

I couldn't believe the temper tantrum Veronica was throwing or the position she was putting Riley in. I saw the agony on his face.

"Never mind," I mumbled. "I can handle it by myself. Sorry to interrupt."

I hurried from the apartment to my van. The last thing I wanted was to ruin a relationship. Riley and Veronica were a perfect pair. They should be together, living out their ultrasuccessful lives.

I'd thought Riley and I had a lot in common, but obviously not. He wasn't the simple, down-to-earth neighbor I thought him to be. He deserved someone like Veronica.

I pulled into traffic and wove my way around town until I reached James O'Connor's house. I expected the building to be extravagant like his ex-wife's. Instead, I found a simple brick ranch.

Before I lost my courage, I rang the doorbell. A man with a full beard and bald head answered. Not the kind of man I pictured Barbara with.

"James?"

"Yes? And you are?"

"My name is Gabby. I was hoping you'd answer some questions about your ex-wife."

"Is she okay?"

"She's fine. I'm investigating the murder of Michael Cunningham and need some more information."

His gaze darkened. "She had an affair with him. Is that what you want to know?"

"It's a start. What else can you tell me?"

He shrugged. "He's the reason we split. Barbara insisted he was going to leave Gloria for her. I told her to dream on. I moved out, and they continued with their fling."

"When did it end?"

"As far as I know, it didn't."

"You don't seem very upset about your split."

He rubbed his beard. "We hadn't been happy in a long time. Barbara has some emotional issues. And she's spoiled, used to getting what she wants. Let's just say life has been peaceful without her."

"Thanks for your help, Mr. O'Connor. I appreciate it."

I hurried to the van and started down the road. Now I had to prove Barbara O'Connor was guilty.

I grabbed my cell phone from my purse. The battery was dead. I threw the phone on the seat. I needed to call Parker. After doing a quick mental calculation, I decided to go home instead of to the station. I could call Parker and let him take over from here. For once, I wouldn't do anything stupid.

It seemed like I caught every traffic light during the drive. I bounced in my seat, trying to dispense my pent-up energy.

At my apartment complex, I threw the van into park and rushed into the building. I fumbled with my keys, trying to find the one to Sierra's apartment. Finally, the latch released, and I rushed through the beads. I ran to the phone, thankful I knew Parker's number by heart.

I heard the door open as I dialed.

"Sierra, I know who . . ." I turned around and dropped the phone. Barbara stood in the doorway, the gun in her hands pointed directly at my head.

CHAPTER
THIRTY-FOUR

Barbara's eyes were wide and crazed. Her hair, once pulled into a ponytail, now framed her face like a lopsided mop. Sweat covered her brow.

She closed the door and stepped closer. "At first, you were helping me make Cunningham look bad. Now that he's dead, I have no need for you."

The phone lay at my feet. If only I could reach it, call for help. Barbara kicked it and the receiver slid across the wood floor. "Don't even think about it."

The gun gleamed. I licked my lips and pictured Gloria Cunningham's skull plastered into the wall.

"Don't do anything crazy."

She laughed and grabbed my arm, shoving me toward Sierra's bedroom. "It's a little too late for that. Come on."

"Where are we going?" I tried to keep my voice steady. My heart beat like a trotting horse.

"Move," Barbara demanded.

"Can't we talk about this?"

"There's nothing to talk about."

"Why'd you kill Gloria?"

"Michael said he was going to leave her for me."

"But he didn't, did he? It would have hurt his career too much."

Barbara scowled. "I knew I had to get her out of the picture."

"So you killed her but made it look like her husband was guilty. You knew where he kept his gun. You knew how to make him look like the killer."

She snorted. "Then the police didn't even find it."

"So you had to burn the house down, knowing the gun would be found."

"Only you were in the house. I thought you had left with your assistant."

I glanced at the gun. "One thing I don't understand—why kill Michael? Wasn't he in on it with you?"

She snorted again. "Not a chance. This was supposed to hurt his career. Then he'd have no reason not to be with me. But what happened instead? People began to feel sorry for him. His poll numbers actually went up."

"But your affair was over, wasn't it? Why would he be with you?"

"He would have come back around. We had something special. We both knew it. I left my husband. It was his turn to leave Gloria, but he chickened out."

"You expected him to come back to you after you killed his wife?"

"He didn't know it was me. I wore a disguise. That was the beauty of it."

"How'd you get the gun back into his house?"

She chuckled. "Easy. Michael passed out after I shot him. Not very heroic for a former college football star, huh? I slipped the gun back into the closet where I knew he kept it. Then I waited for the police to arrest Michael. Instead, they arrested that other guy."

"So, why try to kill me? Why send me a pipe bomb and lock me in a car trunk?"

"To make it look like someone was trying to shut both of us up because we knew too much."

"You weren't the one who put me in that car."

"No, a little blackmail will go a long way, though. That poor mechanic didn't want his wife to find out he'd not only cheated on her, he'd also gotten the other woman pregnant." She smiled. "Amazing what you can overhear at the gym."

"Then you sent me the pictures, hoping I'd release them to the media and ruin his career, right?"

She scowled. "Except instead, you tracked down the woman in the pictures and gave her the evidence." Barbara raised the gun. "Now, enough talk. I have to figure out a way to get rid of you."

"The police know it's you, you know."

Barbara shoved me, and I stumbled toward the back of the apartment. I kept talking, desperate. I could see my short, sad life flashing before me. Live. Get old. Die. That was the cycle. Survival of the fittest. Did it boil down to that? Or was it like Riley, Harold, and Lela said? Did I have a purpose on this earth? I had to keep talking. I wasn't willing to die before I had an answer to that question.

"I found your hair in my apartment," I said.

"Shut up and move."

"Killing me won't do you any good."

"Neither will keeping you alive." She jabbed the gun into my side. "Now listen. I'm thinking electrocution—something that will seem like an accident. Or maybe even suicide. You do have a lot of pressure on you right now, with your assistant being in jail and Michael ending up dead in your apartment. Everyone will understand why suicide seemed like a good option for you."

"Anyone who knows me would be suspicious. I've been through a lot in my life already. This wouldn't be enough to push me over the edge."

She nudged the gun toward me, her eyes hardening. "Start the bath water. And don't make a sound, or I'll kill you now. Understand?"

I nodded. Her eyes said it all. She was going to kill me if I didn't stop her.

"Say it," Barbara hissed.

"I understand."

"Good. Now move."

I walked toward the bathroom and opened the door, the barrel of the gun still pressed into me.

Please, Lord, help me. If you really are up there, like my friends say you are, I want to know you.

The weapon jarred my ribs, and I continued walking. Following her instructions, I turned the water on.

"I need a radio. Where's a radio?"

"There's one in Sierra's room."

Barbara stepped into the hallway. I seized the opportunity and slammed the bathroom door shut. My fingers flew over the lock until it clicked in place.

Barbara pounded on the wood. "Open this right this minute."

I glanced around the bathroom, searching for something to give me a clue what to do next.

"Unlock the door!" Rage singed her voice. I'd really made her mad now.

I could wait her out. But what would happen when Sierra returned home? Would Barbara take out her anger on my friend?

I shuddered.

Suddenly, it quieted. What was Barbara doing? Waiting me out? Finding something to knock the door in with?

I sat on the edge of the tub and tried to formulate a plan. My mind blanked. No windows offered an escape route. I had no choice but to sit here and wait for Barbara's next move.

Why was she being so quiet? I rose and looked through Sierra's cabinets. Maybe if I found some hairspray I could blind Barbara. I saw a small city of cosmetics but realized that Sierra didn't use aerosol. It was bad for the environment, she'd said.

I found a couple of razors. I could use them if I needed to. A travel-size bottle of cornstarch baby powder seemed another good option. I slipped them into my pockets.

A shot fired. Wood splintered. I jerked back.

Another shot cracked. Was Barbara trying to shoot me through the door? Would it work?

I screamed at the top of my lungs, praying somebody—anybody—would hear me.

The lock shattered, and the door flew open.

"You didn't think you'd win that easily, did you?" Barbara aimed the gun at my forehead.

Lord, please. If you're real, help me. I'll . . . I'll check out church. I'll give you a chance. Last-minute bargaining. I'd vowed never to do it. Desperation did funny things to people, though.

I reached for the baby powder. In one motion, I pulled it from my pocket and squeezed. White dust clouded the air.

Instinctively, I kicked at the gun. It blasted. I wasn't sure if I'd been hit. I just knew I had to keep moving.

Metal clanked on the tile by my feet. I grabbed at the weapon. My hands trembled as I aimed it at Barbara.

Before I could make any threats, someone tackled Barbara. Riley. He pinned the woman to the floor. She thrashed beneath him, screaming threats and insults.

Riley looked up, gasping for breath. "Are you okay?"

I nodded and placed the gun in the sink; shaking so hard, I was afraid I'd drop it.

"Gabby?" a masculine voice called.

Parker.

"I'm in here."

"Let me go. They kidnapped me." Barbara flailed on the floor, trying to escape Riley's hold. "They're trying to keep me here!"

"Barbara O'Connor," Parker said, pulling his handcuffs off the back of his belt. "You're under arrest for the murders of Michael and Gloria Cunningham, for arson, and for the attempted murder of Gabby St. Claire."

Parker knelt beside the woman and Riley stepped back.

"I didn't do it," Barbara spat out as she writhed on the floor, struggling against Parker's restraining hands. "You're out of your mind."

Parker snapped the handcuffs on her. "No, we have evidence." Parker looked at me. The concern in his eyes startled me. Maybe I'd imagined the accusation in his eyes earlier.

Two police officers read Barbara her rights. Parker, Riley, and I stared at each other.

"How'd you know?" I asked both of them.

"I heard everything through the vents," Riley said. "I snuck into the apartment and waited for the right time to take her down."

I looked at Parker.

"The hair you turned in is Barbara's. We got a search warrant for her house and found evidence of the pipe bombs and arson." Parker pulled me into a hug. I didn't resist. "Are you okay?"

I nodded, the reality of how close to death I'd been, hitting me. "Yeah, now I am."

"I need to take you to the station for some questions. You okay with that?" His smoldering eyes searched mine.

I nodded, and he began leading me away.

"Excuse me one minute first." I turned back to Riley. My heart did something funny as I looked at his familiar face. I would never forget him—or Veronica, for that matter. "Thank you, Riley. Again. I'm sorry about all the mean things I said about you."

A strange emotion swirled in his eyes. "I'm sorry I let you down."

Veronica must be worried sick about him. I didn't blame the woman for not wanting me around. I'd almost gotten him killed several times now. Still, my heart felt like it weighed a hundred pounds when I turned from Riley.

Parker slipped an arm around my shoulders and led me into the flashing lights that filled the nighttime sky outside. It was over, I realized. It was finally over.

CHAPTER

THIRTY-FIVE

Parker grabbed my hand as he walked me up to my apartment. It had been one month since Barbara had been arrested and Harold released, and three weeks since Riley had moved back to California.

"I hate to cut this date short, Gabby." Parker's pager had gone off, and he had to rush to another crime scene. I nodded. In the two weeks we'd been dating, I was already getting used to it.

Parker's lips brushed mine in a brief good-night kiss. Then he stuffed his hands in his pockets and sauntered down the stairs. I watched him and smiled. He'd been such a support to me since Barbara's arrest. A definite blessing. Especially now that Riley had moved.

Every day, I stared at Riley's vacant apartment door and wondered who my new neighbor would be, wondered if I'd like them as much as I'd liked Riley. I wondered when Riley and Veronica would get married and if I'd be invited. I had no plans to attend if I were.

Parker turned and fanned his fingers in a wave before exiting the apartment building. After he disappeared outside, I stuck my key in the lock and turned it.

A familiar squawk froze me.

I turned around. Riley stood in the doorway to his old apartment.

"Riley?" I resisted the urge to throw my arms around him and tell him how much I had missed his company. "What are you doing here? You moved to California."

His sparkling eyes met mine. I'd missed those eyes.

"Veronica and I called it quits. Neither of us was happy. I'm not ready to be in the limelight. I just wanted to get away from that scene."

I swallowed, regretting the joy I felt at his announcement. I was dating Parker. I shouldn't feel this way toward Riley.

"So, you're here to stay?" I asked. It seemed a safe enough question.

He smiled that same smile that always melted my heart. "Yeah, I am."

"Glad to have you back."

"Glad to be back." He nodded toward the front door. "You and Parker together?"

Why did I suddenly want to deny it? Parker and I were happy. The past couple of weeks had been really nice. "We're giving it a shot."

His grin seemed to dim. Or was it wishful thinking on my part? He looked to the ground before meeting my gaze. "I just wanted to let you know I'm back. We'll have to get coffee sometime and catch up."

"How about church instead?" I asked, remembering the promise I'd made in a moment of desperation. I wasn't sure there was a God out there, but just in case there was, I had decided I should keep my promises to him. Besides, I wanted what Harold and Riley seemed to possess. I wanted the truth, the whole truth, and nothing but the truth.

His eyes widened, and he grinned. "I'd like that."

I would like that too, I realized, slipping inside my apartment. I really would.